Kylie!
Enjoy 2. "Keep
dreaming!"
Jodie Swanson
21 '14

Another Day

Book One

Jodie M. Swanson

Special thanks to both of my kids, and my friend Kim,
for making these memories come true.

CHAPTER 1

Another day. Adjusting my crackled leather boots to get the kink out of the material, then I grab my long trench coat. With a flick of my hair I pass through the small portal of my small dumpy home. Should I even call it that? Doesn't a home have "things"? The newspaper mat and stainless steel mirror I can live with, but…doesn't a home have things like warmth, love, a family?

As I start up the few mist dampened steps leading to a walkway, my companion is there. "Any news?" It's not really a question, just an acknowledgement of her phantom-like presence.

"No messages." She sits on the stone wall, watching me.

"No changes then," I mutter freeing the strained hair strands from my coat's confines. "Another day. Thanks."

"Why does it still bother you?"

I pause, step down again to look at her. "Why not? I see him every day. I see him watching me." Seeing some locals approaching I wait. My teeth gnash seeing them hug the wall opposite me, eyes wary. "Morning." *How can I sound so calm when I'd rather beat them about the head for their behavior?* They only nod, rushing to be away from me, from what they fear, what they can't understand.

"He must care then."

Facing her, anger lights my face. "What 'father' allows himself to be seen, but never touched nor talked to?" Glancing about, wondering if he was already watching me, "He fears me too."

"Ignore him then."

Again, I start up the stairs. "Wanna walk with me?" At the top of the stairs, I turn right along the side of the road. No destination in mind. Every day I did nothing as I have no job, no family, no life. Even in my own eyes I am pathetic, but too proud, or stubborn, to admit defeat.

1

"There he is," my shadow states.

Following her finger, I see him to my left, up the wooded hill. There he hid over a hundred feet away. Squaring my stance, I return his flat-faced look. He just stands there, like he usually does, bland faced or wary.

"Good morning, Sir." Somehow my voice doesn't crackle with vehemence.

Not acknowledging my words, he turns away, deeper into the trees.

"Coward."

I turn hearing that, wanting to laugh. "Whatever," I mumble. "His problem."

"His loss."

"Nice try." His snubbing me always stings, and I once again turn back to the water. Taking the stairs I had only just climbed, I descend, passing the room I live in, down farther, until I am on the wharf that takes me to the beach. My shadow never follows. She knows better than that.

The lapping waves beckon me closer, so I sit within a few feet of their reach. "I'm back," I greet the water. I blindly stare across the blue water. After a few minutes, I glance at the people who ventured on the beach with their kites in tow. So very few brave the beach when I, the outcast, am on it. A smile curls my lips seeing a small family trying to get the wind to grab their small kite.

Again, I close my eyes, concentrating. I hear and feel the sound of the water pushing the granules of the beach. The breeze plays with my hair, tickles my face, and fills my nose. *Aaaaah.*

Recollections, memories of another day, come to me.

"Wave!" echoed through the beach-goers. Panic followed upon hearing that word. Screams and people running

"Daddy!" Quickly I ran to him, grasping his firm hand. Tears streaming down my face, I tried to keep up. Turning I see the wave about to strike. The beach walls were rapidly rising to fend off the monster. But not quick enough.

The water flooded over the walls and beach effortlessly, taking my feet from me.

"Daddy!" I gripped my father's hand harder, holding my breath. Sand stings my eyes for only a second.

It's like a cocoon.

A call snaps me back to the present. *What?* Glancing to my feet, I see the water receding. I jump up. *Where?* The moist sand falls from my trench coat as I scan the area. Off a ways I can see it now. *Damn.*

"Wave!" A frantic scream. A man running with his wife head towards

2

me as they race for the steps. The woman clutches something tightly to her chest as she runs. *A baby. A son.* Tears of panic stream down her face as she gets closer.

Looking back to the water, I clearly see it coming. *Another monster. Rarely do they get so high.* Calmly, I stand before this giant as it approaches the walls designed to break it.

"Help!" The cries fly over the sand
For an instant I look at the scurrying bodies on the beach, then back to the wave. *Too late.* The newly designed wave wands were emerging from the sand. Those who knew they'd not make higher ground in time quickly head to the nearest wands.

The family stops at a wand ahead of me. Together, the man and woman clasp to each other, their son between them. I can almost feel their desperation and fear.

"Help me!" Quickly I turn. *Where?*

A man runs from his wand to scoop up a young girl, perhaps seven. In that instant, she reminds me of myself with a wave like this years and years ago. The man wraps his torso around a wand and molds the girl to him. Her head is tucked into his shoulder and held there tight with his arms holding either side of her torso down to where he locked his hands between her legs.

"Good luck," I whisper. With my right hand, I take hold of a wand. With legs braced for impact, I tilt my head back and close my eyes.

Water stings my nostrils and eyelids as the wave first meets me. Then there's the so familiar cocoon. Bringing my head forward, I open my eyes to the wave's fury. Before is the couple, struggling hard to keep a grasp of the wand. Again, I almost empathize as I watch them. Glancing down, I calmly watch the onslaught of water, seeing the sand and surf war.

A gargled scream makes me look up in time to see the family's son swoosh past. *Goner.* Looking towards the parents, the pure anguish expressed on their faces moves me. The husband is preventing the mother from going with their babe, his face contorted both by strain and fatherly pain. The mom is still gargling her useless pleas, arms still reaching for what she had held.

Damn. I let go of my wand, and seemingly slow turn to find the infant's direction. Spotting his tumbling form I control myself, move like lightning and ease to intercept his water muffled cry. "Got ya." Holding him close now, I see the wave has begun to die off. "That was fast."

With the water now swirling at my waist, I turn towards the family some two hundred or so feet away. The baby's mother clings to her husband's waist as he tries to keep her face out of the diminishing water. Striding towards them, I hold their precious gift safe. He turns first, a look of horror, then disbelief. Cautiously, I step closer and stand beside them.

3

Water at my ankles now, I get down on one knee beside the horrified mother. She whispers, "I lost him."

"Ma'am." My precious cargo is revealed to her.

"Oh my God!" She snatches up her little bundle, bestowing motherly loving kisses about his face while unwrapping him to check her babe fully.

Stepping back, *No "thank you" yet.* A couple more steps back. Both parents just look at me with their odd expressions. Pursing my lips, I nod and turn away. *No "thank you" at all. Should've let it drown.* Mentally I kick myself for the thought.

Briskly, I head towards my haven. Sparing only a glance toward the man who had clasped the girl so snuggly to ensure they had fared well. He is comforting her tear-filled face as another man raced to their sides.

They are well. And I need to hide, to rest.

Sweat coated, I sit up. The chill of the night makes me recline into my blankets again.

The dreams are so real.

I blink at night's shadows reflecting on the walls and ceiling.

The urge to pee is too great to ignore, so I rush to the toilet. As I flush, I can almost feel the wave's power.

"Hon?" I crawl back into bed. He's asleep, dead to his own dreamland. Cuddling to my husband for warmth, sleep soon consumes me again.

Shivering, I awaken. Guess I hadn't slept long as my hair is still damp. I sit up. The urge to relieve myself is strong. As is the sense of déjà vu.

CHAPTER 2

"Kids! Get over here!" I rub my forehead for wisdom, and patience. Perhaps my belly would be better, like the Buddha. "Kids!"

"Let 'em go. Gives us a break, and a chance to gab." Kim smiles. "Besides, maybe someone will take 'em for us." Placing a hand to her mouth she gives a mock call, "Kids for sale!"

Raising my eyebrows in doubt, I return my friend's smile. "Who would want our kids anyways?" With that I turn back into my Blizzard.

"I don't know about your kids, but mine are adorable. Oh...and your son just did a cannonball on your daughter." Kim emphasized the "your" each time just to give me a heart attack as she stresses her point. "Careful, people can see you," she teases. It's a lasting joke between us two, as I have a neighbor who kept falsifying information, slanderous information really, regarding my parenting. "Wouldn't want the cops to come get you."

"Oh, ha ha." My eyes fly back to the kids as they run. "Let 'em play rough. As long as they're having fun, don't break any bones, or bloody any noses, I'll let them kill each other." At my friend's raised eyebrows, "What?"

"Bloody any noses?"

"Whatever." Making a face, I shovel in another scoop. "Your ice cream is melting."

"Yes, Mommy Dearest." Kim laughed taking a bite of her own. "So how's school going? Still doin' good?"

"Really good. It's hard with the kids and going to school full time, but I am managing." The sound of the kids playing and calling for help triggers the dream to replay in my head. After a few more bites, I ask, "Remember earlier I told you have some...bizarre dreams?" At Kim's nod I continue. "Do you have any like mine...that are so...real?"

"No." Kim raises an eyebrow, "But you are an oddball. Nobody's

5

quite like you."

"Nice. Ha, ha." Hissing I threaten ice cream to the face of my good banter loving friend. For six years she had endeared her way into our family with her comments and neighborly love.

"Just kiddin'! So tell me about your freaky dreams, Weirdo."

Finishing the last of my ice cream, I stand up. "Dork." After tossing my Blizzard container in the trash, I sit back down. "Glad I can talk to you about this. Some people would say I need help, or wouldn't bother even listening, to my...." Seeing her pretending to ignore me, I loudly clear my throat.

She smiles, "Shoot Girlfriend, after what we've been through? You know we can talk about anything!"

Kim referencing our past trust and friendship means a lot. "Thanks. Well, they're still really weird. Sometimes I can't tell if I'm dreaming or...if this life is a dream and that's my real one. It's usually continuous, episodic, complete with this other world's memories and everything! Some start as soon as I go to sleep and will last all night. And they're so real! I can feel the cold, heat, and rain. I can taste, and even have to pee."

"Have to pee?"

Seeing my friend's eyebrows go up yet again, I wish I hadn't opened my mouth. "I don't pee in bed, just in my dreams."

"Uh-huh." Her and those darn eyebrows.

"Whatever! Guess you don't understand."

"Oh, loosen up! You know I was just kidding!" Kim lightly punches my shoulder. "You've been talking about these dreams a lot again. Kinda strange, I guess. But I do think you're nuts."

"Nice, thanks," I mutter.

"You're welcome!" she carols back.

Snot. My eyes roll.

"Hey! I heard that!" Kim feigns hurt. For the next fifteen minutes or so she listens to more of my dreams, the details, and my feelings when I wake up. "Gosh, they do sound real. What do you think they mean?" When I shrug, she shakes her head. "Told you that you're a freak." Kim then looks at her watch. "Oh crap! Hey Girl, I gotta go! Hubby's getting' off work to come home for dinner. Guess there better *be* dinner there when he gets home, huh?" Her laughter is contagious. "Where's Vandy?"

Glancing around, we find our children buried in the ball pit. After the many minutes of "I don't want to go" and "Leave me alone", we were mentally ready to head back home. A few more minutes of struggling with disagreeable children and car seats, and we were capable of heading home.

"Hey Girl," I hear from behind me. "Thanks for lunch."

"Notta problem." We give a brief hug. "Better get home before the hubby does."

"What's Chase say about these weird dreams? Is he calling the insane asylum?"

"Nice. You could only hope. Nah, he says it's part of my 'dramatic nature.'" Passing off a feigned look of hurt, "Whatever could he mean?"

"Oh, I have no idea," Kim teases back. "You know, you should write all of these things down. Do any of your dreams have you as an author?"

"Cute." I open my door. "Maybe I should write them all down. Who knows, maybe it'd be worth it."

"Hey, ya never know. You might end up famous! Or thrown in the loony bin."

"Nice. Your vote of confidence is overwhelming."

"Have a good one Girlfriend," Kim carols as she opens her car door. "Call me later."

We part there. Kim heading her way home, and I mine. I can't help but wonder if I'm the only one who has these strange dreams. *At least Kim's lively comic nature helped me not feel so strange.* Sometimes after these "episodes", I feel like I am sick, drunk, or suffering from a monstrous migraine.

While driving I have a sense of "double vision." I am alert to the road I'm driving on, but am able to "see" my dreams as they replay in my head. Faintly, I can hear the water, feel the sand, and smell the place I call home in those dreams. Visions of the wands appearing from the beach, the baby, the....

"Mommy?"

"What Buddy?" Seeing the look on my son's face, I realize I must have snapped. "I'm sorry Little Man. Mommy was thinking. I didn't mean to hurt your feelings." Seeing his wary look, I offer a big smile. "What's up Dude?"

My son starts talking about this and that, ice cream caking the corners of his mouth. His sister throws in her penny here and there, making only toddler sense. Their jibber-jabber fills the car until we arrived back to our house. Their talk then turns to when their daddy will be coming home.

"Soon." It's so vague, I know. No one ever knows when Daddy gets home until he comes through the door. Knowing "soon" is sometimes half an hour up to three hours after his so-called "shift", the kids and I are rarely content. Yet tonight, involving them with their toys allows them distraction and me a chance to think.

Is this real? The spatula stirs the ingredients in the frying pan, sending out delicious smells. *Is this live? Or is it Memorex?* I idly make the motions of preparing tonight's dinner. Thoughts of the "dream" keep coming back with every turn of the spatula, every scent, as I see the wispy trails of steam rising. Mentally I curse myself, *I hate it when this happens. I can't concentrate when I'm like this. He'll be home soon, and I'm still off in la-la-land!*

Well, you wanted to tell him about the dream.

True. But not when I'm still freaked about it.

Maybe you should write it down, like Kim said. That way you know and remember everything better.

I've been playing it in my head all day. I remember it like it was "yesterday", and this is the "dream".

That's the door -- he's home.

Be quiet. You're no help. Smacking the spatula against the side of the frying pan, I turn to greet Chase. "Hi Hon! How was your day?"

"So what do you think?" *Pause, give him a chance to reply.* My eyes meet his as I scrape potatoes from the pan. "I'm not crazy, right?"

"No, I don't think that you're crazy." Calmly, Chase brings over his plate. "I find your dreams are interesting, as you know. They're probably based on your childhood or dramatic nat-."

"Nature, I know." Another few seconds pass as I collect my thoughts. Some of his dreams used to sound familiar, so I ask, "Do you still have those 'water place' dreams?"

"Once in a blue moon, and I usually don't remember them like you can remember yours." Chase finishes the last of his remaining juice, and hands me the glass. "But then again, *no one* can remember like you."

"Oh, ha ha." My husband is threatened by a snapping towel.

"What I mean is, you tend to remember so much. What people have said, clothes people have worn, and even songs played. Whereas I cannot remember some things you say I have done even a few days ago." Chase sits on the counter next to me. "So how was your visit with Kim?"

"Good. Kids played. We ate ice cream, which is great for our diets. Kids played. We talked. Kids ran around. And as we gabbed, I told her about my dreams again." I pull the sink's plug. My eyes focus on the moving water, and the dream is replayed in an instant.

"And what did she say?"

"That I'm crazy of course." My smile gives away the fact that I didn't believe her poke at me. "She asked if you had called the men with the jackets at the asylum yet." I pretend to be guarded, "Have you? Hmmm?"

"Yeah, they're on their way. Come on, stop thinking about it, and let's go to bed." He reaches for my hand.

Following, I nod. Once in our room, I head for our bathroom. Slowly I go through the motions of taking a shower, and it feels like déjà vu, like I'm someone else, or am I imagining? *Stop it! You're driving yourself mad!* Taking a deep, steadying breath, I reach for a towel. Drying off, I notice Chase is reading.

"Uncle Walt or Uncle Bob?" Chase turns the cover to shows it's Walt

Whitman's <u>Leaves of Grass</u> again in his grasp.

After brushing my teeth, I climb over Chase as he reads, sometimes silently, sometimes aloud. Chase finds serenity and intellect in reading poetry, I know. And I feel bad, thinking he's reading after what I've said. Part of me knows he just like to, and not to twist things around, that he enjoys it. Mentally nodding, I admit that sometimes I enjoy it too. But tonight hearing it does little to calm my fears that I know where I'll be once I start to dream.

Jodie M. Swanson

CHAPTER 3

My shower has refreshed me, somewhat. I don't feel as...afraid. Of what, I am not certain. Going through the motions, I brush my teeth and the tangles of my hair.

"Yooo-hoo?"

A smile comes to my face. "Come in."

There she is, my not-so-silent shadow. "Morning! And what are you up to today?"

"Five foot, nine."

"Cute." She sits down on my bed of worn newspapers. "What did you do last night?"

"You act as if you don't know."

Shadow snorts aren't becoming. "I never follow you to the beach."

"Very well." Starting with my awakening from a power nap taken after the wave incident, I told my companion about watching the "Surf-ival Festival" that had lasted for hours.

"You went? Why? To see him?"

"No. More like to give some parents a chance to say 'Thank you'." Seeing her perplexed look, I explain. "Yesterday when the wave hit, this infant was swept from the mother's arms. I recovered him before he was hurt. When I approached the couple, they never said thanks, or even acknowledged my presence. The mom just checked her baby over, and he just looked at me."

"I'm sorry."

"Why? People usually don't, so it's on me." The buttons on my khaki shirt seemed tough this morning.

"Did you...use it?"

Facing her, I nod. "It was like I've never stopped. The energy there was amazing." Turning, I grab a worn pair of jeans and socks. "I know I

11

did the so-called 'right thing', but...."

"They didn't say so." She is staring at me. I can feel it. "Did you wish you hadn't?" It's almost like an accusation. My silence was the answer. "Oh, I'm sorry." Straight faced to her silence, I continued to dress. "Would their thanks have changed anything?"

"Who knows now," I sigh, grabbing my boots.

"But you went."

"They weren't there." A look in my stain-glass mirror stops me. "Sometimes my face isn't my own."

"Excuse me?"

"Nothing." With one last look at the steeled-reflection, I face her again. "I went, and did start something." A deviant smile lit my face.

"Oh no. What did you do?"

They're not here, the cowards.

Continuing along the wooden wharf, the sound of my footsteps seemed calming. Shoulders squared, posture proud, stance challenging, I approached the locals. My looks were met with disbelief, horror, and surprise. With fear of my presence being challenged, I press further into the crowds. Luckily, most of the spectators are watching some dancers on the wharf. It looks like they are having fun, and the crowd keeps cheering. Some spectators have drinks in their hands, and I'm curious to know what they have. And what it tastes like.

The dancing again catches me eyes. Watching the choreography before me, I want to get closer. Making my way, I catch the eyes of one dancer. It was the man who had saved the young girl.

I bet he received thanks.

His eyes keep coming back to me. They're not really challenging, nor afraid. They rarely leave me though, and as that dance ends, I'm a bit more nervous. I stop, watching, taking my eyes from his at times to assess the locals around me, and view the change of dancers. He is given a tuxedo-type coat and a hat. Only four male dancers remain on-stage, which is actually the dock.

The music begins again, and this time the flow of dance is changed somehow. Not the exuberant couples dancing, but just the four of them, and different.

The feel of eyes on me, his eyes, makes me look towards him again. Raising an eyebrow, I challenge his look. My mouth drops as he motions for me to approach.

Not likely me. More like someone else.

We'll see.

Occasionally taking my eyes of him, I purposefully stride to the center set of stone stairs leading down to the docks, and through the crowds. Slowly, carefully, I make my way down the steps until I stand on the dock.

Shocked gasps and a few screams are heard, but I move not. Still I face the dancers who seem not to care I'm there, except for one. He sashays closer, until I'm within his reach. Then he takes my hand. More gasps, sounds of outrage and fear, fill the area.

Let's give them something to gasp about.

Following his lead, I feel like I am flying. I check to be sure that I'm not.

So this is dancing.

One of the other dancers engages in our dance, so I'm to take turns between them. Trying to remain natural, I relax, finding the energy there, asking.

Okay.

Soon, I feel it flow. A little bit. The four men are now dancing with me as the "centerpiece", and I feel light. Controlling myself, as the feel of flying is close, I now know the music, feel an ending coming. A thought comes to mind. Energy flows in an instant, the thought conveyed.

Here it comes.

With the last musical notes, the last measure, my idea materializes. With a final swirl, my positioning is such that I am parallel to the audience, in a false dip. The man stands directly behind me, holding me, his hands around my waist, like an embrace. Two of the dancers stand in an adoring pose on either side of him, as if wanting to be close to me. The fourth dancer had come to slide between my legs, to rest upon one, back arched, his right hand reaching towards the heavens. It was perfect. It was almost erotic. I looked like I was wanted, desired, adored.

The applause was a surprise. As the dancers stood and took their bows, I felt stunned.

Did I do that?

I gazed around.

Standing ovation?

Well, they were good.

Overwhelmed by this scene, and uncertain of its direction, I raced up the stone steps to the wooden ledge I had stood upon before. The crowd moved, shied, but applauded still the dancers. Tears swelled my eyes, and with no comfort from the water available, I rushed to hide in my haven.

A hand grasped mine, pulling me to a stop.

Oh crap. Now I'm in for it.

"Where are you going?" The voice wasn't accusatory, so I slowly turned. It was the man. "Well?"

"What?" Still his hand was there, firmly holding my arm. Feeling his energy, "Please let go." A thought came that he might not.

"Alright." His hand fell to his side, and I felt a loss. Tonight was the first time I'd felt physical contact in years.

Tread carefully.

"Where were you going?" His question was asked gently, like…a caress.

"You shouldn't be near me. People will talk." Already his actions had drawn notice. Whispers and stares filled my senses.

"Why?"

Poor man had no idea he was talking with an outcast, a freak. "I'm not…I'm different. People fear me," I whisper. Turning away from him, I race up the steps to seek refuge. Nearing my little home, I stop. He was behind me, his energy said so.

"And?"

A soft sigh. "What do you mean, they 'fear' you?"

"Are you nervous for being seen with me now?" My tone's accusing, and I half-way regret it. Still without turning around, I crack. "Wondering if your social reputation will recover?"

"No."

Slowly I turn, and take in his features. Blue eyes, startling blue, framed in a serious face topped with sweat layered hair. He'd definitely pass as cute. Maybe not handsome, but cute. "You're not from around here are you?"

"Why would that make a difference?" he insisted.

Delay him. "Why'd you save the girl today? Is she family?"

"No, just thought she needed help I guess." He paused. "And why did you? How did you?" His frown showed he was confused, remembering.

"Why are you here?" The challenge was loud even to my own ears.

He seemed taken aback. "Here, as in this area? Work. Here, as in this area? You. Why are you so defensive?" He stepped closer.

Stepping back, "Me?" Hearing voices coming, I pull away more. "Please leave me. No one talks to me. They are afraid of me." He wasn't leaving, and people were getting close. "Are you daft? Get away before they see you with me!"

"No."

No?

"No?"

He sat down on a stair, and pulled me into sitting next to him. "No. Let them see me. What do I care?"

This won't do. "Good-night." *A touch of magic.* "And I'm sorry."

The bushes concealed me from peering eyes as two couples came in view. They stopped seeing the sleeping man slumped on the steps. "Poor guy must be drunk. Greg, help me take 'im back to the other dancer-types,

14

would ya?"

"Hurry!" One woman looked about quickly. "She lives near here."

"You don't think she killed him do you?" replied the other woman.

"Nah, he's breathin' jus' fine," said Greg checking him before grabbing his half of the man. "Now les get goin'."

"Fine show tonight, even though she showed up," remarked the first man as they headed back down the stairs. Their voices faded into the blackness.

When I was certain they were gone, I slipped into my hole of a home. Preparing for bed, I thought of all that had transpired that day. The energy warmed me as I laid upon my mat.

Again, strange images filled my dreams: children, a man, friends, work, learning, a life.

Jodie M. Swanson

CHAPTER 4

"Hel-*lo!*"

Startled, I come back to the present.

"You did *what?* Are you insane? Someone finally tries to get close to you, and you 'knock' him out and leave him stranded." She waves her arms in exasperation. "I don't get it."

"I was *pro-tec-ting* him. He was only acting that way because of the dance. It wasn't *real.*" Grabbing my trench coat, I head for my little door. "It wasn't anything at all. Besides, people would snub him, like they do me. That wouldn't make me feel better I assure you." Seeing her disapproval with my actions and thoughts clearly displayed, I sigh. "I'm leaving."

"But you said he was cute! *Aaagh!*" She follows me now.

Afraid to head to the comforting beach, I head up the stairs. My friend mumbles to herself about idiots, blindness, and empty-heads, yet I pretend not to notice. She and I have been through a lot together, so I let her rant and rave. Continuing up the stones again, thoughts about the bizarre happenings of the previous night venture forth. It had been fun to "mingle" once again with the "commoners." Times were few and far between when I made such a spectacle, in all senses. Guilt over my usage bothers me.

I shouldn't have played with it.

But it was fun.

It's not necessary. Gives the locals more reason to fear me.

So what?

"If you're going to engage in private conversation, mind if I eavesdrop?"

Slowly, I face her. "As if you can't hear what I think! Ugh! Sometimes I think you try to irritate me on purpose."

"But maybe I'm the other voice you hear?" She's grasping at straws to make me laugh now.

"Actually, when you *do* intrude, you 'sound'…whiney." My eyebrows lift for effect before I turn back up the steps.

Her sputtering is hysterical. "Well I never!" and "I can't believe you said that!" is mixed with her huffs and mumbling. She reminds me of someone somehow. The person's identity seemed elusive. Thoughts of that, a someone else, entranced me. So lost in thought am I about who it could be, that she has to hit me in her attempt to get my attention. "There he is."

And she is right, as usual. My father stands at the tops of the stairs, leaning against the stone wall. He looks like he has been waiting for me to come. Or at least someone. Cautiously, I continue up, ready to pass him by if he wasn't waiting for me, or willing to be civil. Nervousness mounted, and with each step I rise closer. Again I look towards him, only to find his eyes on me.

"He's not leaving," she states.

I see that.

"What are you going to do?"

Be civil. And now within two steps, I stop. Allowing him to size me up, I watch his features for reactions. Sparing a cursory glance I take in all of him. Blandly, "Good day, Sir."

"Is your imaginary friend with you today?"

Looking down a bit for a second to recover, "She is."

"Where was she last night when you were carrying on so?" He snorts. She shrieks, "What a crock of…."

"I don't know. She's not my keeper, just a friend." Pausing in the tension, "I didn't see you there, Sir."

"Maybe because you were cavorting so." He stuffs his hands into his coat pockets. "Why'd ya do it? Thought you might have more sense than that."

"Nice. So happens I was looking for someone, someone I had helped." *Stay calm. Don't let him get to you.*

"Heard about some lady who 'flew' through the wave and saved a baby from being washed away. Knew it was you." He shook a finger now, before thrusting his fists back into his pocket. "So don't bother denying it."

"I won't."

"What a jerk! I can't believe…," she sputters.

"Is that all you came here for? To try and criticize me?" At the anger on his face, I throw up a hand. "Oh, please. For over, what, at least fifteen years, you say nothing to me. Now you want to act condescending? No thanks." He gasps. "If *this* is all I've been trying to accomplish, this hostility, forget it." I step closer. "You're not worth it." Pushing by, turning right along the road, I force a brisk stride.

"Oh my gosh, I...," she begins.

"Quiet. Please, just be quiet." My eyes close.

Unreal, years of my hoping for reconciliation, for nothing. My wispy companion was wrong for once; he didn't care at all. The urge to look back is great, but I won't do it. Too much is flooding through me: pain, hurt, anger, and loss. The energy is picking up on it, so I need to concentrate, focus, and relax. *Breathe, no energy, breathe, relax, serene, breathe.* The energy resides a bit, but the feel of it coursing is still strong.

"You're more of a man than him." She keeps pace with me.

"Shush, not yet." Hearing her apology, I nod. Sighing, I glance around. To my right is the water, beckoning me with its calmness and beauty. To my left is the wooded hill where scattered homes of the locals hide. Ahead, many miles of road lay before me. The road winds around the hills and borders the shore here and there. The canopy of trees almost gives the appearance of a checkered pattern, splotches of dark contracting the lighted areas. It will be a welcomed walk, a calmer to frazzled emotions.

"You're going to be awhile, aren't you?" To my nod, she sighs. "Guess I'll wait here. Maybe I'll pick at your father a bit. "She laughs for effect, so I smile.

Hearing her departure, a deep hollowness consumes me. A feeling I'm sure many others have had as well. It is unfortunate that people can feel this wretched, and have no ailments or injuries. Betrayal, anger, defensiveness, loss of hope, and isolation feed this hollowness. Part of me feels it has died, and maybe Hope should be considered part of the human anatomy. My emptiness is emphasized by the sound of my boots as they crunch on the small stones and sand of the road's shoulder. *Such numbness would better suit the small rocks, for then they'd not feel the force of my treading upon them.*

Many miles later, I spy a small grassy slope off to the right of my path. It is filled with small flowers, bugs and butterflies, and who knows what else. Sunlight filters gently through the trees bordering this mini utopia, lending a welcoming quality. The grass is ankle deep in some parts, and mid-knee in others. Grasshoppers leap to avoid my intrusion, and the air cackles with the sound. The whisper of butterfly wings mingles, and the Orchestra of Nature begins.

Lying down in the soft grass, the musical energy comforts me. With the sun warming my skin, and the sounds of nature warming my soul, I rest. Butterfly kisses and grasshopper trespassings go virtually unnoticed as visions of a dream world now play my senses.

"Have a good day at work Babe." He kisses me back. Then he's gone.

Snuggling into the covers again, I realize I've just had another dream. Luckily the kids are still asleep, so I quickly write down a few notes of my dream.

Notes: Father (name?) tried to put down my saving a child
Remember the festival, the dance (man's name?), and wave,
HISTORY
Shadow, what's her name? Does she have one?
I go to sleep when I wake up
Know the "energy", and when I awaken I almost remember, I can feel it

Tired still, I cover back up, praying for another hour of sleep before the kids wake up. Sleep comes instantaneously.

Stretching, I realize I've had another one of those funky dreams. *Too bizarre by far.* I have memories of a husband, a family, some friends, and a real bed with blankets. Slowly, I sit up and assess the possible length of rest. My nap mustn't have been overly long, as the sun's position hadn't changed much, perhaps half an hour.

My stomach gurgles, and the thought of needing to eat has me heading home. Long walks like these are rarely prepared for, yet I can manage. Today the miles back don't seem as hard on a grumbling stomach. After a couple hours the town comes into view. I look for my friend.

What's her name? Does she have one?

The dream's thought stops me right there. *Déjà vu, again. The energy around me is going into overtime.* Quickly I hurry to my home, hungry and confused. The dream had been short, I recall. In this dream, though, I had awakened and wrote things down about myself.

"Ah, there she is," my companion's voice calls out.

What's her name? Does she have one?

As she approaches, a frown crosses my features. "I have a question." My tummy's growling in protest. "I have lots of questions. Care to join me for dinner?" Smiling, she shrugs and we head to my house.

She senses, as usual, my turmoil. "What's wrong? I'da thought you'd feel better by now."

Opening my door, we go to my cupboards. Opening one, we pull out a jar of pickled herring, some packaged noodles, and crackers. I pause, realizing I had food. "Where do I get the food, if I don't have a job?"

She turns and faces me, a look of disbelief on her face. "What do you mean, where do you get the food? We always get the discarded stuff from the grocers. Why'd ya ask?"

Memories of the boxes of non-sold excess, outdated, dented cans, and torn packages come back as if they'd never left. "Never mind. Just forgot is all." Shaking my head, I reach for my dented pot.

"Just forgot? Just forgot!" She approached with a limp carrot to add to our noodles. "Forgot." Her head shakes in disgruntlement.

When younger, I tried to work at the local grocers just for sustenance, but had been fired. They said their sales had suffered since I had started. Many customers had even stated that if I wouldn't go, they'd have shut the grocery store down completely. I refused to leave, saying I needed to live too. After only a second, the owner told me I was fired, and that he was sorry. He'd never spoken to me since. But once or twice a month I received a box of grocery store "leftovers" placed by my little door, discretely out of the view of any passer-bys. Pity gift, but I'd take it, like I had taken the job.

Seems everything I have is either a pity gift or trash.

My clothes are from the local trashcans. People didn't throw away nice things, so I have very little attire to be proud of. Two pairs of men's pants, one with a small hole in the crotch, and a pair of jeans with below the knees cut off made up my leggings collection. A couple overly large flannel shirts with a button missing on each, a faded tank top, and three stretched out T-shirts with the lettering faded compose my tops. A few mismatched pair of worn elastic socks, two ugly bras, and three pairs of "granny undies" make up my undergarments.

My toothbrush is old and worn. My hairbrush is just as bad. "I'm a mess."

"You're acting strange", she starts. "You keep muttering to yourself, and looking at yourself. Are you upset the guy didn't fall for you?"

"Actually, it's something else." Lighting a match, some twigs become my stove. Placing the pot of noodles and limp carrot onto the contained pieces of branches, I sigh. "I'm having strange dreams again. I'm somebody's wife, mother, and friend."

"Good! That means you're going to meet someone!" She hugs me excitedly. "I'll bet it's that man from the festivities."

"You don't understand." I shake my head. "It's a complete life of somebody else, and it feels like it's...me. A different me, but me." Seeing her perplexed look, I tell her the dream about the notes I have just had. Then, rambling on, "Like I said, my husband was kissing me before he went off to work. As I laid there, in my bed, I remember wanting to take some notes on my dream, which is this...my life! Things like my father, wanting to know his name."

Jeffery Randal.
"I wanted to know your name."
Shadow Danza.
"Shadow?" The thought of her name actually being Shadow doesn't surprise me, yet my saying it does.

"That's the first time you've said my name in years!" Shadow looks shocked. "But yes, that's it. So you remember me in your dreams? I'm flattered."

Giving her one of those, "In *your* weirder dreams" comments, my eyes roll. "Just seems strange, saying it after the last...what...ten years or so?"

"Closer to twelve, since you said it made me sound too 'phantom-like.'" Shadow sighs in retrospect. "Guess I missed it a little. But go on."

"Sorry." Stirring the 'soup', I think some more. "I have this other person's whole life memories when I dream of her. She looks like me, I think, and is as tall. She's my age, but is...well, she's wanted, loved, more than I have been. I think I...she...has two children."

"Do you think you are her?" Shadow prompts and points to the mirror. "Or could it be that your dreams are a reflection of any 'wishful' thoughts you may have about a life you'd like to be having instead?"

"Probably only my 'wishful thinking'," I comment. "It's just so... real."

"Not surprisin' with the power you have."

Stirring the pot another time, "Yeah. You're probably right, as usual." Blankly, staring as the noodles and carrot dance in the pot, "You're probably right."

Shadow retrieves the chipped bowls from the closet, and places them by the pot. "You haven't asked if I did anything to your father."
The knowledge that I wasn't, nor hadn't thought about the encounter, seem comforting. Curiosity about Shadow's statement starts eating at me. Smiling, "Okay, I give. What'ya do?"

Listening to my friend's tale of stalking and 'whispering' is indeed funny. She has me almost feeling sorry for the old man. Numerous times during our short dinner she retold parts of her short story, and her role, emphasizing the funny things. She really must have had him freaked today. Her blowing in his ears, giving him a pinch, and even hissing, "Loser." And she did it for me, the good friend that she is. Gratefulness for the day her presence comes to me. And all too soon, she is leaving for night comes.

Now I lay upon my newspapers, thinking of the comfortable bed of the strange dreams. And energy flows.

CHAPTER 5

The padded sound of kid feet prepares me for their ambush. They jump onto the bed, roaring and screeching like fierce dinosaurs, clawing at the covers I've thrown over my head. "Aaahh! Help me! Help! There's bad dinosaurs trying to get me! Help! Aaahh! Help!" Playfully, I continue to call out for assistance. Their giggles reinforce my calls for help as I continue to maneuver the blankets and sheets to better hide me from their reaching hands.

My protection is successfully pried from my grasp, and I am forced to take drastic measures. "Tickle tackle! Rooaaarr!" Two screaming kids duck for the covers. Laughing, I grab my squirming son and pretend to nibble on him between kisses and tickles. My daughter jumps into the fray, not letting Brother get all the attention. Somehow the bed has become a free-for-all, and I feel like I'm losing. "Rooaarr!" I call out again, hearing their giggling increase to full power.

Another ten minutes of their game, tears of laughter still streaming down our faces, we make our way to the kitchen for some cereal and morning children's television programs. For some reason I don't feel very hungry, almost like I've just eaten. But the kids' appetites are enormous. "Good heavens, you guys are eating a lot!"

Some days I feel as though I have a hard time playing the Mommy Role, but other days are so much fun. As I reenact the character's singing, I feel I tend be a good mom just because of the giggles my kids emit while they copy me. "Bur, bur, burrr!" And the munchkins laugh some more. Even within days, moods swing constantly from bad to good and right back to bad. Right now was one of the few times in a day I could enjoy my two young children.

Jay is almost six years old, and the elder of the two terrors called my kids. His loves are dinosaurs, big trucks, crafts, and cars. He's the light on a dreary day when he wants to be. He's an instigator when his sister seems to get more attention. But my love for him would be hard to ignore. He's a treasure.

My younger child is Joanna, well into the terrible-twos. She was almost named Angel, and far from that is her temperament. Trying and succeeding to be the center of attention with her temper tantrums and screaming fits, she can be hard to be around. Yet her charm is certain, so when she turns it on, she can be quite sweet and proper. She wants to become and do so many things, and as a mother, I hope she can do it all.

Both kids take after Chase in appearance, more than me. Wanting the best for my kids, their having Daddy's looks seems okay with me as Chase is blessed with striking blue eyes and a bright shade of blonde hair. He's tall and on the thinner side, built, but not Arnold Schwarzenegger by any means. His facial features are nice, and in his thirties, he could definitely be called cute. Maybe he's not overly handsome, but cute, especially to me.

Me? I'm plain with pale skin, lazy brown hair and dark brown eyes. One of my two saving graces are that though I'm in my late twenties, I am mistaken for being twenty-one or younger quite a bit. The other is per Chase, and it is my rump. Yep, Chase is constantly saying that if Joanna has my rear, he'll be fighting off the boys.

Still, despite my plainness, I'm hoping to make something of myself. Funny that Chase finally got me going back to college after years of doing other work, and now staying home with the kids. My goals have changed so much during our last eight years together.

We met by accident; him not really looking, and me never hoping. He had come into the restaurant where I had been a waitress, and we hit it off. Guess that's why we've worked so well. We've had our troubles and fights, and still do, but they seem so small in the larger scheme of things.

I'm lucky, I know. Growing up with such a loving childhood, somehow I wonder how I got so lucky. My parents had what most would call a perfect marriage, and three talented children, myself included. Never tormented or hurt, real-world nightmares of any kinds never plagued me. This is the life both Chase and I are striving for with Jay and Joanna.

Part of me now wonders what visions my kids see when they sleep, as I watch Jay recline on the sofa. He is often wrestling with Night Terrors. He has since he was born. The first few nights of his life he'd startle me awake with his infant screams. The comforting I gave seemed like no comfort at all to him. The nurses kept saying that babies don't have nightmares. But I disagree. What more reason to have a nightmare than to leave a warm womb, through a tiny space that makes you hurt, only to come into a bright, cold world?

Still an interesting thought.

Reaching for my homework, I see my notes from my dream earlier this morning. Strange, I almost didn't remember writing them down. I think about the first, "Father" note. Images float inside my head, and I can almost hear it.

"Aagh!" Clearing my throat, my test that afternoon became more important. Distracting thoughts tried to intrude, but the value of an A for this Sociology class was stronger.

Coming home from class, I listen to the sound of "Beat It" by Michael Jackson. Few people enjoy his music like I do. But with the car stereo's volume near its peak, my voice drowned out, I enjoy his music quite a bit. A few more good songs, strange for this time of night, and the car's pulling into the driveway. Turning down the volume to not blow out the ears of the car's next occupants, I bee-bop through the front door. Coming up next to a cooking Chase, "Hey, Hon." A kiss finds his cheek.

"I'll take it you did well on your test?" Chase smiles as he hands me a glass of water. "Here put this on the table. Dinner's ready."

"Yummy!" Jay and Joanna are shrieking as they run around the table.

"Yep, I done did good on that test." Paper towels are folded as napkins as I continue, "And then some!" I feel I have solid A's all around still." Dancing to the kitchen I retrieve the necessary silverware. "So what we having?"

"Hamburger Helper."

"Yummy!" the kids are still caroling.

"So it looks like you're feeling better. I guess that means you didn't have any more dreams?" Chase brings over his culinary concoction.

Sitting down, "I did too. Then fell right back asleep. Then some monsters came into my room..."

"Nnnoooo!" laughs Jay as he sits next to Chase.

"...and they tried to eat me! Big ferocious monsters."

"Nnnoooo!" my son laughs. Joanna just giggles.

"Alright, calm down you guys. It's time to eat." Chase ladles a scoop of the noodle mash for each child.

Between blowing on the kids' plates, I relay my dream. "I was there again, same person and everything. Like the person I am in my dreams, her father had some not nice things to say about the wave incident." Nodding to my son repeating of my sentence, I continue. "I told him off and went for a walk. Along the road was a...like a grassy spot and I took a nap. But when you came in to tell me good-bye, I woke up, and wrote down those couple of things. Then I fell back asleep, into her." Chase fills my uplifted plate. "In my dream I remember the time I was awake and the notes I wrote."

Chase makes an "interested" face and nods as he piles his dinner onto his plate. "Sounds interesting. So you say that you were the same person, again?"

"Mmm-humm." Nodding as I reach for my water. "I'm even more convinced it's like…a version of me, or my thoughts. That's exactly what it feels like." Taking another bite, I wipe Joanna's chin. "I was going to ask your mom about what she thinks."

Chase nods, and helps Jay with a fallen napkin. "Bet she'd like to hear more of your dreams. I was going to call her this weekend anyway, as they'll probably be back from camping then. They went to see Shane and Betty at the lake."

"Mommy's silly," Jay laughs out. "She was singing like on T-B." Jay doesn't say TV, so we calmly try to correct him, which soon has him laughing hysterically.

"Come on, Dude," Chase coaxes. "Settle down and eat your dinner."
Life here is so varying.
Life here? Now why did I think that?

Somewhere nearby, a young man stares at the message on the computer screen. Hitting a few keys and scrolling through functions, the man stops. Fear outlines his features. Holding his lower lip between his teeth, he runs some more checks. "This is not good." Looking for his manual, he flips it open, scanning for the desired pages. "Escape, Escape again." He flips another page, and follows the required prompts, "This is not good at all."

He gets up, and goes to another computer terminal. After logging on, he runs through the series of commands again. Picking up the phone, he dials.

"Confidential Line, Captain Roberts," the bland voice states.

Taking a deep breath, "Sir, this is Sergeant Michner. We have a Level II situation."

The pause is long. "Say again?"

"Captain Roberts, we have a Level II, Sir."

"I'm on my way." The phone goes dead.

Adam Michner rubs his forehead. *Of all things to happen on my son's second birthday. Damn!* He goes back to his terminal and punches the keys some more. "So how long have you two been playing together, hmmm?" A series of codes and notes appear, and he curses again. "This is really not good." Adam positions the mouse over the print icon, and clicks. "Damn."

Hearing the doors and "Room, tensh-huh!" Adam turns. He greets

Captain Roberts by handing him the documents laying in the printer catch. "Sir."

Captain Roberts reads through the three pages, and tightens his jaw. "Two days?" Receiving a nod from Adam he continues. Finishing the last page, he rubs his chin. "Two days." He takes a couple of steps and then returns. "Is there a way to stop them?"

Adam points to the pages Roberts is holding. "Sir, countermeasures have been deployed, but the connection is stronger than they've ever been. See?" He points to the top of the last page. "Full memory recall by *both* sides."

Roberts reads again. "This has happened to these two six different times now? What's happened the other five times?"

Adam sits back down by his computer, and taps away. "Ah, the first was when they were approximately three years old, and it was dropped to both as a dream." More fingers flying and screens popping up. "Second and third time occurred during puberty years, a fairly normal occurrence, Sir." Adam relays. Backing out of that folder and pressing forward, he finds another incident. "The…ah fourth time was in reference to one of the two having her first sexual experience, also fairly normal."

Roberts pulls up a chair and sits next to Adam, watching the commands being given. "Do they realize it, that they've done this before?" Adam pauses. "I don't know. I'll check after this one comes up." The folder for the fifth opened. "Oh, creeps. They felt it for about a month, on and off. No trigger. That was only a couple of years ago."

"What? A month!" Roberts covers his mouth, thinking. "What stopped them?"

Adam continues to scroll through the information. Shaking his head, "None given…nothing. They just stopped."

"Do we know what was passed? Thought beyond self-awareness?"

Adam shakes his head, "No Sir. Our systems can't detect or track all thoughts and messages relayed. There is a reference, here, to 'power or energy' on all six incident files though." Adam sighs, "Other than that, we don't have anything."

Roberts stands up. "I need a classified copy of all you have on this matter within an hour." *Damn, there went my chance for lunch.*

Adam nods, standing up. *Damn. There went my boy's party.*

Jodie M. Swanson

CHAPTER 6

Adam stands gathering his thoughts, clutching the folder in his sweaty hands. Taking a deep breath, he raps once upon Captain Robert's door. *Damn, this job sucks*, he thinks hearing the hollow sound.

"Come in." Roberts sits at his desk. Piles of folders monitor his progress.

"Sir, I have the information you requested." Adam drops the folder onto Robert's desk. "It's not looking good Sir." Adam stands erect, waiting for Robert's reactions.

Captain Roberts pauses to read Adam's stern features before opening the file. Seeing no facial messages to be read, he opens the folder and starts. His eyes keep lifting to Adam's unwavering face as he takes his time reading through the contents of the file. After about ten minutes he tells Adam to sit, reading further.

Sorry Son, Happy Birthday. I tried. Damn, need a new job. Adam fights the urge to rub his forehead.

After the minutes cruise by, Captain Roberts sighs. "Says you are the lead on certain cases, including this one."

Adam recognizes the tone. "I am, Sir."

"How do you explain all this?" Roberts' has his back to Adam.

Adam looks down into his hands. "Sir, I can't. There's no explanation for all of these things to happen. We have no programming to interpret such volume on an individual case like this. This is too bizarre. No other records document such a find, or such retrieval." Adam relaxes, hoping the hard part is over. It wasn't his fault, none of it. "Sir, what do you recommend?"

Roberts seems surprised. "What do *I* recommend? Ida thought you'd have an idea on how to face this." Glancing at Adam's shocked look, Roberts waves a hand. "I have called a meeting with the 'Uppers' on this."

Roberts sighs. *Damn, this isn't going well at all. There goes Major.* He tries to organize the file before him. "We brief in three hours, in front of the Pentagon overseers."

"Sir?"

Roberts turns, and solemnly stares at the calendar upon his desk. "Sorry, Sergeant, but you need to be present for this. It's considered a matter of National Security."

Adam nods and steps out. His face contorts in both thought and anger. He goes back to the elevator and then back to his desk. *No rest for the weary.* Once there, he reopens his computer screen. *I hate this freaking place.*

Adam opens and saves files concerning "Rebecca." He hates this job, though many would have no clue. He has been signed into a Top Secret military field. At first he had thought the job a breeze. Be assigned a few "characters" and feed them certain programs at certain levels of their lives and document all possible aspects of their life and lives. He has been able to do the "homestead" thing, get equity in the home him and his wife and had bought. His eldest son is now enrolled in elementary school, and has lots of friends. His wife has a promising career in the Army and Air Force Exchange Service, and enjoyed her work. He never really cared about how he messed with others until lately. Morals and "should we" thoughts started getting in the way. Seeing the effects of implanting "false" dreams of an unfaithful spouse was disheartening. He knows the government was at fault for nearly four hundred military divorces. He himself had caused nearly forty, and that thought still makes him sick. His wife didn't know what he really did for his career, couldn't obviously, and that has added a strain for Adam. He hates the lies and deceit at home more than those of work. It just makes the job come home, on a personal level. Many times he wonders if that was what the government really wanted of him.

From experience Adam knows the military has the means to do a lot of controlling. *They can mess with weather. Heck, that's how they were able to rid themselves of a financially troubled Homestead Air Force Base. Cause a freakin' hurricane, and poof! Tinker Air Force Base and the lucky misses by tornadoes, please! Certain airline accidents, and the Space Shuttle explosion…the jerks.* Files of information had been laid before him upon taking up this job in order for him to "fully comprehend the severity and responsibility" of his tasking. *Who the hell wouldn't and can't understand that we fuck with people's minds?* Many files, many instances, and Adam is a part of it.

Seeing the base's Mental Health personnel on a regular basis does little to ease his guilt. Adam knows it is part of his job, and understood his obligations, put feels like crap inside. His joy in knowing his family would not and could not participate seems to be the only thing that kept him suiting up in his BDUs and Service Dress.

Taking a deep breath, Adam begins the menial task of going over his copy of the "Rebecca" file and starts taking more notes along the margins. With a few quick keystrokes, he opens up the computer's file to view the status, and hopeful of some changes. The "countermeasures" were usually nasty germs released in the home to allow distractions and redirection through dreams or nightmares. This time the illness sent was different, more powerful, and directed toward the family together, as a whole. It is a nasty flu this time, sometimes leading to pneumonia, which has been released into their home. Adam almost laughed at how easy it has been done. An experienced "part-time mailman" had delivered the mail that day. In no time, there was an open vial and the pouring of the contents onto the mail and the mailbox itself.

Phone calls and internet "tapped", all Adam has to wait now to see what would become of this. "Maybe she'll discount all of this as coming down with the flu." Adam shrugs, then rubs his face. "One can only hope."

While watching the information being transcribed on the computer, Adam stares blindly. The ring causes him to jump. With his heart pounding, he answers. "Sergeant Michner."

"Hi, Honey. Is everything okay?"

Exhaling a calming breath, Adam blinks. "Sure Cathy, everything is… well you know…hurry up and wait. How was the party?"

Listening to Cathy's voice babble on about the highlights, Adam mellows. She had such a calming quality about her when she knew he was stressed or unhappy. Many times she had instinctively known, as loving spouses sometimes do, when Adam had been on his last stress leg and tried to cheer him. Adam never knew how she did it, but counts his blessings daily for such an understanding wife.

"And Blake helped Jacob blow out the candles, by the typical spitting all over the cake." Cathy's laughter rings in Adam's ears. "I think you started something all those years ago with Blake. Doesn't seem a birthday cake can survive a party without a saliva shower. Jessica's girls were mortified!" More laughter echoes, and Adam feels compelled to join in. "Well anyways, you can watch it when you get home. Jessica taped it for you." A slight pause follows, "Adam?"

"Hmm?"

"Any idea when you'll be home?" she asks cautiously.

Adam takes a deep breath. "Nope, some bigwigs are coming down for that surprise-type inspection now. We're expecting them soon though. I was thinking you were the warning call." Adam forces a laugh.

"Oh, well, better not keep you then. I'll kiss the boys for you. Jacob's already passed out. Oh…wait."

"Daddy?" Blake's soft voice pulls at Adam.

"Hey there Sport. How was Bubba's party?"

"I spit on the cake for you."

Adam can't help it. Somehow between the laughing and coughing, he manages a "thank you." "That's very nice of you to keep tradition going Bud."

"Yeah, but Leslie started crying." Blake sounds so grown up. "She was saying the cake had boy germs." The boy's side of the line was quiet for a second, listening. "Daddy, are you laughing at me?"

"No!" Adam coughs out. "Not at all. It was just eating a sunflower seed and it's tickling my throat." Adam hears the "harrumph" on the other end. "What did you tell Leslie?"

"That they were better than girl germs." Blake is wise now to the sounds he hears on the phone. "It wasn't funny Daddy. She didn't want her piece, so her mommy had to eat it." Adam continues to choke while his sons adds, "Mommy says I gotta go. She says it's bedtime. Night-night."

"Night-night Sport." Adam holds the receiver until he hears the click, then hangs it up. "Night-night." Hand still poised above the phone yet, Adam is quick to pick it up during the first ring. "Sergeant Michner."

"Captain Roberts. They're here."

"Sir? Where are we meeting?"

"We're on our way down." The line goes dead.

Adam looks at the time on his computer screen. *Forty minutes early. Dang it!* Quickly, he reorganizes his copy of the "Rebecca" file, and stands for when they arrive. He just lost any joy in talking with his son, snapping back to the military bearing required. Sweat starts seeping from his hairline as he waits, watching the door. He hates the waiting, the not knowing who and what to expect.

The door opens with Captain Roberts leading the way. Standing at attention, Adam takes in the full entourage of an Army General Gurness, Air Force General Niler, and two civilians. Their critical eyes seem to scour the area, and then accuse as they rest upon Adam.

Captain Roberts approaches, and stands next to Adam, almost like support, as he introduces him. "This is Sergeant Adam Michner. He's the individual who has been working 'Rebecca' for eight years, and brought the matter to my immediate attention." Then he turns and introduces the four in turn.

General Gurness is overseeing any military mind experiments. To hear Gurness talk, he must have thought he invented Freud, Carl Yung, and Socrates. His introduction speech is prepared and to influence those he needed. He is obviously in charge as he introduces General Niler as his counterpart and liaison. Gurness then introduces the civilians as Daniel Maxwell and Jay Strebeck, the specialists who have been updating the programs and experiments to be run, the retrieval programs, and the all-around program gurus.

After the introductions, Gurness faces Adam. "We read the file on our way here. We understand you released a stronger countermeasure?"

"Yes, Sir. I felt the subject was too close to the other side, and a severe alteration may be achieved using the illness. It was delivered this afternoon. In experiments concerning this flu-measure, subjects seemed to respond more quickly, and easily, to redirecting programs administered in REM." Adam feels a bead of sweat trickle by his ear.

Gurness turns to Captain Roberts. "We also understand your shifts were up hours ago. Go home, and relax. We'll maintain vigil in shifts with you. Maxwell and myself will take over here until Sergeant Michner's return. Niler and Strebeck are to be on shift with him, starting at…?"

"Sergeant Michner's shift starts at eight, Sir," Roberts offers.

"0800 then. Goodnight gentlemen."

Adam nods and follows Roberts' lead. Once they were out of earshot, Roberts addresses him. "They are in control now. Do your best to follow them but don't counter them. These sons-a-guns are bad news."

"Yes, Sir." Adam feels that certain uneasy queasy all over again.

"Go home, and get some rest. Maybe this will be over in the morning."

Adam doubts it, but nods anyway. Together they walk through the underground corridor leading to the main building. OSI (Operations of Special Investigations) is there to do a random routine frisk to both men as they leave to ensure secret information isn't being removed. The inspections happened on and off, done by either OSI or Security Forces, so it is nothing new to the men.

"My bed will sure feel good tonight." Adam pulls out of the parking lot. Ten minutes later he pulls into his driveway. Cathy is waiting up.

Jodie M. Swanson

CHAPTER 7

"Chase? Would you stop on your way home and get some more Motrin for the kids. And maybe some cough medicine or something?" My head feels fuzzy. It's hard to make out what my husband says. Guess it's not important as I know he'll get what I've asked for anyway. Seems hard to focus as my head is still pounding despite the numerous Tylenol, Motrin, and aspirins I've consumed the last few days. "When are you getting home? I'm not doing well. I can't even stand up without having to lay down a few minutes later."

"I'll be home in little over three hours."

The rest Chase says is lost as pain racks my skull some more. Just the sound of his voice as he tries to reassure me that I can make it penetrates. "I gotta go. See you when you get home." *Help me!* I hang up hearing the dial tone take over the line. The walk to my bed seems horrendous as dizziness takes me. *Please help me, Hon. This has to be the worst I've felt in forever.*

My daughter lays next to me, her fever still in control of her little body. Gently, I pull away the sheet she once again has clutched in her hands. "Need to cool off Baby. You're hot." Her whimper hurts me some more. "I know Honey. I know."

Thankfully the day's been overcast again. On sunny days the light burns through the blinds and sears the back of my eyes. Still, the blinds are down and looking around seems painful. Closing my eyes seems little help with the throbbing going on.

A soft knock makes me open an eye. My son stands in the doorway, peeking in. "Mommy?"

"What Buddy?" Somehow I manage to smile through my grimace.

"Are you still hot?"

"Yeah Buddy. Mommy's not feeling good at all." The covers come up on me even though I keep them from my feverish girl.

"Do you want juice?" Seeing my head slowly shake, he tries again. "Do you want a cheese sandwich? Or some medicine?"

"Nah, no thanks Bud. I took some already. Do you need anything?" It hurts sitting up, but I want to make sure my son doesn't need me. *Oh please don't need me.*

He beams with pride. "Nope! I made a cheese sandwich and got my own juice. I'm watching a movie." Carefully, he starts shutting the door. "Night Mommy."

Smiling a bit, I relax into my pillow again. Pride fills me over my proud son's actions. *Coming in here to check on his old lady. Bragging about his ability to fend for himself. What a miracle kids can be.*

Now my head hurts too much for any more pride. Rest is what my body needs. *And about twenty more Tylenol.* My eyes feel like they are about to explode as I pass under the power of this illness once again.

Strange visions fill my feverish sleep. Images of fairies trying to help me through mazes trying to help me feel better comfort me. Following their whispers, I almost believe they are helping me fight. They seem to guide me to health, and pull me in different ways. But then again, I am feverish.

Then throughout these "sickmares" there is the feeling of falling, and demons. Their hot breath in my face sweat cakes my hair and makes my own breath stink. Angry hands grab my skull and squeeze. Then they pull painfully at my skin. Chains pull my body across the racks and my back cramps in pain some more.

Faces of strangers and of another place compound my migraine. Symbols on computer screens and bright lights hurt my eyes even as I dream. Angry voices and bright lights, a cruel place I wish to leave. *Will this nightmare ever cease?*

Hours pass in seconds, and seconds pass in hours as I see strange places, images, and people. A foot curling into my stomach as soft whimpers catch in my ears and pull me awake. She's still warm, and asleep though tossing her arms to fend off the awful images and things which recently visited me. "Poor little baby," I croak. Flailing an arm, my clumsy hand finally comes in contact with her sippy cup. "Take a sip Sweetie."

"Mommy?"

Glancing up, I see my son again in the doorway. "Hey Jay. Whatcha need?" My elbows feel like they are about to collapse beneath me.

"Daddy called and said he's coming home."

"Thanks Bud. I didn't even hear the phone ring." My elbows give out.

Soft padded feet make their way to my side. A cool hand gently touches my forehead. The contact hurts, but I don't flinch too much. "You're still hot. You need some more medicine." A pulling back of the covers guarantees I won't be getting away without taking something.

"Yes Doctor Jay." Sitting up against the dizziness, I force a smile towards him. He gently grabs my hand and "helps" pull me to my feet. "Thank you for your help." Another smile is bestowed upon a beaming face.

The few steps to the bathroom make me few nauseous. My hand raises to steady my head as I sit on the toilet seat, slash Doctor's care chair. "This one?" Jay holds out another bottle of Tylenol for me. Rummaging through some more containers, he comes up with vapor rub and cough medicine as well.

Heeding doctor's orders I take the pills and the syrup as he rubs the vapor rub on my back and neck. "Thank you Doctor Jay."

Crying in the room next door causes me to sigh. "Sister's up."

"Does she need more medicine too?" His expression is overly hopeful.

"Daddy needs to buy some more. She's out already. But thank you for offering to help." His hair gets a tousling. "Besides, we don't want you to get sick with this. You got lucky with being sick just that one day. Let's not jinx you okay?"

Jay nods as he heads back towards the living room. "Night Mommy."

Gently, I close my bedroom door. Joanna is soaked with sweat, as is the area all around her. Her sunken eyes flitter open and shut. Soft cries are coughed out of her chapped lips. "It's okay Honey. Mommy's right here. Daddy will be home with some more medicine in a few minutes." Gently running my fingers through her tangled hair, her cries quiet some. "It's okay."

Once Joanna mellows more, the covers beckon me. *What can I do?* The warmed blankets lure me back into "sleep". Again time seems changed.

Jodie M. Swanson

CHAPTER 8

Lying on my mat, I think. Meditation comes easily, like a dream, allowing time to pass for my small minutes. The energy flows around me, a warm blanket enveloping me. Branches of my mind twirl and twinkle, reaching out and in. Thoughts of purpose and being fill me, and I am almost aware of all things.

But this time I have a definite purpose, to find out about my dreams. My images are lacking again, and I feel a loss, and a...pain. Something feels cut, severed, and I know I must find out why. The dreams have stopped, and perhaps that is the reason of loss. Perhaps not. Gut feelings are important, I know, and the energy calls to me.

Slowly, unlike the dreams, I can make out the other world I seem to visit. Sweat pools on my brow, and I realize I am her. My form is ill, buried under blankets, wild hurt curling me. Deciding to take control, I open my eyes. A little sweating girl is curled beside me, covers off of her shivering form. The knowledge that she needs to stay cool comes to me as the reason, spoken as a hurt whisper. "Who are you," the whisper comes again, louder this time.

Slowly, I ease in a thought, *I am us. We are one.* The tired sick mind seems accept this as fact, letting go to the fever so I again affect control, sitting up. Pain is a new feeling, a true discomfort not known before. Somehow it feels as though it's not new, just forgotten. Making my legs work, I see where I live. Upon entering a room filled with a screen showing pictures, a sleeping boy greets my eyes. His gentle features bring a soft smile to my face. *Oh, we have so much love here. So much potential.* Kneeling, I brush my fingers across his face, and trace the falling hair. "So beautiful." Backing away so not to disturb the form, I watch the images on the screen.

39

Time flies as I watch drawn images portray live angles and possibilities cross with lights. Some humorous thoughts contrast any of negative insight. *How interesting.* So lost in this I don't notice a man approaching me.

"How are you feeling?" The voice weighs of concern.

This is what I've missed. Look at the concern and love there. Wistful thoughts flicker for a second, before I refocus on the man before me. I have to think to hear what he said. His movements are more noticeable and discerning. *Not back to bed. I'm learning.*

My body almost struggles, until her voice comes forward through me. "I feel strange Chase."

Gentle hands still urge me back to the bed. "Come on Babe. Let's go." Before I know it, covers are on me. So calming with their softness and comfort. The feel is nice, and I am lost in it for a few moments.

Mustering more energy, I leave the body to journey more into its mind. Vivid memories come forward like the pictures on the screen. Different screens appear, different memories, and I stay transfixed. It's like looking into a mirror at times, seeing the images and knowing I've had such similar dreams on and off. *Bizarre.*

The energy speaks to me, calling me back into myself. My time is coming to an end here. The withdrawal is careful, and almost sad. *So much potential.*

My breathing is shallow when I wake. Closing my eyes again, I let the feel of my experience wash over me. After a few minutes I sit up. A smile comes to my face. "I am two." *How odd.*

Feelings of enthusiasm race through me, and I long to share my "meld" with Shadow. Briskly I step through my little portal to the stone steps, and look for her. She is resting her head back upon the wall where she usually greets me each day. Not caring if anyone was around, I call to her. "Shadow!"

She looks at me with a tentative smile. "How'd it go?" Her movement is fluid as she jumps down to stand beside me. Taking a look at my face, she smiles. "Well, spill the beans."

We climb the remaining steps to the road. "It was amazing! If you hadn't suggested I try it, I probably never would have thought it!"

"And you think you are so smart."

"Nice." My eyes roll for emphasis.

"What did you say? 'Nice?'" Shadow coughs. "Is that how she speaks?" At my nod, she laughs, "Oh brother." After a few more chuckles, she's ready to listen.

"It took a lot of concentration. I could feel the energy fill me and move me. It was so exhilarating! When I was aware, I was her again, as if I were dreaming. She was in bed, sick I guess."

"Sick?" Shadow seems concerned.

"I guess. We talked a bit, when she felt me and my thoughts. It was so neat! There was her daughter, sick also, shivering, and she told me that the covers were off to help the girl fight the fever. Then she asked who I was."

"And?"

"I think I told her we were one." My thoughts try to focus. "She let go of herself, somehow, and I kind of…controlled her body."

"Controlled? How?"

Pausing in mid stride I wonder. Glancing at her I offer, "I just did. I got up and looked around her domicile. Her son was asleep, and I touched him. It was wonderful."

Closing my eyes, I can still feel the warmth of the young boy's skin and the silky feel of his hair. Hoping Shadow may feel this, I allow her probing thoughts. Not feeling her presence, I open my eyes. She just watches me, so other "memories" come forth. "There was this screen that had drawn images of light moving, telling…stories, I think. I watched, and then her man came in." Shadow probes some now. "Such emotion there in him. Concern and love. I wanted it to go on. She answered right through me too."

"You mean herself."

"My control of her body form." Shrugging, I continue. "I felt her, went into her and her mind. It was like looking at me in a different life." A thought comes again. "There was so much potential for her, for them. It felt stifled."

"Like the people here?"

"Yeah, like that, but different. She knew, or knows, of it." Shaking my head I wonder if I'm making sense.

"Not really," Shadow offers.

"Nice. Don't even get my thoughts out."

"You picked up some new behaviors. Interesting." Shadow reads my features carefully. "Are you jealous?"

After a moment's reflection. "No, I don't think I am. I just enjoyed it so. Seeing her son, touching him without a single flinch, and the touch of a concerned man." Sighing, the jealousy comes. "Maybe I am some. But there wasn't… the energy, like…not what I have now." Frowning a bit, "But there was the potential, just…I don't know."

"Was the energy displaced, as love, or what?" Shadow is trying to help extract meaning.

"Some love, some seemed lost…undeveloped." My head seems to become a swirl of thoughts. "Yes, undeveloped would best describe it." After a few more steps, "That's all I guess."

"Do you want to do that again?"

Without hesitation, "Definitely." Looking around, I see it's much later than I had first thought. "My, the day is late. Hadn't thought it'd take that long."

My shadow laughs. "I was beginning to wonder if I'd have to break in and rescue you." My laughter is the only one heard to the man we pass. I nod anyway, still chuckling as she continues. "Who knew if she had you captured, or if you got lost. I mean, if you had, then who would I bother?"

"My father?"

Her phantom-like shoulders shake. "Ugh! No thanks. I prefer intellect."

"Oh-ho! A compliment? How unlike you, Kim."

"Who?" Shadow is still. Her face is grave.

"What?"

"Who did you call me?"

Taking a few seconds, I recall the name. "Kim." My frown keeps her quiet. "Kim. I don't know. It just seemed right." Seeing Shadow's frown, I apologize. "Sorry, guess Rebecca's got a friend like you around."

"Nice," she mimics now with a smile.

"Pugh! You! And I truly thought you were offended." Putting my hand up, "Whatever!" My stride seems to pick up.

"'Whatever?'" Her laughing is contagious. "Such a vocabulary! You really did join with this other world didn't you?" It's a rhetorical question, and I know it. It feels nice though to banter with her. I almost feel like...a real person. "It is nice, isn't it?"

Smiling, I pause to gaze across the water. "Sure is." The sun's colors reflect patterns as the water moves. The normal feeling of calmness felt when gazing at the water seems intensified, and mixes with some joy. "Hours went by though."

Her phantom form stands beside me. "Many." Quietly we watch the locals on the beach and the movement of the water. "There is your father." Taking a calming breath, I follow her gaze to see him sitting alone on the beach looking across the water. "I don't think I've ever seen him there before, have you?"

Not that I can recall.

"Want to chat with him?"

Not really. Let him be. Sighing I lift my gaze as the breeze plays with my hair. *Let him alone and let him feel how desolate feels.* Soft whispers of birds tickle in my hair-teased ears. Closing my eyes, I feel content, calm. *Peaceful at last.*

"It's you!"

The voice brings me about with a start. *Oh my.*

"Is that him?" Shadow asks knowingly.

It is. Glancing around, I see a few locals glance towards me. "Hello."

"You are a hard woman to find. I've asked for you, but one knew how to find you." He takes a few steps closer until he is within a few feet.

"But you did warn me, didn't you?"

"He's cute."

Sssshh! You're no help at all. "People here don't want to know about me. I am not...up to their standards."

"Yeah, you're higher," she snorts.

"Yeah, you're higher," he says in turn.

"What?" Hearing Shadow's voice with my own reinforces the belief that I heard him correctly. This time alone, "What did you say?"

"That you're higher." He seems perplexed. "None of them would have tried to save that baby. At least it didn't look it to me."

"You tried to save the girl. So why wouldn't others do the same." My stance is guarded, ready to run or fight.

"It seems that they were more into...I don't know." He gazes pass me towards the water. "I don't know." His eyes come back to me. "It just seemed the thing to say. I'm sorry if I startled you."

His presence is making me nervous, but my phantom is watching me squirm with great relish. *Keep quiet!*

"Didn't say anything." She laughs.

"Why have you been looking for me?" My voice cracks a bit, but my stance is unwavering.

"I don't get it." He looks towards the water again. "The night of the festival, I have some questions." Shadow stiffens with me. "Are you a witch?"

Blinking, I try not to laugh. "I've never been asked that before." Thinking of what to say without lying, I decide the best course of action is to question him. "Why would you say that?"

His eyes bore into mine. "The baby at the beach. Then when we danced, it felt...off, yet planned. Then when I followed and tried to talk to you...I felt it, the words...'a touch of magic'. Are you a witch?"

"Be careful Rebecca."

My eyes turn in surprise to my shadow. *Rebecca?* It seems so long ago, and so coincidental that the lady from another world is named as I am. My shadow just nods.

"Well?"

Squaring my shoulders, I fully meet his look. "I am known to do what is called magical things. I do not consider myself a witch." Pursing my lips I forge ahead. "I told you I was different. I didn't mean to offend, and therefore apologize." A curt nod, then I turn my back. *Water, comfort me. Serenity, please.*

"What do they call you?"

Laughing I turn back to him, "Strange, weird, scary, a freak." Tears begin to well in my eyes as I say these things aloud. "That is what they call me."

He makes a face, turning his lip, eyes still on mine. "I'm Derk." His hand comes up as if friendly.

"He wants to shake hands!"

Sparing a nervous look towards my companion, I hesitantly reach out. "I had the name...Rebecca, years ago."

His hand takes mine, and begins to pump it in the normal hand shake fashion I had seen from afar. But my thoughts are on the feel of his hand, the warmth and power there. *Potential.* Looking into his eyes, then back towards Shadow, and back again. Touch, for me. The feeling is so... comforting, I don't want it to end. The release of my hand by his causes me to look at my again empty palm. His strength still ebbs there. *Nice.*

"So, Rebecca, if you are not a witch, what would you call yourself?" Looking towards Shadow all I receive is a phantom's shrug. "Is there something or someone you're waiting for?"

"I beg your pardon?"

His glance isn't on me though. It is scanning the area where he had seen me look. "You keep looking this way, and I was wondering if I'm keeping you." His eyes again. Such interesting eyes.

"I...I have a friend. A single friend here, that...can see you."

"What are you doing?" Shadow throws up her hands in disgust. "Don't ruin this! He likes you, at least a little."

It's not good for him. Better to scare him away. "Her name is Shadow, and she stands here beside me." The challenge is there before him and I stand awaiting his response.

"An...an invisible friend?" He snorts.

"You take me at my word my name is Rebecca. You have seen things you cannot explain. And yet...?" My words hang, another challenge.

His eyes again pierce mine. "Shadow, huh?" At my nod, he shakes his head. "Strange is right."

Tears threaten, and I turn back to the water. I hear movement behind me, the sound of retreating feet on the gravel. Blinking, some moisture begins to fall.

"Why Rebecca?" She tries to comfort me, but it doesn't help. "He hasn't left yet." Slowly I turn towards where she faces, and see him about fifteen feet away, watching me. "I'll show him!"

Seeing her march off, I call out aloud, "No, don't! Shadow, stop!" My mouth snaps shut as he shakes his head. *Oh, he's in for it.* Transfixed, I watch my phantom friend kick Derk in the shin. His doubling over to grab the offended leg makes me laugh. But apparently my friend has a point to make. She pushes him as he tries to balance himself and this injury. The result is him falling over into the small stones. "Stop Shadow. It's not his fault." Briskly, I walk over to where they are. *Stop this now,* I look sternly at her.

"He needs to know you are telling the truth." She tosses back her mane of hair, and dusts off her hands.

And what if he thinks I did that? Then what? Reaching down I offer to pull him up to his feet. "I'm sorry. She usually doesn't do that."

He sits there on the ground, gingerly rubbing is shin. "Invisible, but vicious."

Jodie M. Swanson

CHAPTER 9

Adam looks around nervously. His decision has been hard, but he feels it a necessary one. Across him is his wife, dressed for going out to dinner. Her calmness is just a façade he knows. He had told her he needs to talk to her, about something important, and to get a sitter. She has no idea what he was going to say, but none-the-less she is here. He has to get this off his chest. With one last look, he takes the fortifying deep breath. "Let me start with…I love you Cathy."

Tears well in her eyes. "Did you have an affair?"

Stunned, he pulls back. "What?" Disbelief crosses his features.

Cathy sits up in her chair, trying not to let the tears fall. "Are you having an affair?" Her eyes meet his briefly.

Adam shakes his head, and takes her hand. Feeling her pull away, "No Cathy. Look at me, Babe. No. This is…," he looks around some again, "…concerning work. I can't hide this anymore." Seeing her questioning look, he adds, "My job isn't exactly what you've been led to believe." He leans forward, and whispers, "It's a top secret type job I have. Please laugh for appearances. I don't know if I've been followed." He sits back a bit. "I always wonder if I am, or if you are. I can't live with these secrets anymore. I work as…well, like a Behavior Mm…Manager. I adjust people's behaviors with…implanted thoughts."

Cathy sits, mouth parted. "What are you saying?"

Adam can't meet her gaze. "I fuck with people's lives." Hearing her gasp he continues. "The government controls some fifty thousand or so individuals, all American citizens that I know of. It started about thirty years ago with the idea of mind control, and has continued some. Mostly now it's the monitoring and…programming that's done."

Cathy glances around in disbelief. "Mind control? Having an affair was better." She stands up. "I want to go home."

Adam gently holds her hand. "It's the truth, please believe me. For the last...many years, I am in charge of about eighty...minds. Half of them I had to implant things which caused divorce. I am not happy, have hated doing this. My only comfort has been knowing they haven't done anything with us." He catches her doubtful look. "Any of us. I have checked files, and know it for certain. I also know what to look for, and we don't have it, thankfully. But you have to believe me in this. It could get me a court martial, discharged, the whole nine yards, just for telling you."

Cathy sits back down. "Why? Why have you hide this?"

Adam sighs. "It's the job. A horrible job." Seeing the waiter begin his approach Adam smiles. "Please act natural, just in case we are watched." As the waiter stops at the table, Adam let go of her hand. He silently applauds her ability to control her facial features while they place their orders. Once the waiter left for their drinks, he reaches for her hand.

Cathy doesn't give it. "How? How did you cause those people to divorce?" She feels angry and hurt, and it reflects in her hissed whisper.

"By...implanting ideas when the subj-...people were in REM. They have little like...radio transmitters in which we...code things and send them out. It's fairly easy, but we really shouldn't have. So many people." Adam fades away as their waiter approaches bearing their beverages. "Thank you."

Cathy glances around, taking in some of the other patrons. "We really could have been followed? At any time?" She glances back to his face. "Even at home?"

Adam frowns. "Probably in some areas of the house, like the office. The living room, and stuff like that. Just to be sure I'm doing my job and not talking about it." Seeing her red face, he reaches for her again. "I'm sure we're okay. Besides, that's what I need to also tell you. I want out of this. My enlistment is up in four months. My CJR rip came down a few months back, and I haven't decided for sure what to do...or say."

Cathy looks down into her lap. "What happens if you do leave? Will we still be watched?"

"I don't know. I can't even say for sure if we have been. But I need to include you on this so you know what I feel I'm up against. I really don't think I can do this for much longer than four months. Something's happened, above and beyond what normally happens. That's why I missed the party two weeks ago." Adam nervously sips his water.

"One of yours?" Cathy whispers. At his nod, "Suicide?"

Adam chuckles. "No, far, far worse, though that has happened to me, twice." At Cathy's shocked look, "Only one was partially my fault. I caused a bad childhood memory, and well...I lost him." Adam's face reflects a genuine sadness. "That was two years ago. He was a…lost case." Adam shrugs his shoulders as he meets Cathy's eyes. "Anyways, this is actually a matter of national security, so I'm told. I think I need a favor, or a friend's favor. I need to reach one to of mine, out of work bounds, so to speak. She lives two lives, sort of. The mission with her is…controlling, and learning of…energy, and potential."

"What do you want to do?" Cathy leans forward a bit.

Adam smiles. "I need to talk to her in person, and see if she knows… things. I'm thinking I'll ask about an approach approval. I know it's done, but rarely. Usually things are set up, and…I don't know if they'll let me, being short."

"But they don't know you're short, do they? You haven't told them you don't want to reenlist, or have you?"

"No, they don't really know." Adam runs his hands through his hair.

Cathy smiles seeing their salads fast approaching. She smiles to Adam. "Thanks for suggesting dinner Honey. It's been awhile."

The next half-hour is spent conversing on the subject of the process of the actual implanting. After that, Cathy turns the discussion over to family and recent happenings that Adam has been missing due to the extra hours put in. As she fills him in on regular table talk, Adam feels as if he'd been relieved of a great burden. The scorn in which he'd braced himself for had come and gone, better than he had hoped. He smiles in retrospect over the idea of him cheating on her. As he listens, she runs down some options for job searching for either of them. He hasn't realized she'd been involved with searching for these kinds of things before, and says so. She shrugs her shoulder, "Well, one never knew when you were, or if you were, coming home."

"Funny," Adam pretends to take a fork to her person. "Soon, you won't be able to keep me away." He smiles back at her. *It's going to be good being near her and the boys.*

After paying their bill, Adam bends to kiss her. He whispers first, "Just in case, no more on this." Then he opens the door to head for the car. *I feel better.*

Reaching home, Adam is surprised and nervous to see Strebeck waiting for him. Cathy questions who the man is, and Adam offers for Strebeck to hear, "Oh, that's Jay. He's the new guy at the shop. What's up man? Wife kick you out for moving her here already?"

Strebeck quickly jumps on the explanation, "Kind of. Seems I forgot something at work that I had for her, including my keys to get back in…my office. I remembered where you said you lived, and have been waiting for you to see if you could help. I only got here about ten minutes ago, and was told you'd be along. Sorry to interrupt your night off. "

Cathy now understands. "Go ahead Adam. I need to help Blake with his homework. Let me know if I should stay up or call a locksmith for you." Cathy chuckles as she heads up to the door. Then she looks back. "It was nice meeting you." Turning to Adam, "See you soon." Then she is through the door.

"What's up?" Adam rather likes Jay, as he seems personable, and not a lover of the program either. Jay Strebeck has been told to stay another two weeks to ensure no more problems arose. The three others had left after a week of surveillance.

Jay just approaches. "Your car or mine?"

"I guess mine. Hop in." Adam feels butterflies as he fastens his seatbelt. He waits for Strebeck to close the car door, then starts the engine. After a few blocks, "What's up?"

"They aren't supposed to be…entered. I've never seen anything like it!" Strebeck throws up his arms. "Completely new!"

"What do you mean, 'be entered'?" Adam relaxes, his paranoia at being busted at ease.

"Rebecca, she was like…entered. Remember when we described how her case dealt with energy and expanding the mind's potentials. Her half made contact, somehow, and seemed to…mix with Rebecca."

"What?" Adam tries to focus his thoughts as he drives. "Two is playing in One's realm? She got 'here'?"

Jay slowly turns. "Exactly."

CHAPTER 10

Roberts regards the two men before him. "Are you sure this is a good idea? Few actual meetings have proven beneficial towards the overall mission." He stands, arching his back. "Shoot, at this point I guess we should consider everything." A hard look is passed to the men. "Are there any other feasible options?"

"Sir, I think this may help us get an idea of what we are actually dealing with," Adam states. "Perhaps we're not needing to go any further with this pursuit if the subject doesn't fully comprehend what's happened." Pushing forward, "Besides Sir, we may learn more of what the subject interprets this way."

"How so?"

"By actually finding out what we cannot via the system. We might be able to find out what actually is happening when they connect. Then again, there may be nothing to find at all. I feel we won't know for sure unless we at least try this route." Adam states the last with emphasis.

Roberts turns, "And you agree with this?"

Strebeck nods. "Nothing like the systems is showing has happened has ever happened before. The best way may be to do a one-on-one study with the subject. Perhaps we are all at wit's end for nothing. Then perhaps, it could be something." Jay opens his briefcase. "In this circumstance we are thinking of using an easy, non-obstructive approach. If the subject can see past a ruse, complicated scenarios may result. Here's favorable list of choice the two of us came up with." A list is brandished from the briefcase. "Of course the final say here is up to you. Or it can be with those above you, if you prefer."

Roberts snatches the sheet of paper. "I'm hoping to avoid that gentlemen." Glancing through the short list, he rubs his upper lip. "Not many to choose from. Which did you two think would work best?"

Adam waves the question to Jay. "We think either the sales call for a personal survey, or the 'new to the neighborhood' idea, or a combination of something similar. There aren't many choices we think are operable in this case without more details from the subject."

"Befriend her?" Roberts sits down heavily. "Would I need to involve outside help? Or is one of you interested?"

Adam darts a look. "I may, but it'd be easier for a female, I think." He tries to pass off a feigned chuckle. "My wife would probably like this."

Roberts looks up sharply. "You're not to discuss any of these things, and you know that."

"Sir, I understand. I was just thinking aloud that my wife tends to take to meeting new people better than I."

"Meaning?"

Adam sighs. "I'll give it a shot."

"Better. Now, I want all of this kept at our level for the time being." Roberts takes in the list again. "You two come up with a way to meet this lady, and let me know what happens. I expect to be kept informed. Dismissed."

Both men mutter their thanks. Jay opens the door and leads the way. Adam closes the door behind him, then shakes his head. Remaining quiet, the men head back to Adam's terminal.

Once there, Jay reopens his briefcase and pulls out some notes. He scans for location information on the subject "Rebecca." Taking another piece of paper, he writes it down, then looks up to find her phone number. Recognizing the area code, he reaches for a map. The thought takes him by surprise, and he looks towards Adam. "She lives only fifty miles away?"

Adam just sits staring at the computer screen before him. A smile crosses his now relaxed face. "Yep." He taps at a few keys before facing Jay. "That close."

Jay blinks back. "That could work out even better! Your family wouldn't even miss you. You can do the trips during your shift. And I'll maintain the helm." He scribbles this down on the notes. "I can monitor if anything happens while you are out with her."

Adam hides his surprise. "You're not coming with me?"

Jay shrugs. "No need. I can call to do the actual setting up for you two to meet, if you'd prefer."

Adam nods. Butterflies start playing in his stomach for the first time. He had felt so sure about doing this until now. "What way are we going with this? The sales call then?" Receiving a nod, he continues, "For what purpose?"

Together the men try to work the issues of the purpose of their call, questions to be asked for the survey, and how to record the information. The idea starts seeming harder than they had originally thought. Most of their questions seem legit for the purpose of the survey, but they both had to agree, the ability to ask the necessary lead questions was getting hard.

Realizing they had missed lunch, they decide to take a break. Taking Jay's car, the two men arrive at the base's Burger King a few minutes later. After receiving their orders, they sit in a quiet corner.

"Why did you mention wanting to do this?"

Adam is startled by Jay's question. Taking a moment to reflect, he decides to answer with some honesty. "It's my responsibility. She's one of mine." He stuffs some fries in his mouth.

Thoughtfully Jay sips his Dr. Pepper. "Why volunteer to...?"

"Meet her?" Adam shrugs. "Guess curiosity about seeing her in real life versus via the computer screen's interpretation of her life. I've never met any of my cases." Adam smiles. "Hope I don't blow it. Cathy's so much better at this than I am."

"Is that why you said that earlier?" Jay takes a bite of his sandwich.

"Yeah. Cathy always seems in tune with people, especially in tense situations." Adam takes some more fries. "Maybe I'm not the best, capable person, but...."

Swallowing, Jay nods his understanding. "Why not let someone else do it then? It's not too late. I mean, if you're overly nervous about all this."

"She's my case. I don't want someone to mess up anything. I don't want to feel regret over it later."

"Like with Larry?" Jay says softly. Seeing Adam's surprise, he offers, "I had to be briefed on you and other cases. I was given authorization to find out more about you and some of your cases." He takes a sip before starting again, seeing Adam's downcast look. "What do you think went wrong there?"

"They didn't judge him right before...they implanted. He didn't have anything to offer." Adam sighs. "He wasn't a good candidate."

"Maybe that's why they used him, to see affects," Jay offers. "It wasn't your fault."

Adam shakes his head. "For two years, two years, I've been thinking of that day. He was mine for three years, so I felt like I knew him."

"Did the counseling help?" Mentally Jay kicks himself for letting that one slip. "Sorry."

Adam bit his lip. *Damn snoops.* "Not really. I was still the one who pressed the keys. I was the one who sent the command to send those implants." Adam stuffs some sandwich in his mouth, signaling he wants to stop talking about it. *Damn snoops, in a damn job.*

Jay takes a couple fries, feeling seven times a fool. He knows he has just lost some ground with Adam, and feels bad. Thinking for a while as the silence hangs, he wonders if Adam liked his job. Or if he wants to continue it. "Do you like this job, Adam?"

Adam practically snarls. "No! Causing divorce amongst honest relationships? Losing cases? Lying to my wife?" Adam thinks quickly. *There could be leading here.* Putting a fake smile on, Adam counters with, "At first it was neat! Having so much control, and the secrets. Staying here we have been able to get some equity in our home. The boys are able to have steady friends, not being moved every couple of years. The job has neat computer systems to work with. I've been able to make rank, somewhat. I don't know. Guess I'm still...upset about Larry. It's not too bad." Adam shrugs again, adding a smile for affect.

Jay studies Adam as he takes another few fries. He'll have to check to see if Adam has already applied to re-enlist. He'll also check that with Captain Roberts later today, as well as past evaluations. *Maybe you aren't the one for the job.* Jay does understand all of the emotions Adam had just portrayed, feels them too, but knows there is job to be done. If Adam is trying to sabotage the subject, then something needed to be done. He'd also have to check the files and notes more carefully. He decides to change the subject somewhat. "How did you meet Cathy?"

Adam takes it for what it is worth, hoping his recovery was bought. "Through a friend. She was working, had started going to college. We were introduced one night, and she kept telling me she wouldn't date a military man. She said she was a 'career-orientated woman.' I just think she didn't want to pick up and move all the time." Adam smiles as he crumples the sandwich wrap. "Somehow I convinced her to see me. The rest just came along the way." Adam finishes with a genuine smile. "How about you? Married?"

Jay polishes off his fries. "Was once. I found out she was part of the system afterwards." Jay lowers his voice. "I knew she seemed so smart, so in-tune with things. Her dreams were always so vivid." Jay shrugs in memory. "One day she found out what I really did...."

"How?" Adam prompts.

Jay meets his eyes. "I told her. I felt overwhelmed, maybe a lot like you're feeling. I just came out and told her one night when we had been fighting." Jay looks out the window. "She had called me the next morning saying she couldn't live with me any more knowing what I did. I thought she meant divorce. But, I received a call while I was still at work saying they found her body. She wasn't as strong as I...we all had thought." Jay lowers his teary gaze.

Adam reaches across the table. "I'm sorry."

Jay shrugs, saying it had happened three years ago. "Guess we have things in common after all, huh?" Jay sips again at his soda. Maybe he wouldn't check Adam out after all. If he wanted out, Adam has the right to. As long as he is doing his job, which Adam is, then there should be no reason to go further. "Guess we also better get back."

Adam nods as he collects his trash. Mentioning he wants a refill, he parts for a moment to get it. *Who would've thought Jay would be so involved with the system after such an experience? Poor man. Luckily I can leave, and I will.*

Jodie M. Swanson

CHAPTER 11

Don't hang up, don't hang up! Running to grab my cordless, I stumble again on Joanna's toys. "Gall dang it!" On the fifth ring I press talk. "Hello?" My breathing haggard, I hope that it's not some telephone company trying to get me to switch that has almost cost me my life.

"Yes, may I speak with Rebecca Stewart?" the man's voice asks.

"Speaking."

"I represent a surveying company. We are in your area taking surveys on everyday issues. Your name and number randomly appeared using our system, and we'd like to see if you would have any objections to completing a face-to-face survey?"

Recent e-mail messages come to mind concerning men forcing their way into women's homes or vehicles, attacks, etc. Cautious, "I'm not sure I understand. Who is this survey for?"

The man's voice seems robotic. "Miss Stewart, I am calling to represent a small government agency whose focus is the quality of life for everyday citizens. If you do not wish to participate, we understand. Please take into consideration that all information, including yours will be kept confidential, as we are an independent consulting company. We only offer a first name so the surveyor will know who to expect, for the survey. However, the agency does offer that the survey can be done in a few places. Some participants do choose the comfort of their own home. Would you consider this as a possible option Miss Stewart?"

No way am I letting a stranger in my house! "I'd rather not."

"Ma'am is that a not participate, or not in your home? Please remember that we represent a government agency, professionals dedicated to everyday quality of life issues."

The phone line goes quiet, and I feel put on the spot. "Are there other places you have the interviewing done?"

"Ma'am please hold as I look up certain public interviewing areas." There is the sound of keystrokes before the voice returns. "What day would be good for you? That way I may be able to narrow down a search for you Miss Stewart."

"Why can't I do this over the phone?"

The man seems like a robot. "Ma'am, I am not able to do phone surveys. As I mentioned, my job is to see if a selected nominee is willing to participate, and schedule a session." There are a few more keystrokes heard. "Is there a day and time that would work best for you? And keep in mind that I'm looking up information for public surveying areas, as that is what I'm detecting you'd prefer."

Thinking if I have anything planned, "I guess Wednesday afternoon I'm free." I hear some more keystrokes. "If that isn't available...."

"Actually-," the man's voice cuts me off. "I'm showing a two o'clock available at the Lotta Expresso Coffeehouse. Would you like that one, or would you like me to keep looking?"

"A coffee shop?"

The robot begins again. "Yes, Miss Stewart. This agency has their surveys done in relaxing atmospheres, to help relieve any tension a participant may feel prior to conducting the survey. And I'm sure the local businesses don't mind at all, considering the patronage they incur during surveys." His laughter is the first sound of human-like emotion from this man.

His responses make sense to me, so I agree to take that survey session. In the back of my mind I am making a note to see if Kim can tag along that day, just in case. She has mentioned the possibility of getting together that day anyway. Half-heartedly, I write down the necessary directions to the Lotta Expresso Coffeehouse. My nervousness about this causes me to ask. "And if I cannot make this for some reason? Say I get sick, or there's an emergency?"

"No need to worry ma'am. The surveyor will be there regardless, so you won't need to try and contact him. His name, so you know... is... Adam. If you'd like I can give you the number I have here for the Lotta Expresso Coffeehouse."

Indicating that I would like it, just in case, I jot the given numbers down. His voice still sounding robotic, the man goes through the thoughts of thanking me for my time. Thanking him, I hear the phone line go dead. Deciding better now than to forget, I quickly dial Kim's number.

On the third ring she answers. "Hello Bec!" Her caller-id gives me away every time. "What's up?"

"Not much. Just got a call to do a quality of life type survey

Wednesday afternoon, and was wondering if you were doing anything?"

"You too? I was called about ten minutes ago. I'm slated for something like 1:30. I was going to blow it off, but if you're going! Heck, we can get a sitter and go shopping afterwards!" She sounds so excited, so I agree and ask where she was having her survey done. "Some place called the Lotta Expresso Coffeehouse. Sounds cheesy, but guess we'll see."

"Glad you are going too. I wonder how many people they asked," my tone neutral. "Thankfully, I know someone else going. Who would have thought we'd have the same type call and be surveying at the same place? Seems too funny."

"Or weird," Kim hints. "What did she say to you?"

"It wasn't a woman. It was a man who had acted like he had said the same thing to hundreds of people all day." My curiosity is piqued, "Why?"

"Well, I guess nothing. I was kind of wondering if we had the same caller. If we had, that really would have been fishy. At least your guy seemed to know what he was talking about. This lady stumbled more times than I don't know what."

"Poor lady was probably on her first day and had to call you." I'm laughing until tears came to my eyes. "Poor thing! She probably wants to quit now!" My laughter continues as she counters.

"Hey, hey-hey! I'm not that bad. It's not my fault she kept stumbling over her cue cards!" Kim snorts with indignation. "You make me out to be some...witch."

"Nah, I just know you, ya meanie," I say before I laugh some more.

"Knock it off," she teases. "So? What time are you slotted for?" After hearing my time was at two, she feigns a suspicious tone. "Two, eh? Hmm. Do you think they suspect we're friends?"

Laughing, I dissuade her from that. "With the way you put me down? No. No one would ever make that mistake."

"I'm hurt!"

"Nice, it's about time!" My laughter blends with hers. "Besides, I was told I was randomly selected as like some sort of nominee."

"Sure, you got the one who knew what he was saying. This lady just kept rambling 'I'm sorry' and 'Let me ask my supervisor'. I was so ticked." Kim's disgust is obvious.

Still laughing, "I'm surprised you even agreed then."

"Told you," she sounds so stern, "I was going to blow them off. But now! It's an opportunity for a lady's day out!" Her voice sounds happier than she really is, I know, but it's still funny. "Well, I better run. I need to get Vandy some medicine. I knew Chase should have put you out to pasture or put you down when you were so sick. Just seeing you the other day she picked something up."

"Sorry, but we had been over it by then." Not really sure if she's kidding or not, I sound sincere anyway.

"Uh-huh. Whatever."

"Brat!" Knowing now she is joking, I let her have it. "There I was on my deathbed, having demons and fevers tear at me for days on end, and you're conspiring to have me put to sleep!"

"Yeah, basically." Her laughter is contagious.

"Nice. You better get going then." Hanging up the phone, I shake my head at my friend. *What a meanie.* Smiling, one of our other conversations comes to mind when Dennis had called Kim mean. She told me she couldn't believe that the two people who knew her best had called her that. Dennis had told her to take the hint. Still chuckling, I get back to trying to clean up the house, and Joanna's toys.

Jay sets the phone down and takes a deep breath, exhaling loudly.

Adam pats him on the back. "That was good! Ever think of working for those magazine sales people? Or the phone companies?" Still laughing, Adam stops the tape recorder. "You sounded like you knew what you were doing."

Jay offers a small smile. "Thanks. Hopefully she'll show." He runs his fingers through her hair. "Did Sergeant Trevor get her call out?"

Adam smiles as he rolls his chair closer to Jay. "Yep, but she kept stuttering so badly over her lines. I felt so sorry for her. I was thinking if *you* couldn't do it, *I* wasn't going to show." Tapping a few keys, Adam looks to check the Stewart phone line. "Call going out, to…Kim and Dennis Lewis. Bam. Bet it's a done deal."

Jay looks at the number and smiles. "That's what we were banking on." Tapping his fingers on his briefcase, "Good, good, good. Now let's get *you* ready." He gets up.

Making a face Adam shrugs, "I guess a deal's a deal. Why did we go through with this?" Adam's dry laughter denotes his tension, but he follows Jay.

The men go into another office. Once there, Jay opens his briefcase and takes out the third draft of their makeshift questionnaire. Together they go over questions again, making sure they sound legit, and will serve their intended purpose. The process takes longer than the two had originally thought, and they jump when they hear a knock at the door. Adam glances at his watch, "Oops. 'Briefing time.'" He gives his best Captain Roberts before opening the door. "Hello Sir, we were just about to brief you."

Roberts lifts his eyebrows, indicating he has heard what Adam had said, prior to opening the door. Offering a small smirk, he enters, closing the door behind him. "Good. Did everything go as planned?"

Adam nods. "Sergeant Trevor first contacted an acquaintance of the subject in order to establish rapport and an interview, a survey actually. Then Jay contacted the subject to also get an interview. The two women actually scheduled for the same day, Wednesday, and around the same time. We monitored the Stewart phone line hoping she'd make contact with her friend as some sign of 'guarantee' that the subject would indeed show as she agreed to. A call was made. We feel confident that the women will be there."

Roberts nods in response. Turning to Jay he questions the validity of the survey in acquiring the desired data. He listens as Jay and Adam go over the entire survey, highlighting the purpose of each question. After about an hour of discussion, he claps his hands together once. "Hot damn! You may have it here! If she does show, I believe you two did indeed find a good way to measure whatever you call it that you want to measure." The twinkle in his eyes gives away his joking. Standing up, he nods. "Let's keep our fingers crossed for…Wednesday, is it?"

"Yes, Sir. We're looking for a show time of fourteen hundred," Adam offers optimistically. "Jay and I will brief you after we organize the results."

Roberts nods again, then heads for the door. "Good work gentlemen. Let's keep our fingers crossed that everything is as it should be." The door closes behind him.

Jay relaxes a bit before the computer screen. Going into a database program, he quickly designs the "survey", and print up thirty copies.

Adam looks perplexed. "Why so many?"

"Well," Jay begins. "If your Adam the Survey Collector, you should have some surveys, as well as some completed, don't you think? Here." Jay hands some to Adam. Start filling them out, mostly the tops and front part, as they'll be in folders. Let's put red X's on the last one, in a lower corner, so we know these are dummies." Taking a red pen from his briefcase, Jay starts doing just that. Then he hands the marked surveys to Adam.

Adam glances at his watch as he grabs a pen. "Okie-dokie." After about thirty minutes he is finished. When the dummies were in the "completed" folder, he has to agree that this looked pretty legit at a glance. A separate folder holds some of the empty survey forms.

Jay smiles as he stands up, cracking his back. "Not bad. Tomorrow we'll go over the stuff you'll be doing one last time." Seeing Adam's "Whoop-tee-doo" look, he laughs. "Hang in there. Who knows maybe you'll get another Oak Leaf Cluster for your Achievement Medal, or something." Then he leaves the office.

Adam nods, taking a deep breath. *I just this over and done with, then I want out. Keep the stupid medal.* He has to admit though, this is the most fun he has had with this job in years.

Jodie M. Swanson

CHAPTER 12

Kim and I belt out our slightly off-key rendition of the song on the radio. Nearing the Lotta Expresso Coffeehouse, Kim finds a parking spot, but doesn't turn off the engine, so we can finish singing the song. At the last note, she turns down her volume, then turns off the engine. Taking a deep breath, she looks at her watch. "Well, it's almost 1:30." She reaches for her purse.

"Do you still think this is legit?" My voice seems to quaver a bit with doubt. "I mean, it is odd we both were called and are here, don't ya think?"

Kim shakes back her shoulder length hair. "Well, if it's not they are in for a piece of my mind. And either way we got a day without the kiddos. Come on. Let's go have a cappuccino." With that she opens her door, purse in hand. Following suit, I wait on the curb as she hits her remote keyless entry to lock her doors. The werp, werp signifies her car is secure. Together we head in.

Upon entering, we look around for a possible sign or booth or something. Not noticing anything overly obvious, we look at the people present. One man stands out alone, sipping his steaming drink as he looks through a few folders. He glances at his watch, and towards the door. Seeing us, he tentatively smiles then looks down at his folders again.

"You're first." Nudging Kim forward. "I'll get the cappuccinos." Discreetly, I watch Kim stride toward the man. Seeing her sit down, I take it she's found the surveying Adam. While ordering, I occasionally glance their way to see Kim is now appearing relaxed. Thanking the server, I head towards the table and carefully set her warm cup near her. "Here ya go." Kim thanks me. Adam smiles up at me, before turning back to the survey. Backing away a bit, I take a seat by the small television to wait out my turn.

Generally, I don't watch much television, but CNN is okay as I find the headlines and sub lines interesting from time to time. Today a disturbing sub line about a young teenaged boy charged with assault against his teacher catches my eye. I wonder if the surveying agency watches CNN. "They could learn a lot by just watching this, and judging their own reactions," I muse aloud while sipping.

Glancing towards my friend, I see they are still taking the survey, even though it's nearing my time of two o'clock. Deciding on another cappuccino, I go towards the register again.

"So, what's the deal with that guy?" The server cocks her head in Kim's direction as she makes my drink.

Smiling, I reach for some more money. "It's some sort of quality of life survey, I guess. We got called a couple of days ago." Handing her the money, "Have many been in here?"

She shakes her head. "Nah, he just showed up about an hour ago, organized his folders and ordered some coffee. He kept looking at his watch, and I was beginning to wonder what was up. Here's your change."

Thanking her again, I make my way back to my seat. Her words came back to me. "Just an hour ago?" Checking my watch proves it to be just past two. I wonder if he was supposed to have a person show at one o'clock. *Guess lots of people ditched this.*

"Completely painless." Kim's voice gives me a visible start. "Re-lax!" Chuckling she sits across from me. "Just some mumbo-jumbo about life, goals, and dreams. Piece of cake."

"Thanks for the encouragement, 'Mom.'" Standing up, I reach for my cup. "Brat. Can't take you anywhere." Shaking my head, I turn towards the man sitting filing Kim's survey. Reaching him, I say that I'm supposed to have a two o'clock with him.

He searches a list of people for the coffeehouse for Wednesday, at two. "Is your first name Rebecca?" At my nod, he smiles. "Please have a seat." Reaching into a folder, he pulls out a survey. "Okay, my name is Adam. I'm a representative of an agency collecting information about the quality of life issues, as well as everyday issues.
The agency feels honesty is better achieved by face-to-face type surveys." He adjusts the survey before him. "You two friends?" He indicates Kim reading a newspaper where I had been waiting.

"Actually, yes."

"How odd! Randomly done survey, and both of you are called, and meet the same day? Right after each other? What are the odds of that happening?"

Adam seems genuine, so I agree. "We thought it odd ourselves." Shifting in my seat, "And as for honesty, she probably wouldn't have shown up if I hadn't called her to come along with me."

"Well, thanks for coming. Not many show up. She did say she almost didn't."

"Yeah, I heard you've been here since about one. A no show, huh?"

Adam covers his surprise. "Yeah, I was to meet someone at one, and one at three. We'll see if they come or not." Placing his folders aside, "Are you ready to begin? She said at the end of her survey that I'd find yours more interesting." He chuckles lightly. At my nod he reads a consent to interview for benefit of the surveying agency, then asks for my consent to continue. Receiving it, he marks the appropriate box.

Some of the questions he asked were easy. What kind of neighborhood do you live in? Do you work outside the home? Do you have a home-based business? Are you married? Do you have kids? Blah, blah, blah. Feeling sorry for the poor man who had to read through these questions to anyone who actually showed up, I relaxed with these.

Then there were some different, more personal questions. Have you lied to someone you trust? Have you ever cheated on a spouse or significant other? Do you like making a spectacle of yourself in public? My face must have given away my surprise for each question, as he smiled at my indignant "No" each time.

Some of the questions seemed almost psychiatric. Do you have fanciful dreams? When I asked what that meant, I was told it was wanting what wasn't real, or couldn't be real. Shaking my head no, I wasn't ready for the next. "Do you have dreams of different lives?"

"What?" Confused, I look at his calm face. "What do you mean? Like reincarnation and that stuff?"

"Sure." His pen was waiting to make a mark.

"Sure, I guess you can call them that." Nervously, I shift again in the seat.

"Do you remember your dreams?"

"Vividly."

His pen marks my answer. "Do you dream in color, or black and white?"

"Always in color, though I know it's not the norm."

Again, the pen moves. "Do you hear voices?" At my negative response, he indicates he's to skip a few questions. "Do you have sequential dreams? Your friend made a mention that you would find this one interesting."

My eyes find her, still on the newspaper. "Did she? Yes. I have sequential dreams. A lot."

"Off the record, care to share?" Adam offers a genuine smile.

"Nah," I offer back as I catch Kim's glance. "Not much to share. But I think I'm going to have to kill my best friend."

Adam chuckles with me. "She didn't say anything more than that, honest. Okay, next question." His pen says "Property of U.S. Government" on it, I notice as he marks my answer on the sheet. His voice rattles some more questions, and as I answer I keep darting "I'm gonna kick your butt" looks at my friend who starts laughing. "Okay, only seven more to go. Do you wish you had secret powers?"

Laughing, I said, "Sure to read my husband's mind. And to find the things that I've lost."

Smiling, he reads the next question. "If mind control was possible, should the government be authorized to do it in an effort to better life?"

"No. They keep botching things up."

Adam's eyebrows raise, yet he rights it down. "Have your parents ever taken bribes for self-betterment, that you are aware of?"

Searching his face, "Are you serious?" At his nod, I shrug. "I don't know."

"Have you ever received bribes for self-betterment?" Hid pen is poised.

"Definitely not." *Some people may have, but not me.*

"Are your parents your biological, foster, or adopted?"

"Biological."

"Do you think life is fair, why or why not?"

Speaking slowly so he could write as I talk, I express that life isn't fair. So many avenues and choices, and vicious people and minds are out there. *Manipulators and con-artists seem to rule the government, and therefore the world. Of course it's not fair.* Seeing he was short on space, I stopped my angry ramblings.

"And finally…why did you decide to complete the survey?"

His pen awaits, and his eyes are on me. "Felt maybe could help out, I guess." He starts writing as I continue. "There's enough crap out there to realize the quality of everyday life isn't that full of quality, though. Just watch CNN, and stuff. There are always bad things being done. It's a scary world we live in now. I wish I had the power to change it."

"If you did, would you?" His face is curious.

Gnawing at my lip, "That's eight. You said seven more."

He shrugs. "So I did. You win." He laughs. He stands up and shakes my hand. "Thank you. We appreciate your input."

Getting up I look around. "Guess you have a wait until your three o'clock. Well, have a good one." Picking up my cup, I return to where Kim waits. "Nice."

"*What?*" Her voice reflecting the feigned innocent.

Shaking my head, I smile. "Let's go. I can't believe you told him I'd find that question about having sequential dreams interesting!"

Reaching into her purse, she laughs. "I thought you would is all. I thought of you as soon as he started talking about dreams. I kept thinking to myself, what 'til Bec gets this one, and this one, and this." She follows me out the door. "Kind of a funny survey. Makes you wonder what they're really studying, and for who."

"Well, his pen said 'Property of the U.S. Government' on it. Probably for the 'We have to do paperwork to get our paychecks Agency.'"

Kim laughs as she werp, werps her car again with her remote entry button. "Yeah. Waste more of our hard earned tax money on $300 toilet seats, $100 for screwdrivers, and now weird surveys. I wonder about people who make surveys too. What questions are the real ones, et cetra." Opening her door, "Get in! Let's go shopping!"

Pausing for a second to look back, *Real ones?*

Adam watches them leave, then writes "Rebecca" on the survey still in his hands. Pleased that Rebecca had showed up, his face lightens. Exhaling loudly, he brings out his cell phone. Pressing a few numbers, he calls his desk.

"Strebeck, this is a secure line."

"Survey complete." Adam smiles listening to Jay's enthusiasm on the other end. "I'll be on my way shortly."

"Sounds good. Your wife called earlier. I told her you were at some appointment and would call when you had a chance. See you when you get back."

Adam thanks Jay before the line goes dead. He'll call Cathy in a few minutes. Right now he is content to have finally met one of his cases. Unfortunately, some of the things Adam had hoped to answer weren't overly clear, but at least they knew she had vivid sequential dream recollection. That is both good, and bad. Good that she is honest and is able to recall. Bad if she recalled what she isn't supposed to.

Something nags at Adam though. When cases are assigned, usually they were given a mission statement. With a select few, including Rebecca, in the remarks it only stated "Energy." He doesn't really understand this, but has a feeling Jay does.

Jodie M. Swanson

CHAPTER 13

Adam enters his area, and grabs his file on Rebecca, his eyes lighting on Jay. "Come here." Without seeing if Jay is following, he heads for the back office. His annoyance is tenfold. All the way back he realized he knows so little of what he has done for the last nine years. Sure, he knew he hit keys and played mind games. That was about it. He has no idea what some of the symbols Jay had shown him the other night actually meant until Jay had explained them. Jay had the also explained different functions and commands, and their purposes in better interpreting such information.

Adam did realize that having met Rebecca has changed a lot of things. It ha complicated his involvement tremendously. He feels like an inexperienced puppeteer putting on a performance before professionals. The thought galled him the past sixty-some-odd minutes and counting. His is ready to throw military bearing out the window, and knock some heads until he gets answers.

The closing of the door almost startles him, as Jay speaks. "So, how'd we do?"

Jay's hand reaches for the completed survey.

Adam holds the folder tightly. "I have some questions first."

A look crosses Jay's features as he takes a seat. "What questions?"

Opening his own file on Rebecca, Adam points to the word. "Explain this more to me." At Jay's confused look, he continues. "Most cases have mini mission statements or agendas. Most parents were asked to complete a consent to perform infant experiments at time of implant. Other cases seem to act as controls. What else is going on here?"

Jay reflects a moment. Looking up he sees that Adam isn't going to budge on this. "Why the concern about all that?"

69

Adam leans forward, his hand pounding the file in anger. "Information on this case has been withheld from me, or isn't complete in the system, and I'd like to why. What is it?" Realizing his voice has raised, "Something's overly different here, and I'm so stupid that I've just figured it out. Something isn't in my version. I have a feeling you and Captain Roberts know."

Jay gnaws his lower lip for a second. Again looking at Adam, he opens his own briefcase. "Not all of the people have a real purpose. You are correct in that some are dummies, if you pardon the expression. Others, were...selected. Rebecca is such a case. Ever notice certain cases had numbers assigned in the name or statement of implant? The special ones, like Rebecca here don't. Her only code is 'Energy,' and for good purpose." He takes out a much bigger file than that Adam had been collecting for years. "Here. I'll give you a few minutes alone. You aren't supposed to see that, but I'm going to the candy machine. Need anything? I'll knock before I come back. I'm locking the door behind me." With that Jay set the file on the table and walks out.

Adam pauses for only a moment, then reaches for the file. Quickly scanning the first few pages, he comes across some information that surprises him. "Electrical interference?" Quickly his eyes scan more. "Unbelievable."

Before him is the main letter of purpose dated over thirty years ago. It was a doctor's belief that some of the problems with pirate radio waves and transmissions were caused by electrical interference. Upon further study, they surmised these interferences were indeed a factual, but not stemming from weather, as first thought. It was from people. Some of the people exhibiting this phenomenon in the United States at that time were adults, and easily "controlled" by the thought of extra money for their cooperation. Sometimes, though very rarely, testing proved it to be the infant capable of emitting energy frequencies.

In Rebecca's case, she had still been a fetus. Rebecca's mother had agreed to undergo some testing for $200, a nice sum twenty-nine years ago. When the tests didn't show what was expected, the doctors and researchers were dumbfounded. After the baby was born was when they had the discovery of the interference's origin. Trying to keep a hold on this new case, they had offered another sum. Rebecca's parents had been resistant this time, unsure of the continued interest in their daughter. The promised $1500 came as a big surprise, and the family felt the power of money. Their financial future was now in good hands. They had signed the contracts, and the deal was done. For one day a week Rebecca was seen at a clinic and monitored. By six months of age her "energy" had faded slightly, but hadn't gone away, the doctors had felt there was little choice but to place an implant. Her parents had been outraged at first. The doctors repeatedly told them that Rebecca was still healthy, just traceable. As another consolation, they were told she didn't need to keep visiting the clinic.

Some of the experiments with Rebecca were to see her full potential in her dream state. Such interpretations and analyses were not made available to Adam as she was of the highest category of security. Other such cases had resulted in 'inmates', so to speak, unable to leave, bound by contracts not of their choosing. Luckily Rebecca's parents had thought ahead more than other parents, and had ensured no captivity would come to Rebecca, at any time.

If they only knew, Adam muses.

Reading on he shakes his head at what early programs had tried to distinguish and implant. She had effectively rejected many programs and implants through her years. Adam now smiled remembering a time or two when she hadn't taken his efforts either. *Tough cookie.*

Hearing footsteps scuff to a stop, Adam pauses. Slowly he closes the flap, listening. "Of course, Captain Roberts. Adam's preparing his brief now, I think. I just went to get something to snack on." The knock came, and Adam quickly opens the door. Briefly meeting Jay's eyes, Adam gives a quick nod. "Sir." He addresses as Roberts walks through the door. Once the door is closed, he again retakes his seat.

Roberts looks at Adam. "I hear we have the survey." At Adam's nod, he presses. "What have we learned?"

Adam takes the survey out. Slowly he opens the folder, composing himself. "The subject was not aware of any conduct by the government in the area of mind control, though she is against it. The subject also has 'vivid sequential' dreams, though she didn't offer explanation at the dreams when offered a chance. In the area of...if she had the 'power or ability' to do certain things, what would she want to do with I, she joked at the ability read her husband's mind, do better than the government at helping society, etc. When asked why she wanted to complete the survey, she said hoped her input helped as society is chaotic, my word, not hers." Adam shuts the folder, and shrugs. "Her basic results show she counts her dreams as only that, dreams. I feel based on this, that she is not a threat, and shouldn't be considered as such."

Captain Roberts asks to see the survey. Quietly he scans the remarks and comments. Upon finishing the last page, he turns the page face down, and rests his chin on his hand. "Adam, could you leave me and Jay alone please?"

Adam nods. Standing up he catches Jay's eyes. "Of course, Sir. I'll be at my terminal." He opens the door, then exits.

Captain Roberts shifts a bit. "Was he wired?"

Jay nods. "He didn't know that the pen I gave him was bugged. He did nothing out of the ordinary, only what was expected of him. I have the tape here, if you'd like to hear it." Jay hands the tape over to Roberts' outstretched hand. "As I listened, I found the subject's answers normal, as if any Joe or Joan would answer. I also listened to the friend's answers. There is a part where it may sound funny, but mostly because of our bias. Listen as a normal person, and you'll see it's normal talk."

Roberts looks at the micro-tape in his hands. "Let's go over it, to be sure." His eyes fix momentarily on Jay. "Where's there a recorder?" Jay opens his briefcase. "Damn Jay, what don't you have in there?"

Jay shrugs off a smile. "I was a Boy Scout. You know, 'Be prepared,' and all that." Withdrawing his own tape from the machine, he then hands it to Roberts. "Volume's all the way up, so you may want to turn it down before you press play. And it's already rewound."

For the next hour Adam looks at the closed door, wondering what was happening. His fingers go through the motions of going through the cases and the programs for each. Upon reaching Rebecca's again, he pauses. His mind wonders what ability she still may have, and what the government was hoping to do learn from it. The movie Firestarter comes to mind, and he shivers. "I'm not the shop."

Are you sure?

The thought startles Adam a bit. In the movie, the government and a secret bunch of doctors had run tests on people. "Just like me. I am. Oh my God." Adam shakes his head slowly. His features go stern, and he flips through her screen information, and eventually comes to a personal information page. He reads through the information with a fine eye, and notices, as if for the first time, that the information has typos, as if words were missing. "Or deleted."

Hearing the back office door open, Adam escapes until he is on the main screen. He starts flipping through a few command options as Captain Roberts and Jay walk up. He passes a cursory glance at them if unconcerned, and reaches for his logbook. He opens it up, flipping to the last pages. He acts like he's verifying the information on the screen against the log. His nerves sizzle with tension as they near.

Roberts peers over Adam's shoulder. "What you doing?"

"Verifying log entries against the computer. Nothing else is happening right now." Adam sets the log down, still open. "Why? What do you need, Sir?"

Roberts shrugs. "Nothing. Just curious if there were any more developments on this?"

Adam shrugs in return. "Nothing at all, Sir. Normal weather pattern. Normal all around." Adam taps a few keys until the main screen comes up.

Roberts leans forward, then backs away. "Very good. May I see you in the back office now please?" He leads the way, Adam in tow. Once the door is shut, Roberts signals for Adam to have a seat. "Okay. We've reviewed the survey and have some more issues to discuss. First, if this subject has another cross-over, another breech, what are your suggestions?" Roberts reaches for a piece of paper in the printer, then sits.

Adam looks around the room, searching for a good answer. "Sir, perhaps just monitor her, and record what we find."

Roberts jots this down. "Interesting, but maybe a valid option. Second, what is your impression of her after meeting her?"

Adam makes a face. "I don't know. I guess for all the hoop-la, she seemed like an everyday lady. She was casually dressed, and curious, cautious. I guess, a lot like my wife might be in a circumstance like this."

Roberts continues writing as he asks, "No weird expressions or faces. She didn't make you feel uneasy, or did sense anything odd?"

"Nothing, Sir."

The pen continues to move. "Would you be willing to meet with her again?"

"Sure, I guess."

"Is there any chance that the two women switched timeslots for the survey?" The pen hovers in the air above the paper.

"I don't think so. Everything seemed to line up with what we have on file on her. The two look a little similar, but not enough to match her friend to Rebecca's information." Adam shifts in his seat, getting more comfortable feeling he'd be here a while.

Jay watches the closed door, aware that Adam is being drilled. He feels bad for the man. Adam had done everything he was asked, yet he was to be questioned like everyone else, for sake of covering all the bases. "What a crock!" Jay's dislike for this field flares for a few minutes.

Bored, he taps at the keyboard, gaining access to files from his office via a secured link. Hesitating, he slowly taps methodically, then looks at the screen. His wife's file comes up, for what seems like the billionth time. Slowly he traces her face with his fingers. Biting his lips, he stares at the screen. "So many regrets, Angela. I'm so sorry." He wonders why he has stayed in this long, and knows he feels obligated to make it up to her. "I'm so sorry." With one last run of the fingers, he wipes her image away.

Taking a pen he writes a quick note for Adam.

Adam,
  Hey, I'll be back tomorrow bright and early. I have things I need to do. You have my cell number if you need it.
  -Jay

With that, he grabs his briefcase and leaves.

Jodie M. Swanson

CHAPTER 14

Jay nervously approaches the house, briefcase in hand. He has seen a lady matching Rebecca's profile get out of a car about fifteen minutes ago, bags in hand. He doesn't really know what he is doing, but he knows something needs to be done. Reaching the door he takes a deep breath, then pushes the doorbell. Hearing the ring echo, he steels himself for when the door opens.

"Just a minute!" The voice is muffled by the door. Finally, the door cracks a bit. She takes visual inventory of him, and he lets her. "Yes? May I help you?"

Holding the door firmly, I take in his appearance. He's casually dressed as he holds a briefcase. He has a government nametag on his shirt saying his name is Jay Strebeck, Civil Service. He has a nervous posture about him, though his face seems serious. "Yes? May I help you?"

"Yes. My name is Jay Strebeck, and I work for the government in a... classified department. By my talking to you I may be jeopardizing my career." He pauses, looking unsure of himself. "I think we need to talk. May I come in?"

Still firmly holding the door, I think. "Do you have some sort of identification?" He relaxes, fumbling with his back pant pocket. Carefully, he withdraws a civilian identification card, and passes it through to the awaiting fingers. Not really knowing what to do, I go over it carefully, seeing reflective images in the seal of the card as I move to better light. It looks like it's the real deal, at least to me. "Here's your ID. Why do you want to come in?"

He takes his ID and puts it back into his wallet. "I think I have some information which may interest you about...about a recent survey you took. The one today." His voice is a loud whisper. "Please."

Slowly, I open the door, allowing him entrance. "I need to make a phone call. Have a seat." The dining room table is lit, and he goes there while I make my way to the phone. Keeping my eyes on him, I dial Kim's number. When she answers I tell her I need to come over right away.

"Don't tell them someone from the government is here. Your line is tapped." Again his voice is a loud whisper.

"Just come over, so we can talk. Bye." Hanging up, I warily approach him. "What do you mean my phone is tapped?" Still standing at the opposite end of the table, I jump as he brings up his briefcase.

"Easy Rebecca. Let me explain. Here. I have something to show you." His briefcase is filled almost to bursting with notes and a huge folder. He pulls out a mini recorder. He presses play.

The voice I hear is mine, answering the survey questions from earlier today. My eyes shoot to his. "What's going on here?"

Jay stops the tape and replaces the recorder in his briefcase. "First, everything I'm about to tell you, and show you, can get me fired...or worse. I need your promise that this stays here. And I'll need your friend's promise when she gets here."

Stalling, I glance out the window. "She'll be here in a minute." My actions must be obvious to the man, as he nods, then sits still, looking at his now closed briefcase. He continues to wait silently occasionally taking deep breaths and nervously tapping his fingers on the placemat on my table. Taking a look at his watch, he still says nothing. Hearing a car pull up, he looks with me out the window.

Kim looks at the vehicle parked near my driveway as she comes up the pathway. At her knock I open the door. She comes in, a worried look on her face. Her eyes briefly meet mine. I pass her gaze to the man sitting at my table. "What's going on?"

Jay stands up and walks over. "Hello. My name is Jay Strebeck. I work for the government. You must be Kim?" Extending a hand, he shakes Kim's hand. "Pleased to meet you."

Kim shoots be a bewildered look, and I shrug, making a face. Quickly I whisper, "He showed up at the door. He showed me his government ID, and everything. He's got my interest piqued, but he hasn't said anything so far except that my phone is tapped." With that we go to sit at the table.

Jay's face is solemn. "Ladies, I'm nervous here. I told Rebecca earlier that my talking to her could lead to...my being fired, or worse. But, after some of the things that have happened, I'm willing to take the chance. First, I need to know that what we talk about today goes no further. I didn't want to involve anyone else other than Rebecca, but had a feeling she'd want to talk to you anyway." He looks at Kim's confused face. "Seems you two are close, and share a lot. Better to have you both here so there's no chance for...problems." He stops, exhaling loudly. "Can you promise me you will hold this here, and not share this?" He looks at me while I look at Kim. She seems hesitant, but says she agrees to keep quiet. Meeting his gaze, I agree too.

He closes his eyes, hands braced on his briefcase. Taking a couple deep breaths he opens his eyes, and the briefcase. "Rebecca, earlier today you admitted to having sequential dreams. Lots, of them, with vivid clarity. Is that correct?"

Looking a Kim briefly, I nod. "Have had them since I've been little. Why?"

Using both hands, Jay brings out a huge folder. "We've been watching you, monitoring you, and...implanting things to keep you from dreaming."

"What?" Kim gasps.

"What? Why?"

Running his hand through his hair, Jay opens the folder. "About thirty years ago, the government was running some tests on different frequencies they were finding in random parts of the world, and the United States. At first this phenomenon was thought to be weather-based. Experiments were inconclusive.

"Quite by accident the researches realized that...certain individuals were emitting the electrical frequencies. All of the cases had no idea that they were." Pausing to see how the information is being received, he pushes on. "The government then recruited these people, paying them, to...be lab rats, essentially. Tests were run on the ability to control the electric impulses, the force, if any, and other things. People were rated, toyed with, and some lost."

"Lost?" My voice sounds strange.

"Some became too exhausted by continuous experiments. Others... took their lives, tired of the captivity."

Kim's horror sounds loud in her whispered, "Oh my God."

Licking his lips, Jay continues. "Once in a while, the researchers would find the wrong person, and no harm was really done. Someone would make money for nothing." Jay looks directly at me. "Your mom was one like that."

"What are you saying?" Again my voice sounds far away.

"They thought it was your mom, but they were mistaken. They paid her $200 to undergo some testing which proved they had the wrong person. It baffled them though, as the energy readouts were topped off. Soon, towards the end of their testing, it was brought to their attention that your mother was pregnant." His eyes again come to land on me. "With you.

"The agency put a lot of pressure on your parents, who were

financially troubled at the time. They made repeat offers of a couple hundred dollars to be able to run some tests and watch you grow. Your parents refused, saying you weren't going to grow up in some freak show. After a few more months, the government made an offer your parents couldn't refuse." His face softened. "Your parents were hurting bad for money, though the $200 had really helped them. The agency promised to pay your parents $1500 to be able to run some tests with you. As part of the bargain, you were not to ever be told by them. Also, once a week until you turned eighteen, you were to undergo testing and experiments."

"But I didn't do that."

"You didn't have to. By the time you were six months, your energy-level had only depleted slightly, and you were strong in every test they handed your way. You far exceeded all the other infants and toddlers at the time." Jay ran his fingers through his hair again. "I don't know all the tests done at that time, but I do know that some were quite painful to the 'weak.' Apparently you never 'suffered' as some had. One of the things they noticed though was you REM. Are you familiar with REM?"

"Yes. Rapid eye movement. The part of sleep when dreams occur." My offer of knowledge is weak at best.

"Correct. Well, it gave them the idea to start testing dreams, but they couldn't really do that with once a week sessions. They needed more... exposure to you and your mind, and abilities." He offers his softly. "The next may be hard to listen to." He lowers his gaze to his briefcase. "Your parents reluctantly agreed to an implant, due to some fine print in the contract. At six months of age, you have had an electric...radio collar, of sorts."

"You're lying!" I jump out of my seat, throwing my arms at him. "How dare you? My parents would never have done such a thing! They always took care of me! We were never wanting!"

His gaze remains lowered as he keeps talking. "The implanted device..."

"Shut up!" My hands cover my ears. Kim comes to my side.

"...was designed to listen, so to speak, to what your brain was saying and be the eyes for the researchers." He still doesn't look up.

"Liar!" Tears start welling in my eyes. "This is a lie!"

"I wish it was." That's all he offers before he looks at me. "The agency knows that you have some...bizarre dreams. Your recent... episodes? We've tracked them. As standard protocol, they had to release the flu that entered your home." His gaze is down again.

"What?" Angrily, I stride up to him. "What did you say?"

"The flu released into your home was a plant. A countermeasure to keep you from dreaming." He isn't looking anywhere but at his briefcase. His finger traces the edge of it.

Kim sputters. "The government wanted her to be that sick?"

He briefly meets her eyes. Memories of Angela and their argument playing in his mind. He looks back down, nodding.

"Why?" She goes to him. "Why would they do this?"

"Because she is considered a threat." His voice is now a whisper.

"I'm a threat? *I'm a threat?* You people get me and my daughter sick. Sick, mind you, and *I'm* the threat?" The house echoes my anger.

Kim puts her hands on my shoulders. "What do you mean, she's a threat?" Her voice sounds calm, yet concerned, so I look at her. Her eyes are on the man at my table.

"The government can read the amount of energy she puts off when she dreams." His eyes met mine before going back to Kim's. "Sometimes it's the equivalent of…say an earthquake, tornado, hurricane."

Images of the wave come to me through the anger. "The wave."

My whisper gets his attention. "What did you say?"

"The wave. When you said that just now. I saw the wave I sometimes see in my dreams." Still angry I glare at him.

"Do you cause it?"

The question catches me off guard. While reflecting on this, my voice softens in thought. "No. They were there before me." Feeling Kim next to me, I look at him. "Do you all see my dreams?"

"The government has no idea what your dreams are about. They're only able to measure the amount of energy displaced while you dream, and trace thought patterns." Jay remembers the melding. "Would you like to tell me about these dreams?"

Warily, I shake my head signifying that I did not.

Jay exhales. "Trust me. I know quite a bit about what you are going through, thinking." His eyes meet mine. "My wife had an implant."

"Then they can be removed?" My voice is eager.

"No. I didn't mean that." His fingers again trace the briefcase. "She and I had an argument over my working with this. She said I had lost my morals." He made a face, and tears welled. "She didn't know that I wanted to learn more about the mind. My intent was never to harm anyone." He blinks a few times, fighting tears. "I found out about her implanting and programming after her…"

"She killed herself, didn't she?" Kim adds softly.

He spares a quick glance, and nods. "Every day, I think I should have never told her about what I did." He swipes at the corner of his eye. "But losing her I was able to advance further into the system, as a way to fight the loss. I was given access to files to better explain what had really happened. Deciding to not lose her again, I kept up with the job. I was hoping someday to make it up to her. Guess I am thinking this is it." He looks at me with reddened eyes. "I'm sorry, but after years of being watched, something told me to let you know. Adam wanted to himself, but is afraid of the consequences."

The name clicks. "The surveyor? Who is he to me?"

Straight-faced, Jay holds my gaze. "He's your case worker. Your lead. He's hating his job too. It's affecting his marriage. He's been wanting to meet you since the step-up precautions have been implemented. The survey offered him that chance. I had him wired, as directed. He doesn't know that though." Jay runs his fingers along the briefcase. "When I left him, he was still being interrogated about this afternoon." He tiredly rubs his face. "I'm starting to babble. I'm sorry."

Taking him in, I wonder how I can validate his claim. "You can listen in on my conversations, can't you? I mean with my line being tapped?"

"Yep. Pretty much."

"Is Kim's line tapped?"

He looks at me, then to her. "From time to time."

Kim sputters, as I ask, "Her cell phone?"

"I wouldn't doubt it. Why?"

Straight-faced, I meet his gaze. "I want to call my folks. I want to hear it from them." Somehow I keep my voice from cracking.

Jay meets my look, then opens his briefcase. "I'm not tapped."

Carefully, I take the phone, and tell him I'd like a minute. Kim stays with him as I go to my room and dial my mom's number. When she answers, I realize I don't know how to start. "Mom? I have some questions, and I need to know the truth." Listening to her concern, I press on. "Can you tell me, I mean, have you ever…accepted money from the government in exchange for things…dealing with me?" My heart breaks hearing her gasp. Her tears and sputtering prove that the man at my table is indeed correct. "Oh Mom…how could you?"

Silently, I listen to her relating the story. She pours it all out, and I listen, sadly, to her story. My heart breaks into pieces listening to her. She explains that they were unable to pay rent, and were about to be evicted when the $200 had come along. My dad was still trying to get a steady job to help get ready for my addition to the family, and wasn't having any luck. She told me they fought long about the money, but explained they had felt they had no choice. Once they received the money, a steady job offer had also come, with the aid of the government. When she was finished with her tale, she begs forgiveness, and expresses her love for me.

Anger gives way to grief, and my tears started flowing as I have listened. Sniffling, I tell her there is a man in my house who just told me everything she has. I tell her not to call me about this as my line is tapped. Hearing her gasp, I sigh. Softly I make my excuse to leave, and thank her for her time, and hang up.

Looking in the mirror, I see a stranger. My anger comes back a little, so I swipe at the tears lurking in my eyes. Doing so I catch the time. "Oh no!" Quickly I go back to where Kim and Jay sit. "Kim, it's almost five o'clock."

She nods. "I already called Dennis and told him I'd be late."

A car pulls up. "It's Chase and the munchkins!" Panicking I look around.

Jay stands up. "I can explain this to him. I guess I should."

Looking out the window, I see Chase taking in the two cars in front of the house. As he approaches, I open the door. He takes one look at my teary face, and says, "What's happened?"

Jodie M. Swanson

CHAPTER 15

Chase sits holding me, rubbing my back. He softly kisses my hair. "You okay Bec?" His hand comes firmly around my waist to hold me to his side.

Looking up, I see Jay watching me. For the last hour or more, we had gone over everything. Chase had taken it better than I had, asking questions and pulling me into his lap when he said I was looking teary again. He was outraged, naturally that the government is doing something to play with people's minds. He was also outraged that my parents had done what they had. After Jay continued explaining things, he mellowed though. His behavior was less offended, and turned more supportive. His actions have helped me greatly, but seeing Jay's eager expression, I ask. "Hypnotize me?"

Jay nods. "I may be able to get someone to do it, for a fair fee, without letting the agency know. It's up to you though."

Shaking my head, "I don't know. Wouldn't it just help if I told you about my dreams? You said that that was a key."

"True", Jay agrees. "But do you want to really share them?"

Glancing at Chase, I sigh. "Sure, I guess."

Jay peeks at his watch. "Tell you what. I'm going to go ahead and go. I want you to write down as much as you can remember from your dreams. Use details. I'll come by again, say…in three days for them. Will you do that?" At my nod, he smiles. "And don't worry. I won't share your dreams with the agency. You have my word."

The sun's rays dance along the crests of the near-by waves, looking a lot like golden glitter on black velvet against the sky. The echoes of the remaining seagulls reverberate along the beach as the sky darkens. The smell of water hangs heavy around me as it tries to float on the slight evening breeze. Sighing, I pick up a handful of moist sand, thumbing it through my fingers. "I don't think this place is real."

My phantom friend sucks in her breath. "What do you mean?" She waves her hands about, her nostrils flared. "Of course it's real. How could it not be?"

Casually meeting her look, I make a face. "It just can't be, I guess." The sound of the surf deserves my blind attention.

Shadow angrily shakes her head. "I don't agree. I can't believe you would even say that! I can, we can, feel this sand. I can smell this beach's salty air." Her eyes dart upwards, catching on the noisy birds above. "Can hear those damned seagulls." Again, she shakes her head, almost hissing. "If this isn't real, what is it?" The challenge is loud though she had quietly bit out every word.

Gazing across the waves, "I don't know." Closing my eyes, I again dig my fingers into the squirming sand. Slowly, I open my eyes to examine my resisting catch. Lifting my hand a bit closer, I feel the tiny granules and small pebbles coursing over my skin as they make for the safety of the ground once again. "I just don't know."

She shoots swiftly to her feet, swiping at the rebellious granules lodged in her pants. I understand her upset, can empathize completely. That's why I have decided to come to the beach, for denial, reason, belief, something. For some reason she has come down, sensing my turmoil. Now she is feeling it too. *I'm sorry.*

"What's there to be sorry about?" She snorts in anger. "I refuse to believe that I don't exist. That everything I see…I really don't. What a crock!" Her finger flies to my face. "Since when did you become some all-seeing-and-knowing prophet?"

Taking her hostility lightly, I slowly stand beside her. Carefully I swipe away any remaining sand in my hands. "Maybe I'm wrong."

"Damn Skippy you're wrong," she shouts. The echo is louder than those of the seagulls heading home.

My eyes meet her angry gaze. "Sorry I upset you, but you did ask." Seeing my response did not appease her at all, I glance down. Noting the state of my clothes I shake my head. Smiling I dust my clothes of stowaway sand. "Sorry I even opened my mouth." With a short last glance, I turn away from her, towards my home.

"Is it that man? Derk? Upset he hasn't come back?" Her snide remarks almost hurt, her anger letting loose on me. "Or is it that dream-land person?"

Feeling my feet slice through the sand, I watch the sand shifting between my boots. My head slowly shakes. "No. It's not Derk. It's that other person." My gaze lifts to the stone steps leading to my hole in the wall. "I went to…that place again. I came into it while she was writing things down in a journal of some kind." My hand stays some wind-loosened strands. "I'm nothing but a dream to her. I read while she placed me with so many of her other 'dreams.' I watched for two hours as she wrote notes on dreams she's had, as many as she could remember and write down.

"She knew I had come, and almost dismissed me as a memory at first. Then it was almost like talking to her, through her writing in that stupid journal. She was starting with some of her first dreams, and I was in a lot of them. All through her life she's been having dreams on and off about here, and me." My steps slow nearing the steps. "Two hours of her writing stuff about my personal life, like it is all some dream." Angrily, I turn about, shouting, "It's all some dream!"

Shadow's steadying hand settles on my shoulder. "But you see her in your dreams." Her offer is valid, but also weak. She knows it, and she gently questions, "So, what does it all mean?"

My shoulders shrug as I turn away from her. *This is all a dream.*

"I think I need to go with you next time."

My feet pause a moment so I can look directly at her. "You can do that?"

Shrugging, she smiles. "I can do almost anything you can. So? What do you say?" Her eyes quickly scan my stoic features. "Come on. Let's do it." Her hand still on my shoulder gives me a gentle push.

Now?

"Of course, why not?"

My feet finally reach the stone stairs. Slowly I turn towards the watery sunset. The sun's last rays cast colors across the darkening sky. Night has definitely taken hold of the day. *Why not. And find out about all this.*

"Exactly."

Briskly, we mount the stairs leading to my domicile. Excitement races through me at the thought of "mind tripping" with Shadow. Wondering how it could be done, I turn to her.

"Well, I've never actually done anything like this before. I'm just going off the two ideas of my being able to read your thoughts, and kinda…piggyback them with your abilities. I mean, it can't be all that different, my reading you like that, can it?" Shadow takes a seat beside me on my mat. "Then again, if I can't, well…I'll just sit and watch, okay?"

Verbally agreeing with her, I settle in. Reclining on the wall of my sleeping mat, I close my eyes. A cursory thought of how it may feel having her join me skips in and then right back out.

"Should make none," she supplies.

What do I say about you when she notices you? Wispy mist layers start pooling around me, and I feel it coming.

"I don't know. We'll see if she does, if I can read you."

The energy flows.

"Whoa."

"What?" My eyes snap open hearing Shadows remark. Taking a second to refocus, I see awe etched in her features. "What is it?"

Shadow offers a small smile. "That was bizarre. I could feel you, and it, heavy. Well not really heavy, more like engulfing, all of a sudden. I could almost…see it come from you."

Frowning, "What did it look like?" My voice sounds like a hoarse whisper.

She shakes her head. "I don't know. Almost like steam, but not." Annoyed she swipes her hand through the air. "Anyway, sorry. I didn't mean to interrupt."

Running my fingers through my hair before resettling against the wall, my eyes close again. Almost immediately I feel it, flowing, surrounding. *That's it, surrounding.* Wispy layers and shadows blow past me. The feeling of "here" takes me, and my mental eyes open. This time they feel heavy. *Must be Shadow.*

A snort. "It's not me."

Turning within I look to see if Shadow's here with me.

"I can't get there."

I can feel you. It sounds like me.

"Who's that?"

I'm back. Hope you don't mind, but I have some questions.

So do I.

"Who's who?"

Who is that?

A friend. Is it okay? We all seem to have questions we need answers to. I wait cautiously, hoping I don't lose the connection. "Stay quiet, Shadow."

Ah yes, Shadow. We meet again.

"Your thoughts sound the same. Tell me how to tell you apart." Shadow sounds confused.

She speaks. *I am told I am One, and so the dream me is Two. That is what I do understand. What I don't is how I can feel this much…energy, by being me and then again not at all later. There's so much energy, pressure. I feel it, and almost know the…way to control it.*

I smile in thought. *The energy is what holds us, isn't it? Are you the main entity then?*

Entity? Like a god figure. No! I'm…just me. Her voice rings with a private joke left untold. *There's nothing special about me. At least there wasn't that I knew of until now. I just recently found out about you.*

Where does the energy come from?

I don't know. I somehow think it's always been there. But I do know I have more control of it in my dreams.

Whispering, Is that all I am? A dream? My whole world? A dream?

*No. I don't think so. I believe you are an extension of myself, in a parallel...
world to mine. We are sharing some sort of bond, if you will. I can think of it clearer
like this, when I sleep. And yet, when I'm awake, I lose it, forget it, something.*

Chase can't believe his eyes. Before him is Rebecca asleep, yet she is
carrying on a conversation as if she was awake. She seems to be floating an
inch above her mattress, but he can't be sure without touching her. He
calls her name gently, and she turns her open eyes towards him.

He could swear that it appears to be light coming from within her. The
sight rather startles him. "Rebecca!"

I have to go now. My husband is awake.

I heard him. Is everything okay?

I have to go now. Come again soon.

The energy releases me softly, lowering me softly back to myself. The
urge to sleep now is strong, but I know Shadow is waiting. Slowly I blink.
Rubbing my eyes, I ask her what she thought.

"She's onto something with this parallel place thing." Shadow paces
the precious few feet of my floor, fingers gently playing her lips. "Wow.
Wow!" She turns on me quickly. "The energy you guys were sparking, I
tell ya, I could feel it. Whoa." And she paces some more.

Sitting up, I smile. "Not bad, your idea."

Shadow smiles at me. "What can I say, I'm talented."

Right.

"Oh-ho! Look who's cocky now that she really may be real!"

And that almost made sense. Try again. Standing, my muscles demand a
stretch. "What time is it?"

"Late. Late, late, late." She still paces, now moving around me.

"Calm down. Relax. I think you're working yourself up too much."

Shadow stops in mid-stride. "She says she can't control her energy the
way you do. Why is that?"

"A block."

Shadow looks at me. "Block? What kind of block?"

Shrugging, I offer no response. Instead I make ready to brush my
teeth.

"Block," she mutters. "I wonder if you can help her break this block."

My reflection catches my eye. "Maybe she doesn't want it broke." My
image sends me to a memory of my childhood, and the first feelings the
energy. Shortly after the wave incident people had come to ask my parents

questions. My father had promised my ability to do fortune-telling, palm reading, dream-interpretations, and other things. All things I couldn't do. In a fit of anger my father had hit me for not trying, and the block restraining my energy broke, and the result was disastrous.

The anger in me erupted, and lifted me, literally. Face-to-face with my father, and not realizing it, I wished I could hit him back. Then he was hit, sent sprawling about ten feet away. Blood ran from his nose as he struggled to his feet.

"Little shit! Brat! Look at what…." He had stopped, as I wished him to.

With a wave of my young arms, I tore down the walls of the house. Seeing the walls falling I panicked, thinking of my mother asleep at the far end of the house. Going to her, I realized I had killed her instantly. Passionately, I wished I hadn't done that. That I could bring her back. But it didn't work. My father collected some things and left me there. I started crying, and the crash of lightning echoed my pain. My tears fell with the sudden down pour of rain.

Blinking back tears I again see my reflection, and stick the junky wore-out toothbrush in my mouth.

A soft squeeze and my shadow is sharing with me. "Not all of it has been bad, has it? We could help her redirect it, as you know how to control it."

I don't know. My reflection looks tired, worn. *I don't know.*

"It was just a thought. I'm sorry." Shadow gently pats my back, and says good-night, disappearing through my doorway once again.

Putting down my toothbrush, I touch my reflection in memory. Taking a steadying breath, I take the few steps to my mat. Lying down, I pretend I'm somewhere else, and warm wisps of energy take me there. *Paradise is achievable.*

CHAPTER 16

Adam slowly pulls into the parking lot. Spying a vacant parking spot, he continues humming along with the country song playing through his car. Allowing the song to finish, Adam smiles to himself. "It's going to be a good day. How could it not be after all this Rebecca stuff, which was pretty much over?" Hearing the song come to a close, he takes a deep fortifying breath as he shuts off the engine. "It's gonna be a good day for once."

The interview proved there had been little for the agency to worry about, so all would hopefully relax down to normal. Even the small-scale interrogation Adam had undergone yesterday by Captain Roberts had seemed to signify an end. He had to admit that at first he had been very nervous, unsure of why he was being questioned at all. After a few minutes, he realizes he had nothing to fret about. Roberts had only wanted extra documentation in case the higher ups wanted any updates or further information. Everyone definitely wanted this over, as Roberts had said a couple times.

"So maybe now it is," Adam muses. Taking his hat, he opens his car door. Walking briskly through the coolness of the morning, he offer friendly nods to others on their way to the building in which he worked. Making some mumbled "good mornings" as he goes, he whispers to himself, "Only a few more months. Then I'm done with this freakin' place." He makes his way further, heading for his desk. Once there, he sits down in his chair, and leans back to stretch and yawn.

"Late night?" Jay comes from up behind him.

"Oh! Morning. Nah, just thinking this should be a good day." Adam methodically turns on his computer as he continues talking. "The stress of the last few weeks has been pretty rough. I haven't slept well lately." Seeing his log-in prompt now being displayed on the computer screen, he taps in his passwords. "Guess, you can tell I'm glad it's over."

"I hear that." Jay pulls up a chair. "Let's hope it *is* over."

Adam tosses him a look of feigned annoyance. "Here I am trying to be all optimistic, and you're trying to tear me down." His screen comes alive with the agency's main menu program. "First things first, let's check our little lady, shall we?" The code representing Rebecca's file gets tapped in. "Keep your fingers crossed." He presses enter.

Instantaneously, Adam's screen fills with information and some warning codes. "Oh no." Quickly Adam scrolls down to check the length of the displayed information, and curses. "No, no, no! *NO!*" He hits the icon to print the information, and scrolls back up. Curses still flow freely from his tense lips, ending with, "Crap and more crap!"

Jay puts his hand on Adam's shoulder as he starts to stand. "Guess I'll go let Roberts know what's up."

"No." Adam quickly darts Jay a look before going back to his screen. "I mean, before we brief him, we should know what we're going to brief, right? Let's see what all this cobble-de-gook is about first."

Jay settles into his chair again. He briefly wonders if his visit has had anything to do with what is displayed before them on the screen. In his heart, he knows it has. Uneasy with that knowledge, he carefully scans the information. Seeing the numbers and comments shown, he briefly closes his eyes before rechecking he read it right. "Holy Christ."

"What?" Adam stares in confusion.

"Here." Jay's finger flies to the screen. "Look! It's practically unheard of." His fingers still trace the data line by line. "And here. The level of the readings...so damn high. Rragh!" Jay quickly moves to get his briefcase.

Silently Adam watches Jay's every move. Seeing the briefcase open he asks softly, "What is it?" Glancing back at the screen he asks again. "What's it all mean?"

Without looking up from his task of fumbling through the papers and files in his briefcase, Jay sighs. "If those number are correct, she's just broke the highest levels of energy usage on file."

"Should I call Guinness?" Adam tries for the joke, but seeing Jay's stern face, he offers his apologies.

Jay starts up again, papers moving quickly. "This is serious. The agency will have read that for sure. The persons who have reached close to that have had the agency collect them...for observation.

"Some have slipped into comas following the experiments involved with the agency's testing. Others reportedly lost the energy altogether, either by exhaustion or death. One man, who had been with us awhile, who had really been in control of it, lost it. He went insane one day, destroyed the testing facility, killing five other people. It was labeled by the agency as a suicide."

"Geez." Adam can't think of anything else to say.

Jay nods. "If our Rebecca just did what I *think* she did, the agency is probably already on their way. They won't leave her alone now. That's for sure." The briefcase slams shut. "Damn it."

Shifting in his chair, Adam wonders aloud. "How long does she have?"

Jay waves a hand. "Not long, unless…I need to go."

"Go? Go where?" Adam stands, reaching for Jay's arm. "What are they going to do with her?"

Pausing to see if anyone is near, Jay leans forward, his voice only a hiss. "They'll lock her up, like all the others. They'll run tests on her, try and make her perform tricks for their probing minds. They'll stick wires into her, and when she finally dies, they'll slice her open like a frog."

A light brightens Adam's once confused features. Slowly he stands. "You're going to help her, aren't you?"

Jay stops and opens his mouth. The cell phone ringing in his briefcase causes both men to jump. Quickly the snaps flip open, and the phone is in Jay's hand. "Strebeck."

"Is this…Jay?"

The man's voice sounds vaguely familiar. "It is."

"This is Cha-…"

"Oh, of course Mr. Chase. I've been expecting your call. So good to talk to you again. Can you hold for a moment, please?" Jay looks at Adam. "I'm going to the back office for a bit." Seeing the desired nod from Adam, he makes his way to the office. Looking around a last time, he softly shuts the door. "I'm back, Mr. Chase. What can I do for you?"

There's a heavy sigh before Chase's voice is heard. "Well, it's kind of hard to explain. It's about…"

"Right, right," Jay interrupts again. "I'm partially aware of some of the things that are happening. Is she okay?"

Chase pauses. "I guess so, but last night, she seemed possessed."

Interested, Jay probes. "What do you mean possessed?"

"I mean 'possessed.' Like demonic stuff like on television, possessed."

Jay rubs his forehead. "Did you have a fight?"

"No, no. It's not like that." Chase sounds even more exasperated. "It's different. And you were the only person I thought to call."

"You did the right thing." Jay rubs his face as he paces the small room. "I need to know some things. First, how did whatever it is start?"

"From one of her dreams, I guess."

Nodding as if Jay could see him, he continues. "Was anyone or anything hurt?"

"No."

"Is she aware of what happened?" Jay holds his breath.

"Everything, except she didn't realize she was…like, off the bed. Know what I mean? Off the bed, but over…"

"Stop there. I'm got the idea." Jay runs his hand through his hair. "Okay, I need you to do something. Her best friend, you know who, no names, can you get ahold of her?" Jay's mind whirls.

Another cautious pause from Chase. "Sure, I guess I can. Why?"

The clock on the wall catches Jay's eyes. "I'm sorry, but some things need to happen very, very quickly. I need you to have this friend contact your home. Have the missus pack some bags for the whole family, enough for a day or two."

"What's going on?"

"Mr. Chase, please. If you trust what I've told you, do this. Do it right away. I'll be there shortly to explain.

Chase sputters, "Wait! I don't understand. How can you help us?"

Jay heads for the door, eyes shifting to the clock. "Please trust me. Send the friend, now. I'll talk with you soon. I have to go now. Bye." Jay hangs up before Chase could say anything more. He is actually glad Chase has called. It may help make up some time if the agency has already gotten their collection efforts underway. But the clock is ticking, and he has lots of things yet to do.

Throwing open the door, he makes his way to Adam's desk. He waves his cell phone like a pointer. "I've got to go. If you hear anything, please call me. You've got my number." Jay secures his briefcase. "I've got to go run some errands for the rest of the day, if anyone asks. See ya." Jay doesn't hesitate any further. Hurrying through the halls, he dials a number not dialed in years. Hearing the hoarse greeting on the other end, Jay smiles. "It's me, Jay."

The line is silent for a few seconds. "What's wrong?"

Taking a deep breath, Jay nods at those he passes. "Something's happened. This time I have a chance to help. I need to recall a favor. Can I count on you?"

"Sure Jay. Anything. What do you need?" Quickly Jay gives the man the list. "Geez, this must be big."

Jay smiles as he puts his key into his vehicle's door. "It is. It's also got the agency's name all over it. It might get messy. For once, I may have a chance to make it up to someone."

A silence fills the line a moment. "This 'someone' depart from us a few years back?"

"It is, but I can't talk anymore now. I'll let you know where to send the other stuff when I can. I'll call you within the hour." Jay presses the button to end the call. Talking a deep breath he starts his engine. "Come on Blue, let's go make a difference." Pulling out of his parking place, Jay feels his pulse quicken with excitement.

A few miles later, Jay is off the base and getting on the interstate towards where Rebecca and Chase reside. Putting on his shades against the now-bright sun, he muses aloud, "Guess it could turn out to be a good day after all, Adam." Once on the interstate, he sets his cruise control for a few miles over the speed limit. Checking his watch he groans inwardly. "Come on."

The cell phone gives its jingle. "Strebeck."

"It's me," the hoarse voice confirms. "There's a room at the Sleep Inn for the first night. The necessary paperwork and itinerary are already faxed and waiting for you at the hotel. A new phone will be furnished for each party. The requested money will be in your account tomorrow. The identifications should arrive by five in the evening at the same hotel via AirBorne Express. Did I miss anything?"

"Hope not," Jay jokes. "Have a lot riding on this."

"I have the other phones numbers and will call you only on those from now on." The man coughs heavily. "Better let you go. Good luck, and God bless."

"Thanks my friend. If all goes well...." The line goes dead in Jay's hand. Jay isn't really surprised, due to the government's ability to scan cellular calls with ease. Also, due to the sensitive nature of the call, the length of the call is important.

So much is at stake, and Jay is half-way surprised he is doing something about it for a change. He knows a lot of it deals with his revenge-type attitude, but doesn't care. He has been wanting a chance to make amends for too long to let a perfect opportunity like this slip away. He feels he owes it to all the people the agency wronged, including those no longer around.

Staring blindly at the road, Jay's thoughts go back to his last argument with his wife. Regret fills him again for the hurtful words and taunts they had shared. Her words still echo in his head, "What kind of animal are you?"

"What kind of animal are you?"

"Angela, please stop being such a bitch!"

"Me?" She had whirled on him. "I'm the bitch? You're messing with people Jay. You're letting people die! You work for the people who let people die! And I'm the bitch?" She had surprised him with the swiftness of the slap. "How dare you! How dare you pretend to care about me, when you are letting innocent people in your care die?"

"I don't see the comparison." Jay threw up his hands. "You aren't making any sense at all! I came to release my pent up frustrations, let you know I feel horrible, that I was tired of hiding all this. And what do *you* do?

You rile me up some more! What's the matter with you? Goddamn it!"

"Leave then." Her angry challenge hung.

"I can't." It was weak, but Jay was afraid to leave. "I just can't."

Angrily she had gotten in his face. "So why come to me? Do you want me to feel sorry for you?" She had waited a second, reading his face. "You are sick! I can't believe I am married to a freaking lying perverted animal!" She turned her back to him as Jay's hand reached for her. "And don't ever touch me again. Ever!"

"You're being irrational! Just forget what I…"

"I'm being irrational? Forget you!"

"Will you just shut up? Bitch! I can't get two words in edgewise! You're just as bad as them!" Jay slammed the bedroom door shut.

She had opened the door. "No, you didn't just say that."

CHAPTER 17

"Honey, *please* put your shoes on." My eyes fly to Jay's as he peeks out the front window. "How much time do we have?"

Jay turns towards me. "Not much. Did you start the load of laundry like I said?"

Nodding, I nibble on my lips. After another second I ask, "Why did you want me to do that?"

Jay reaches into his jacket pocket for his pen. "So they will think you aren't gone, gone. That you plan on returning soon. Here." The pen is thrust into my nervous hands. "Jot down a note to Chase saying that you've taken the kids for a walk, and will be back later. Hurry."

Doing as he says, I wonder aloud. "Why are you helping me? Us?"

"I have my reasons. Now, is that everything?" He looks around a bit. Seeing me taking my purse, he stops me. "Wait, Rebecca. You won't need this anymore."

"What? But what if I need it? Some money?" My hold doesn't lighten up on the purse yet. Jay asks how much cash is in the purse. "About seventeen dollars. And my credit cards."

Jay darts another look through the window. "Take only fifteen then, but not the cards. You won't be needing them anymore."

The severity of what's going on finally sinks in. "We're running now, aren't we?" Seeing Jay's nod, anger fills me. "Why? What have I done?"

Jay looks at me, his eyes filled with compassion. "Nothing. But they still will want you. They see you as a..." His cell phone rings, and we all jump with nerves. Jay offers a tentative smile. "Mine." He flips it open. "Strebeck."

Helping Joanna finish with her juice, I watch Jay's face. "Come on, Kids, let's get out in Jay's car." My son again makes a comment on how neat it is having two people named Jay around. Smiling, I whisper, "Sure it

95

is, Little Man. Just goes to show that Daddy and I picked a good name, doesn't it Buddy?" My hands ruffle his blonde hair.

Strebeck waves us to the door, phone still to his ear. "Right, sure Captain Roberts. I'll get right on that after I finish here." A pause mixes with a strange look from Jay, and then he speaks again. "Tell him I'll be back to the office in a about half-an-hour. If anything else comes up, or they contact you, let me know right away....Thanks." He ends his call and snaps his phone shut. "The agency is on its way. We've got a little more time than I had hoped, but let's get going." He opens the door, "Act like I'm a friend leaving, and I'll take the bag. Take the kids out, and head down the street towards the Chevron about five blocks away. I'll be at the convenience store, and you can get in there. Okay?" He smiles seeing my hesitant nod. "It's going to be okay." With that he snatches up my small duffel bag and heads to the car. "Thanks again! I'll tell Chase 'Hi' for ya! See ya later!" He calls out over his shoulder.

"Why'd he do that, Mommy?"

Smiling, I turn to my son. "Mr. Jay is being silly. But now, you heard what he said. We have to walk a few blocks, then we'll see him. We're going to go for a ride."

"Don't wanna go without Daddy." Joanna whines out with a pout.

"Daddy is going to meet us, Honey. Mr. Jay is just going to take us on a vacation for a couple of days."

"Are we going to stay in a hotel?" Jay's face lights up.

"Maybe."

"With a pool?" His face is even brighter.

"Don't know. We'll just have to be good and see, won't we?" Taking in a look of our house I wonder if we'll ever be back. Thinking of all the things we'll be leaving behind, I pause. "Hold on, wait here you guys." Quickly I go to my bedroom. Once there, I grab the heirloom jewelry, and two photo albums. *Not leaving all of these things behind, no matter what.* Making my way to the kitchen, I put them in plastic grocery bags.

Making my way back up to the door, the phone rings. Jay had told me not to answer the phone from now on, but I checked the caller-id. Unlisted. My heart starts pounding, a sick feeling grows in my stomach.

Are you with me now?

No answer.

"Let's go kids." Quickly I make sure the note is in an obvious spot. With one last look, I close the door. "Slow down you guys." The kids are already near the sidewalk. "Wait for me."

Holding Joanna's hand, I slowly look around. No one is around that I can see, and I hope no one notices me. Seeing no one, I begin to relax. The neighborhood would be alive in the next few hours, I guess. The image of cars surrounding a house comes to mind, and I wonder if that would be what will happen.

The five blocks was a quick walk, and we see Jay's vehicle already there. He isn't in the car, so I start to wonder where he is. Standing outside the store, I peer in. Finding him going over the candy selection, I try to get his attention. After a couple more times of waving, he finally sees me and put up a finger to signal he'll be just a moment. I respond in turn by nodding, and head to the car to see if it's open. Finding it unlocked, we pile in.

"I like Mr. Jay's car, Mommy." Joanna fondly rubs the upholstery, and car door. "It's pretty."

Smiling in turn, I look around to see how many people are in the area. Not many. Just the occasional cars passing by, or fueling up, so I relax some. Glancing back towards the store, I see Jay unloading an armful of stuff onto the counter. He smiles back at whatever the cashier says as he pulls out his wallet. His phone must have rung, as a hand quickly dives into his coat to retrieve it. His quick look at the car tells me it's about us. He looks at the cashier, then back to the car. He puts the phone away, and smiles at the cashier again, who is busy putting things into bags. Jay helps. Everything effectively stowed for transport, Jay pushes through the door, bags in hand.

As soon as he gets in the car he starts talking. "While I was waiting, I thought I'd get you some goodies for the next couple of days. New toothbrushes, candy and snacks, and stuff like that. Here ya go." The bags land in my lap.

Turning to him, his face is grim. "Was it bad news?"

The car starts to reverse. Jay pulls out of the parking lot before he answers. "They're going to be here in an hour. That doesn't leave me much time." He quickly changes lanes, speed picking up a bit to stay a little ahead of traffic. "As soon as we get you to the hotel, stay there."

"Yeah-hoo! We're going to a hotel!" My son bounces in his seat with glee.

"Calm down, Honey."

With only a casual smile towards the still smiling boy in the back seat, he continues. "No matter what, do not answer the door. If someone calls, don't answer it. Don't leave the room through the door. If there is an emergency, the room adjoined to yours is vacant. Leave that way." He shakes his head. "I don't know if I'm telling you all of this for nothing, or if we'll have to use it." He gives me a hard look. "I'm risking a lot here."

"I know. Thank you."

"I mean if things fall through, you'll have very little time to move. Understand? I haven't had much time to prepare this. I've never even done this before. I hope I've got everything covered." He seems deep in thought as he drives. "Oh! The phone. If you need to contact me, we both have new cell phones. Yours will be waiting for you at the hotel. Mine too. Only answer the cell phone. Okay?"

The sinking feeling is returning. "Okay." I feel his eyes on me.

"Are you okay?"

Nodding I stare blindly out the window. *How can I be okay? My whole life just got turned upside down.*

"I know. I'm sorry." Jay slowly shakes his head.

My head turns. Carefully, I say, "I didn't say anything."

"Yeah you did. You said something about your life being turned upside down."

Swallowing the huge lump in my throat I wonder what I should say. Luckily, the soft girl little voice in the backseat spoke first. "Mommy didn't say anything. She was just looking out her window."

My eyes didn't leave his face. *Are you there?*

Here and present. What's going on? I feel panic. Her voice makes me realize I had been holding my breath.

"Are you sure you didn't say anything?" Jay's face seems paranoid.

"I'm positive I never said it. But I *thought* it." My eyes don't leave his face. "You heard what I was thinking?"

Jay frowns a bit, and hits his turn signal.

"She's here, right now. The one I have dreams I am."

Jay turns a panicked look at me. "Christ. Tell her to leave or something. They may be able to trace it."

Go away. I need you to go away. Hurry! A feeling of loss for a split second, and I knew she is gone. The lump still sits in my throat. "How?" My eyes meet his for a second? "I mean, how can they trace me with that going on?"

"Because that's going on. You still have the implant in you. I'm supposed to take you somewhere tomorrow to see if we can remove it, but maybe I'll have to step things up." Jay is silent for a few minutes. "Has that ever happened before? When you were awake, I mean?"

"I'm not sure. I just felt like seeing if she was there since you had heard my thoughts. It seemed natural for me to do so." We're nearing the edge of the city. "Don't know how I knew, but I must have. I could feel her almost. Hear her."

Jay gives me a weird look. His eyes go back to the road. "Here we are. Home, sweet home." He gives me a look. "At least for tonight." Pulling up to the desk he says to stay in the car, and puts on a hat. With that he heads into the hotel.

"Mommy?" My son is leaning forward in the seatbelt.

"Hmm?"

"Does this hotel have a pool?"

Fighting back the urge to laugh, "I don't know, Dude. But I think we need to stay in our room tonight. We don't even have swimming trunks for you." Calmly I soothe his upset. "We'll get some new swimming trunks for you later, okay?" Slowly he nods, not really satisfied.

Jay comes out of the hotel and heads for the car. Once he gets in the car, he takes off the hat. "The room is towards the back, luckily. We'll get you in that way." He slowly pulls the car to the rear of the hotel. Once he pulls into a parking space, we all get out. The bags from the convenience store fill my hands. We head for the door and I see the security key in Jay's hand slip in the slot. The light goes green, and Jay holds open the door. We follow him up a set of stairs to our room. He again holds the doors open. "Home, sweet home."

"You said that already."

The room is of good size, and thankfully the kids go right in. Holding my hand open for the key, I wait in the doorway.

"Sorry. I'll keep this. Here's your stuff." Jay hands me the small duffel bag. "I'll be back with the hubby in a few. I'll need this to get back in. Here's your new phone." He tries to make having it sound so sheik. "Let me program my cell number in real quick, in case you need anything."

"Anything else?" Fatigue starts to consume me even though it wasn't quite noon. But I wanted to make sure I had it all straight.

"Please don't sleep. I know it's going to be hard, but we'll take care of that in a bit. I hope." Jay rests a reassuring hand on my shoulder. "Have faith." He smiles broadly at my weak one. "I'll bring some pizza for lunch when I bring Chase."

"Pizza! Yeah-hoo!" My son carols.

Instinctively, I rush to hush him. "We have to be quiet here, Dude. We don't want to be noticed. Okay?" Looking back at Jay I ask when to expect him to return.

"Hopefully within the next half hour." He turns to leave. "And one more thing."

"What?"

"Welcome to the Witness Protection Program." The door shuts.

CHAPTER 18

Jay shuts the door behind Chase, who is holding a pizza above the heads of two excited kids. Ushering the munchkins to the beds, and reminding them of the need to be quiet, I take the pizza from Chase.

"Okay. You are all here. As I have briefed you both, the agency is going to arrive at your residence soon. Before I go I need to give you your new paperwork." From his briefcase he pulls a manila envelope. "Let's see." He rummages briefly through the contents before heading for the bed and dumping them out.

"You are no longer able to have contact with those you have before. I'll let some of them in on what's transpired, like your friend Kim, as soon as I can. Don't try to call family, work, et cetra. They'll be looking for that.

"Also, we have the standard name changes." He looks at and brandishes a new driver's license for Chase. "Here you go, Mr. Michael T. Kirkland."

"Plover, Wisconsin?" Chase remarks on his new license.

"You gotta be from somewhere right? Why not a place you've never been?" Jay peers at it, then waves a driver's license towards me. "Mrs. Tanya A. Kirkland. Also, a cheesehead, for obvious marital reasons." He pulls up some social security cards. "Here and here. These are for the kids. As well as these." New birth certificates are now in my hands. "Here's a map of Wisconsin, and some travel guide information to familiarize yourselves, if you get bored. Here's a Target gift card. It has fifty dollars on it. Also, here's one for K-mart worth one hundred, I think. That's for clothes and other personals. A credit card with a four thousand dollar balance, joint of course." He continues going through the pile. "Oh, wedding certificate," he smiles some more. "Also from Wisconsin."

Chase asks, "Are we moving to Wisconsin too?"

Jay pauses. "Do you want to?" Seeing our bland looks he gives us a wave of dismissal. "We'll talk about that later."

Jay's phone rings, the one still in his coat, and we all freeze. He looks at the kids. "I'm going to take this outside. Hold on."

Chase looks at me, and I rush to his arms. "I'm so sorry."

Gently, he rubs the small of my back. "Guess I meant it when they asked in good times and bad. Good grief!" He pushes me away to see my face. "It's going to be okay. Strebeck comes walking into the squadron with a pair of armed Security Forces guys, and a piece of paper. I about crapped my pants. No one else was about, though. Then Strebeck asked to speak with my commander. After about ten minutes behind doors, I was 'escorted' from work. Poof!" Chase's hands imitate a miniature explosion. "Just like that, I'm done with the military! He said that the last deposit would go into a new, secure account, along with a hefty sum of seven thousand dollars. I don't know what was on that piece of paper, but I didn't stop to ask my commander on my way out either." He chuckles. Then looks for the smiling kids lounging on the beds. "And you two!"

The giggles erupt as two once-quiet kids become animals once again, before my eyes. "Chase, please."

"Michael," Chase teases.

Hearing the door, I turn to see Jay Strebeck's grim face. "Well, the chase is on. I've been requested to arrive at your residence and help interview friends and family if you don't turn up within the next hour. I told them that I'd be at your place in half an hour."

Seeing his unease, I reach for him. "Oh Jay...thank you so much. I know what risks you are taking, and want you to know we appreciate it."

He nods, and takes a few deep breaths.

"We'll be forever in your debt if this pulls off." Chase stands beside me, his voice strong.

Jay almost laughs. "You'll probably regret saying that." He runs his fingers through his hair. "Oh! Reb-, Tanya. Please don't eat anything, or have anything besides water. You have an appointment with me at ten o'clock tonight for that implant. I was able to get a favor returned from a surgeon on the east coast. He'll be arriving tonight. I'll call on the cell before I come up, okay?"

Nodding, I feel the urge to hug him. I take a step towards him.

He backs away. "No celebrations yet. There's a lot to be done before we pop the cork, okay?"

"Mr. Kirkland, Mrs. Kirkland, have a good night. I'll talk with you soon, I hope." With that he is gone.

"Who wants pizza?" Chase carols to the eager kids.

"Me! Me!" The kids call out in unison.

Going to a window, I watch Strebeck get into his car, and just sit.

Jay sags into his car seat. His nerves are strung taut he knows, but he needs to psyched up about this disappearance when he gets to the Stewart residence. He's done this before, the research and rescue. He usually hates being a part of it, but knows it is part of the job. He also knows they rely on those closest to the core of the agency the most. Jay has even half expected to be present when they went to her house. He dislikes the agency's predictability and ruthlessness when it came to collection of people.

Jay pulls out his trusty old cell phone. Pressing a few numbers, he waits for the call to go through.

"Staff Sergeant Michner, this is a secure line. How may I help you?" Adam's voice sounded like a recording.

"It's Strebeck. How are things?"

"Hot. People are swarming everywhere. Captain Roberts is ticked, and sweating like a hog. How go your errands?"

Jay rubs his face. "Good. Getting everything settled here as fast as I can so I can try and help search for her." Jay pauses hoping Adam will back him up. "Do they have any idea where she may have gone?"

"Nope. They say she had left some note, and hasn't returned as of yet. They're starting a watch on the house, I guess." Adam sounds neutral.

"I'll be in the office tomorrow, hopefully. And if she turns up. If it's going to be later, I'll call you at home. Okay?" Jay waits for Adam's response. Looking up at the window of the hotel, he spies Rebecca watching him. "Guess I bet get going. Keep me posted if anything changes, will you?"

"I will. Hopefully she turns up." Adam sounds convincing. "We're all hoping she's okay, and that this will end soon."

Jay nods, eyes still on those watching him. "Hear, hear. Talk to you later." With that said, he ends the call, eyes never leaving those on him. With a last long look, he starts the engine, and leaves.

Those eyes on him have made him nervous. They weren't panicky, nor distrusting. They were just, there, almost probing. "Like Angela's."

Jay slowly pulls around the corner and sees a surveillance vehicle about three houses from Rebecca's. He slows down, as if checking numbers until he sees Daniel Maxwell heading his way. Jay pulls over to the curb. He rolls down his window as Maxwell approaches. "Hey, sorry I'm a bit late. Some bad directions."

Maxwell laughs. "Or bad direction following."

Jay laughs in turn. "You know me." He places the engine in neutral, the shuts off the car. "So what's up? Where is she?"

Maxwell just shrugs. "Dunno. We've been waiting for a couple hours, and she has yet to show up. We knocked when we first arrived, but there was no answer. We checked the door, and it was unlocked. Gurness ordered some to go inside and do a quick check. From the looks of things she was going for a walk, at least that's what her note said."

"Any signs of flight?" Jay gets out of his car, then reaches for a jacket.

"None. Her purse is still in there, money, credit cards, checkbook, and everything. Nothing is missing as far as we can tell. She even was doing some laundry. She had just put some clothes in the wash when we arrived. It just doesn't make any sense." Maxwell shrugs and pats Jay on the back. "Guess it's your turn to have a bash at all of this."

Jay pretends to be stumped. He looks over the neighborhood and notices two other cars. "When did you all get here?"

Maxwell looks at his watch. "Probably two to two-and-a-half hours ago."

"Maybe she takes long walks."

"We haven't discounted that yet. But about an hour after we got here, they had some flash come up for a few seconds on her profile. Gurness was wondering where she was when this happened. He's hoping she didn't, you know, have an accident, or something." Maxwell kicks the loosened pebbles, then looks around.

"I'm sure she'll turn up yet. She could be just around the corner." Jay looks around for affect. "What about this 'flash?' How long?"

"Just a few seconds, barely registered. Not long enough to get a reading on her location either."

Jay nods, and scratches his head. "Do we have any idea what this one was?"

Again a shrug. "Too short to tell." Maxwell sits on the hood of Jay's car. "This is a first. We've never had to camp out on a collection before." He smirks. "I didn't even bring marshmallows."

Jay scans the area again. "Has anyone gone to her friends' homes yet? Checked with her husband? He could be getting off work soon."

Maxwell nods and points to a co-worker. "Stan has been cruising the homes of the friends here, and hasn't seen her yet. No biggie, I guess."

Jay turns. "And her husband?"

"Had some appointment and has yet to return as well. His commander was not very cooperative. Said that he needed some sort of explanation for our asking about one of his troops." Maxwell waves an annoyed hand in the air. "Old pain in the ass."

"Probably wanting to protect his troops, or wondering what his troop and done wrong." Jay sits next to his old friend. "Guess we can wait a bit longer to see if she shows up. If not, I'll start visiting some of her friends, and see what they have to say."

CHAPTER 19

Jay slowly pulls up to Kim's house. With one last look to be sure he wasn't followed, he heads up her walkway. After pressing the doorbell, he waits, eyes still looking about for some sign of being trailed.

Kim cracks open the door. Seeing Jay standing there, she looks around. "Hello."

Jay quickly interrupts her thoughts. "I need to talk to you about your friend. May I come in?" Jay sees a young girl in her pajamas. "I know it's late, and that you may have some questions."

Kim stands clear allowing him access. Once he's in she secures the door. "What's going on? Why did you have me tell her to pack her bags? Where are they?"

Jay puts up a hand to stop the flow of questions. "They are safe. Had things not been done as quickly as they were, she'd be on her way to the agency's testing facilities. I needed you to help me speed things up in a way they wouldn't be able to detect."

Kim eyes Jay sternly. "Where is she?"

"You can't go to her yet. They'll be expecting that. They've been monitoring the neighborhoods for the past three hours looking for her."

Dennis walks in. "Who's this?" Kim offers the introductions. "So you've turned sour on your own job, huh? Why?"

Jay glances at his watch. It shows the time as a little past nine. "Let's just say I have a personal score to settle with some of these people. A few overdue favors that need collecting. And a bad memory I'm trying to heal.

"Look, I don't have much time. I have some very important appointments. I just came by because I wanted to let you know that they are all okay. I'll let them contact you as soon as possible." With that said Jay stood. "I was supposed to check and see if you've heard from her today. That's why I was allowed to come over."

Dennis stands too. "Thanks for stopping by. Kim's been a mess all afternoon."

"I have not!" Kim snorts at Dennis' look. "What?"

"Like I said, a wreck." Dennis shrugs off Kim's huff. "We appreciate you looking out for our friends." He extends a hand to Jay.

"My pleasure, but like I told them. Don't start celebrating too early. Lots has to be done first, so keep your fingers crossed. And pray." Jay opens the door. "Thanks for your time. Sorry to have intruded while you were getting ready to call it a night."

"Hey, Jay?" A voice comes from the street.

Jay turns. There is Maxwell, and he is heading their way. "Hey, Dan. What's up?" Then turns back to Kim and Dennis. "I'd appreciate it if you do hear from them to give me a call." Jay withdraws a business card. "My cell phone is always on." Jay turns feeling Maxwell beside him.

"Evening folks," Maxwell dismisses them. "We have a lead. An elderly lady said she saw Rebecca and the kids walking about an hour before we arrived. The lady said she was holding some bags, like groceries. Said that they were heading towards the bus stop area. We gotta go." He tugs on Jay's arm.

Jay offers Kim and Dennis a smile. "You have a good night. And don't worry. She's bound to be around."

Kim offers a small smile as Dennis shuts the door.

Jay follows Maxwell to the car, checking his watch as he walks. "So what have we done with this tip?"

"We sent a couple of guys to check it out. They should let us know. Hopefully she didn't disappear."

Jay looks incredulous. "Why would she? She had no idea what was going on. I'm sure it is not as it appears." Jay pauses nervously, knowing he needs to leave to get Rebecca for the appointment he has scheduled. "Tell ya what. I'm going to drive around the town a bit. I'll let you know if I come across anything." Jay heads for his car. He glances about the sees another car. "Where are you headed?"

Maxwell shrugs. "Guess I'll call it a night. We've got rooms over at the Howard-Johnson. How about you? You heading back to billeting, or want to bunk up around here? We can get the papers faxed to the hotel it you need."

Jay waves a hand while smiling. "Nah. Think I'll go ahead and head back. All my stuff is in the room. Wasn't planning on being here all night. I thought we'd find her right away and then I could tie up loose ends with Captain Roberts." Jay rubs his face in feigned disgust. "Just lock this one up and throw away the keys. She's been a pain for the agency since they found out about her."

Maxwell nods in agreement. "Sometimes I think they should dispose of freaks like this. Like that one kid a few years back. Ugh. Reminds me of that movie that just came out. You know, the mutants and stuff. It's based on the comics."

Jay nods his head, all the while seething with anger. His blood boils with contempt for people like Maxwell, and the agency as a whole. "I know the movie." Somehow Jay's voice don't relay his inner emotions.

"People like that have no place in our society anyway."

Jay glances at his watch. "Yeah, well I need to get going. I have that long drive ahead of me, and have to back here early. Unless of course you find her during the night. Then give me a courtesy call so I can sleep in, okay?"

Maxwell nods, and offers a friendly wave. "Wish we all could sleep in tomorrow. I'll give ya a buzz in the morning."

Jay doesn't even waste his time or his breath to comment as he starts his car. I was nearing ten o'clock and he need to get Rebecca to have the implant removed. Or so he hoped. Jay honestly knew little of the possibility of removing the implant after so many years. To his knowledge, no one ever removed one from a living person before. He had all the specifications, knew where the implants were usually connected, and what they looked like on x-ray, but not if they could be successfully be removed on a living "host." He knew they will have to try. If not for Rebecca, than for him. *Better to let her die going free, than to die a prisoner at the hands of the agency.*

Jay heads first for the interstate, planning on making a good look of it in case of being followed. Taking an exit, he pulls into a McDonald's. He places an order, then uses the restroom. When he comes out, he notices nothing unusual, so heads for his car. Taking a few bites, he watches the other vehicles' comings and goings. Seeing almost the entire parking refill with new vehicles, Jay calmly pulls out. He keeps checking his mirrors for signs of being followed. Seeing none, he weaves his way to the Sleep Inn.

By the time he gets there, he's a bit ticked with the flow of traffic. Pulling into the same parking spot he was in earlier, he looks up to the window. He half-expects her to be standing there with some, "I knew you were here" look. Instead, the curtains are pulled shut, and no light comes from around them. Quickly he enters the hotel and climbs the stairs leading to the room. With a soft rap, he inserts his key in the lock. The bathroom light is on, with its door slightly ajar. There is no movement, no sound. Jay's heart starts pounding. "Hello?" Jay exhales a sigh of relief hearing the soft exhales from the room.

Rebecca gets in his face with a hiss. "You said you were going to call first." She turns away in anger. "You gave us all a heart attack!"

Instantly, Jay feels like a jerk. "Dang it, I'm sorry. Had so many things on my mind. But we have to go." He reaches for her arm. "I'm late, and I'll only have this one chance."

"Let me say goodnight to the munchkins." Rebecca gives her kids a big hug and quick peck on the cheek. "Be good. I'll be back after you go back to sleep." With a quick kiss on Chase's ready lips she heads towards him. "Let's ski-daddle."

The silence between us is strong, and so is our nervousness. "So?" Fastening my seatbelt, I shiver against the chill of the night. "How'd it go at my place?"

Jay shrugs. "You're gone. They're pissed. They're looking and asking questions." He snorts. "Some old lady said she saw you and the kids heading for the bus station with a few grocery-type bags, so they're luckily busy checking that all out right now. Could take a few days for them to realize they are on the wrong track." Jay shrugs again. "Then again, they could know they were mistaken by now."

"Is that why you're so nervous?" My voice sounds shaky.

Jay turns his head. "I'd rather not talk about it." *It would not do you any good.*

"What wouldn't?"

"Hmm?" Jay gives me a weird look.

"I asked what wouldn't do me any good?"

Jay snaps a look at me. "You're not doing your stuff right now are you?"

"I...I don't think so. Why?"

"The thought. You just read my thought." Jay seems pissed as he shakes his head.

Trying to lighten the sudden tension, "Now why can't I do that with Chase?"

Jay only looks at me, then back to the street.

After a few more minutes of silence, a thought comes to me. "This procedure, has it ever been done before?"

Jay makes a small face while shrugging. "Sure, many times."

"You're holding something back, aren't you?" Jay's face contorts as I watch. "It hasn't been done before, right?"

He shakes his head.

My body sags into the seat. Idly, my hands play with the seatbelt as a numbness surrounds me. My limbs feel heavy, and I know only part of the reason is due to the lateness of the night. "Am I going to die?"

"Christ!" Jay whips a look in my direction. "No. At least I hope not." He runs a hand through his hair, then rubs his face. "Look. Just think positive, and everything will be fine. 'Speak it and so it shall be.'"

The hospital sign catches my eyes. A block later we are at the night entrance, and Jay's parking the car. The building never seemed so eerie during the day. Many times before I had been here, and never felt like this. *Probably because you didn't think you were going to die.*

I'm not going to die.

Well, let's hope not, for both our sakes.

Jay touches my elbow. "You okay?" At my nod he urges me forward like a reluctant foal. "Let's get this over with."

My feet slowly make their way into the building's entrance. Jay is already talking to a nurse who looks about to page someone. Her lips move, and a split second later, "Doctor Redden call the Information Desk. Doctor Redden to call the Information Desk." My feet still shuffle along until they come beside Jay's.

"So? What's up?" My voice sounds weak.

"It's okay, Honey." Jay takes my hand. "I've already called for the doctor to call down to let us up. It should only be a minute." Again he looks at the nurse expectantly.

"Honey?" My voice a soft hiss.

"Go with it, Hon. It'll be okay." His look shows a brief wink, wink.

"I'm okay...Hon." My voice seems to catch to my own ears.

The bleep, bleep of the Information Desk's phone demands all of our attention. Calmly the nurse answers, then listens. Her face takes in the two of us as she listens. "Okay." Her eyes go to something on her desk, then to a folder. "Uh-huh." After another couple of seconds, she smiles. "Okay. No problem." She turns to us. "Doctor Redden is sending someone down with a wheelchair for you." She indicates me, so I nod as if expecting that. "He also said to have you sign the waiver and consent forms." This she addresses to Jay as she hands him the folder she had glanced at earlier. "He also said everything is prepped."

Jay thanks her, so I follow suit. Hearing the ding of the elevator I turn, and see a wheelchair on its way over. The young man pushes it straight towards me. "Hi," he says to me as he pulls up. "My name is Erik, and I'm the nurse assisting Doctor Redden this evening." He looks at Jay. "Everything signed there Jay?"

"Sure is Erik. How have you been?" Jay shakes the young man's hand. "Been a while, hasn't it?"

Erik smiles warmly. "Sure has. But we can chit-chat later. Doctor Redden is ready, and the flight leaves in three hours. We don't want to miss it, if you know what I mean."

I warily look at Jay. He knows so many people it's almost unsettling. But Jay seems at ease as he tells me to relax and guides me into the wheelchair as if I was some ninety year old invalid. Once Erik starts pushing me, I feel ninety. Again I feel heavy, nervous, fatigued, and... alone. No one seems about as they push me to the elevator. The ding seems to echo through the shiny halls. Not wanting to eavesdrop, I concentrate on the muted strains of music coming over the elevator's single speaker.

Feeling a hand on my shoulder, I realize that Erik is talking to me. "I'm sorry. I wasn't paying attention."

His smile is kind. "I said that as soon as we get to the room, you'll need to strip, leave nothing on, and don the hospital gown. Opening to the back please, and don't tie the sashes. Okay?" Getting my nod, he continues. "I'll start the IV right after you're changed, and then start the sedation." The elevator dings signifying we're on the level we need to be. "When's the last time you ate?" He writes down my answer.

"Are you using conscious sedation?" Jay's voice is almost drowned by the sound of the elevator's doors opening.

Erik shakes his head. "He's wanting a combination of stuff, just in case."

Erik's words go on, but I only notice the room I've just been wheeled into. It's cool, and goose bumps are already forming on my arms. Seeing the gown, I stand and reach for it. The sound of the door closing gets only a glance as I quickly verify that the door is indeed closed.

I can't believe that I'm doing this. But it's not like I really have another choice, is it? My sweatshirt comes off, and shortly after, everything else. Soon I am modeling the unfashionable hospital gown and awaiting Erik's return.

"Knock, knock."

"I'm ready."

He comes is with a tray of needles, alcohol swabs, and vials. A bag of saline is over his shoulder. "This won't take long. You'll be out and done before you know it."

Placing my right arm before him like a prize, I glance at the door to see if Jay is around. My eyes catch him talking to a man dressed in surgery garb as they look at x-rays on a light board.

"Slight stick."

My eyes are on the man next to Jay. *Please do a good job.* As if sensing me, he turns and smiles.

"The needle going in."

The surgeon heads towards the room. With a quick rap, he enters. "Hi there. I'm Doctor Redden. I'd shake your hand, but Erik would probably have a fit as he's still stabilizing the needle." He glances at Erik and tells him four ccs of something-or-other, but I still am watching his face. He senses this and looks back at me. "No, I've never done this exact procedure before, but feel like it should be no problem."

"It's going in now. Ma'am, you may start to feel a bit woozy. Let us know when that happens, ok?" Erik sounds so calm.

"Where's Jay?" My mentioning his name, he appears. "If anything goes wrong, tell them I love them."

He takes my left hand and gives it a gentle squeeze. "Positive thoughts."

Nodding, I feel light-headed. "I think… it's working."

With a last squeeze, sleep takes me.

Jodie M. Swanson

CHAPTER 20

Jay spins the small vial before my groggy eyes. "Success. You're almost free."

Slowly, I blink and try to sit more upright. "What is it?"

Jay examines the small piece of metal, and rolls the vial a bit. "Your implant. It was a bit easier than we thought it would be to take out."

My unsteadily hand comes up to hold the vial. The outside of the metal was speckled with blood yet, but I could set three little hooks, and a thin fiber coming from the base. "So this is it? I'm free?" The metal rolls in the vial as I twist it. "They won't be able to trace me anymore?"

"Nope. No tracing, no monitoring. Adam will be pleased to be rid of your information, I sure." Jay sits casually on the bed beside me. "How do you feel?"

"Like I'm still sleepy. I want to go back to sleep." My head falls softly to the pillow. The discomfort is minimal right now, so sleep takes me in its arms again.

When I awaken, I feel Joanna beside me. Her soft breath tickles the hairs on my arm. Confusion hits me, and I struggle to sit up. Doing so causes my head to rebel with pain and dizziness. Groaning, I settle back against the pillows. Warm wisps of steam fill the air around me, and I notice it is coming from the shower. Again I try to sit up. Dizzy, I throw my legs over the edge of the bed. Resting my head on the back of my hand, I sit there.

After a few minutes, Chase comes out of the bathroom, toweling his hair. At first he doesn't notice me as he goes about trying to dress quietly. After he fastens his pants he sees me sitting at the edge of the bed, and rushes over.

"Hey. How ya feelin'?" His hand gently rests on mine.

"Dizzy. Like I want to hurl." Slowly, I rub the grogginess from my face. "What time is it?"

Chase looks behind me. "It's almost six in the morning."

Turning my head, slowly I glance towards the curtains. The first few rays of light were tickling their edges. "How did I get here?"

Chase turns to grab his shirt. "Jay brought you. You were fast asleep in the car, so I needed to help carry you up."

Noticing my clothes are missing, I panic. "Did he bring me up like this?"

"Heck no. You were wearing your pants and the hospital gown, and Jay's coat." Chase bends down to grab his shoe. "He said to tell you that there was a couple night shift nurses who came by and dressed you. He said that he wheeled you out, and put you in the car." Chase sits down beside me to put on his shoes. The motion sets nausea into play. "He said you might wonder." The shifting of his weight on the mattress sends me to my knees and crawling for the toilet. "Are you okay?"

Resting my warm cheek against the cool porcelain, I wonder the same thing. My head is spinning and in pain. Gingerly, I reach for the source of the pain. Finding a medium-sized patch of my hair missing, I squeak in dismay. Tape that binds the coarse gauze to my scalp is fairly small, so I assume the site is even smaller.

"Are you okay?" Chase kneels beside me. He hands me a damp washcloth. "Here. Let's get you back to bed." Carefully, he wraps his arms around my waist in an effort to lift me to my feet. "Come on." He strains against my sagging form. "Help me out some, Hon."

With limp legs and sagging shoulders, I stand. "Where is Jay?"

"Next door. He brought you in about three in the morning, and crashed. He said he'd be up around seven thirty or so." He maneuvers me to the bed. "There ya go." He sets me down and immediately pulls the covers up around me. "Just relax some more."

Sunshine is streaming in the room when I wake again. Blinking against the brightness, I think I feel better. Sitting up proves otherwise, but know I have to try anyway. The pain at the rear of my head has increased and I want it to go away. My groan attracts some attention. "My head really hurts."

Chase is the closest. "Hold on." He turns away, and heads for the bathroom.

Looking around, I see that Jay Strebeck and my kids are watching me. Offering a small smile, I wait for Chase to return. The realization that I'm dressed is a comfort having some man in the hotel room. The curtains aren't spread wide like I had thought, but rather only about half way. The light coming in announces that it is late morning. Chase stands before me hands out. In one he holds a cup of water. In the other a pill. "What is it?"

"Tylenol three, the good codeine stuff." Chase stills hold out his parcels.

Taking the pill, I gaze around some more. Noticing that our bags were gone from the room I inquire about it.

Chase smiles. "They're in the car. Jay helped us secure a used auto to get us out of here. It's not as nice as our Accord, but it'll do." He takes the empty cup from my hands. "But we need to leave soon. Jay's already given me all rest of the paperwork."

"Where are we going?"

"We're going to Wisconsin!" My son runs up to me, and I flinch at the pain that erupts by his forceful landing. "Daddy says it's going to be great. He says he's going to take me fishin'."

"Me too!" Joanna screams.

My hands fly to cover my ears against their loudness. My eyes look at Chase. "Where in Wisconsin?"

Jay comes over. "We need to get going. You can talk about this later." He reaches into his coat pocket and withdraws a worn business card. He hands it to Chase. "This is a friend of mine. Contact him when you are settled somewhere. I'd like to keep in touch, and maybe still do the hypnotherapy."

Chase takes the business card and puts it into his wallet. "We'll let you know." Jay nods. "Guess I better get going. I was supposed to have 'reported in' thirty minutes ago. They'll be wondering where I am if I don't get there soon." He shakes Chase's hand. "Good luck, Chase." He in turn offers me a hand. "Rebecca." Releasing my hand he gives a pat on each of the kids' heads, then opens the door.

"Thank you." My voice sounds small, but he looks back and smiles. "Thanks so much." Smiling in turn, I watch him leave. Standing against the pain I slowly make my way towards the window, but his car is already gone. Catching my son's eager face, I try to smile. "Well, I guess we better get going."

After a few minutes we settle down in our "new" car. Reclining against Chase's jacket I prepare for the jolts and bumps I fear will be on the roads we take today. "Where in Wisconsin?"

Chase shrugs. "I thought we'd check out this Plover. It's near some other cities. One is Stevens Point. There's a college there, and some industry as well. It seems like a good place to start, since we already have some identification for that area, and whatnot." He pulls out slowly, and apologizes for the little jolts.

Offering him a weak smile, I say that it's okay, that I'll survive.

A few miles later we are on the interstate, heading for Cheesehead Land, Land of Moos, and Packer Backer territory. The thought seems remotely funny. Leaving one Potato Land for a Dairy Land. A soft chuckle comes from within me.

"What?" Chase smiles at me. "What's so funny?"

"That we're going from the land of Potatoes to the land of moo-moos."

Chase agrees, laughing with me. "Your head must be feeling better."

Giving a slow nod, I mention that the pain seems to be subsiding. "I'm still feeling tired though." Chase tells me to go ahead and get some more sleep. So I do.

Jay pulls up next to Maxwell's car. "Sorry I'm late. What's the news?"

Maxwell shakes his head. "It's not good. The bus station lead was a dead end. Found out about an hour ago."

Jay is surprised. "That was fast." Seeing a truck coming up behind him, he says to Maxwell, "Let me park." He pulls ahead a bit and parks. Taking a moment to brace Jay cracks his neck.

"I hate it when you do that." Maxwell was already by the door.

"Sorry. Didn't know you were there," Jay teases. "So? What do we do now?"

Maxwell shrugs. "I guess we're waiting for her 'beeper' to go off."

Knowing he's making a reference to the implant, Jay smiles inwardly. *Not in this lifetime pal.* "That could take days. We don't have that long. She could be hurt or something." Jay taps his door showing he wanted out of his vehicle.

"Maybe." Maxwell rubs his balding head. "I just don't get it. How could she just disappear without us knowing?"

One of us does know you prick, and I'm not saying where she is. Jay only shrugs in agreement. "She's gonna turn up soon. I just know it." *But not where you are expecting.*

CHAPTER 21

Standing on the beach, I feel the sun's warm rays blend with the sounds of the surf. The tranquil scene before me does its job completely. My tension is gone, replaces by calm control. Peace. Inhaling, deeply I close my eyes. Beside me is my phantom friend. "She is safe now. Someone helped her." Sighing, I smile. "Guess she didn't need my help after all."

Shadow nods. "Point taken."

"You!" A male voice shouts over the sand.

Turning, I see Derk fast approaching. Confusion lights my face as he stops a few feet away. My hand comes to my chest. "Me?"

Exasperated, he throws his hands up. "Of course you. I have been looking all over for you."

"Why?" He doesn't seem truly agitated so I raise my brow. "What could you want with me?" My stance shows I'm ready for a battle of wits or strength.

He looks about, mostly in the sand. "Is your *friend* around here?"

Wanting to laugh, I nod. "Why?"

"How is it possible? What you can do? And her 'state' of being invisible?" He looks annoyed, and tired.

"By...energy, I suppose." Looking at him, I wonder why he's really here. "Why do you ask?"

He looks around, then shakes his head. "If you're not a witch out there casting spells, how is all of this possible? I mean, I know things are happening, and you are the cause."

Straight-faced, I stare blandly ahead. "What things are you talking about?"

He shrugs. "Maybe not really causing by thought, but by actions?"

"What *are* you talking about?" My voice doesn't hide my irritation.

"He's a nut case. Throw him back." Shadow crosses her arms next to me.

He listens to the gulls overhead before talking. "How is it she can do physical things, and yet not be physically seen? I've done some asking of the people from around here about you and your *friend*."

"And? What rubbish did they come up with this time?" My tone still denotes my irritation.

"They told me to talk to you father."

My chest feels like it's collapsed. "And did you?" My voice gives itself away as a whisper.

He nods. "He said that you started as a normal little girl. He told me about the wave when you started...acting strange. He told me about your wanting to read people's futures, and..."

"He's a liar," I grind out. "I *never* wanted to pretend to read people's minds, futures, hands, or anything else. That was all *his* desire."

"Relax. You're letting him get to you." My phantom's voice offers wisdom.

"He abused me, and the energy that comes to me, for his own gain." My voice is under control again. "When I didn't comply..."

"You lost control and killed your mother." He said it so easily, without contempt.

"That much is true."

"So, what is this power you have?" He takes a small step forward.

"I have no power." Seeing him about to argue, I continue. "I have what most people lack. I have control."

"Nicely said." She champions me.

Thank you.

"Over what?"

"The energy that every living thing has about it, it's being." Shrugging, I try for the appearance of calmness. "I can manipulate it to do as I want, without truly manipulating. It asks me if it can flow through me. I just help direct it." My eyes meet his. "Do you understand?"

He nods, then shakes his head. "How? Can you give me an example?"

"I guess. What do you want?" My curiosity is piqued.

"Lots of money."

"What a dork," Shadow huffs.

"Doesn't have anything to do with the energy your being has to give. Sorry."

"I was wondering why you lived in that hole you call home." His voice is tinged with disgust. "Now I know."

"I'm glad then that you don't call it home." It's all I can think of to say.

He holds my gaze. "Actually, I want to see your invisible *friend*. Can you do that?" His tone is bland, as are his features.

"The real question is, can you?" My eyebrows challenge him. "She's visible to the open."

"How come then I can't see her if I want to?"

Taking him in, I wonder why he wants to see my silent companion, and ask him such.

"I fricken own her one for walloping me the other day." He says it some matter-of-factly, that I can't help but burst out laughing. I hear Shadow laughing, too. "What?"

"You want to see her so you can get revenge?" My laughter is in full force now. "And we had thought you a nice type. Guess I was wrong." His shoulders relax a bit as my words sink in. "That's why I help protect the only person to befriend me."

"Protect? How?" He cocks his head to one side.

"You can't fight what you can't see, right?"

"Let him see me."

Turning, I look at my friend, I say aloud. "Are you sure you want that?"

She nods, and repeats. "Let him see me." Her eyes are on his face.

Slowly, I let the energy flow, softly. Watching Derk's faces as Shadow's veil of magic fades, I see surprise. His mouth parts in awe at the other woman appearing before him.

"She's beautiful!"

His words sting me. My eyes dart to my friend's to gauge her response. Seeing her tears, I wonder at their presence. Her eyes come to mine. "It's the first time anyone but you has seen me in fourteen years."

Nodding, I realize the man is no longer interested in retaliating against her. Nor has he any interest at all in me. Slowly, I step away, further down the beach to listen to the water's song. The feeling of jealousy tightens my heart, but soon a sadness fills its place. The realization that I had hoped someone would like me comes as a surprise, at the wrong time. Casting a quick glance their way, I see a smile light Shadow's face. Trying a small smile, I look across the water. It's receding. "Oh no." Quickly I turn and call to Shadow. "Wave! It's coming! Go!"

She spares a quick look at me, then grabs Derk's hand. She hauls on his arm trying to get him to move. He stands transfixed, looking at me. Her voice pleads for him to follow, and he does so, finally.

Looking back, I wonder when the last time a wave struck at sunset was. *When Mom died.* The thought came to me, and I shudder in remembrance. The shudder triggers another thought. It still in my mind, I head straight for the water.

"Rebecca!" Shadow's call is distant, but strong. Her mental presence enters me. "What are you doing?"

Trying something new. Now at the moist granules the waves had kissed and tickled only minutes before, I see the wave approaching. It's not overly big, not like the last one, but definitely could wash some people away if they were on the beach. My eyes dart back and forth to ensure I'm the only one out here. *Come on, you booger.*

Again, her presence. "Get out of there!"

Nah, I'm going to try and tame the beast. The energy starts trickling, moving. The wave approaches and I sense the wall is already up behind me. The energy surrounds me, the cocoon in the face of danger. My eyes close to get a better feel.

Down you beast. The energy flows from me. *Down I say. Work with me.*

The water surrounds me, from the waist below. The swell now small, almost normal, as it recedes to my thighs. "Good job." My hand touches the water. The water's charge still tickles my legs. "Good job," I repeat aloud. Turning, I see the walls going down. Smiling, I calmly head up out of the water.

"Rebecca!" Shadow is running down the beach towards me. She excitedly screams "Woo-hoo!" as she races over the sand. She jumps on me, happily patting my back. "Oh, that was unreal! Unreal!" She screams again.

Calmly, I look across the water. "It was the least it could do." My try for a point does not go unnoticed.

"Oh, so modest!" She gives me a big hug. "Wow!"

Smiling, I gaze across the water. "The thought just came to me to try." Seeing Derk coming up I pull back, away.

"Do you cause them, those waves?" His question is softly spoken.

"I have assumed for some time that I have some impact on their… comings." My voice is soft, far away, even to my own ears. "But I never knew for sure. I've never been able to ask anyone about the waves. I just remember there being some." Looking across the now normal waves I shake my head. *So strange.*

Hearing the chatter of other spectators coming our way, I excuse myself, and head for my cubby hole of a home. My earlier comment to Derk about my home plays in my ears as I brush past the locals and their weird expressions.

"It's about time."

I know that voice. Looking up I see my father. His face is as unreadable as ever. Not wanting to be bothered by his trivialities I try to walk past him. He reaches for my arm, and I quickly retract it. "Do you need something?"

"I'm surprised." That's all he says as he looks at me. After a few more seconds of holding my gaze he asks, "What triggered you this time?"

"What do you mean?" My look is incredulous. "Are you saying I caused it to come?"

"Are you saying you didn't?" He voice is equally challenging.

Working my lower lip, I wonder if I can ask him about the waves. "Have they always come?" His slow shake of the head prompts me again. "Did they start when I was born?"

"Earlier. When you were still in your mother." He looks across the now calm waves. "No one pieced it together until that day on the beach. People were running and screaming, and then…it hit." His eyes look so distant. "You blacked out I guess, but there was like a big thick bubble around us. It burst when you came to. That's when I knew it was you." His eyes turn back to me. "I believe you do cause them. And I'd wish you'd stop."

He takes a step away, but I hold him there, mentally. "You have no right to treat me this way. You helped cause some of these things."

He looks shocked. "Me?"

Anger fills me. "Pushing, mean, unloving, hurtful. Triggers. I'd wish you'd stop. Then maybe I will." Releasing him, I turn away. The energy doesn't want to be done with him yet, though. Calmly I think, *His time will come. Let him go.*

My feet send sand sprays as they make their way up to the steps. Once there, I quickly jog up the steps and slip through the door. Making for my mat, I relax. My emotional strain lessens until I hear footsteps by my doorway. A soft rap, and I relax, knowing who it is. "Hey Shadow."

She doesn't say anything as she sits next to me. No thoughts, no words, nothing. In silence we stay, companions in quiet harmony. After a while, she shifts.

"What?" My voice sounds tired.

"It was nice having him see me."

Forcing a smile, I whisper. "I'll bet it was." Looking at her, I watch her. "Seemed quite smitten with you, didn't he?"

She laughs. "Maybe at first, but I think it just the surprise of it all."

I sit up a bit. "Why would you say that?"

"He wanted to know if I could do what you could." She scuffs her shoes on the floor. "I told him that everything I had had come from learning from you."

Smiling, "My. Aren't we modest?" I lean back chuckling.

She gives me a sour look. "Come on, Rebecca. You know that you harnessed this for me to better associate with you. I don't have any natural ability."

Shaking my head to show my disagreement, I sit up again. "If you didn't have an ability to listen, to understand, nothing could have helped you. I think that's all some people really need. Besides a big boost."

"Maybe." She still looks troubled. "I don't know." She stands up and paces my room's few feet. "Maybe we should have never done that."

"What? Are you saying you regret my helping you?"

Shadow looks in the mirror. "Maybe somewhat. But maybe I could've helped you more. By letting people see me with you instead of them always thinking you were making me up."

"I don't care what they think." I relax a bit.

"Don't you?" She sits next to me again. "I don't know. I think I disagree. You couldn't wait to get off the beach just a bit ago. You all but ran back here."

Staring straight ahead, I pretend indifference, but know she's right.

"Of course I'm right." She stands up, waving her arms. "Do you know what they are doing right now?"

Shaking my head, "No and neither do you."

Her shoulder slump. "Not funny. Those people are celebrating a possible end to the waves after what some of us saw you do."

"And?" knowing she has a point to all of this.

"I dare you to go out there. I dare you to get up right now and go out there and face them. Take credit for what you did." Her voice has risen, and her stance has become more rigid. "Show them you are not a coward."

"Nor am I prideful." Reclining against the wall, I think.

"Just do it." She gives me a look, "Please."

Slowly, I stand, and make my way to the door. Pausing there, I feel her beside me. "Are you seen by all now?" At her nod, I return my own. "Guess I could be too." With that said, I stride through the doorway.

A few people were making their way on the steps, shying a bit as they go. Anger fills me a bit, and I think of turning back. Shadow's soft "no" pushes me forward some more. Heading down the lamp lit stairs, I see more hesitant faces. Coming around the corner, I look towards the dark beach below. Before me was half of the town, all looking around, some holding torches or flashlights. Someone calls out, "There she is." A few people start clapping. Most just stare. An older man comes up the few stairs that lie in-between us, and touches my hand. The charge I gave off makes him jump a bit, but he smiles kindly. Offering him a tentative one in return, I pass by Shadow and head back into my home.

I had done what she wanted, but am unsure of the response of the locals. Why did she even want me to go out there? I saw no celebration. Despite my annoyance with the individuals who still retreated with distrust, I had to admit that it was nice to be touched again.

Lying on my mat a few minutes later, I am ready for sleep to come. The energy wraps around me with its warm secure blanket.

CHAPTER 22

Awakening at a travel center gas station, I feel the urge to pee. As I stand and stretch, I feel hungry, and a little light-headed. The pain is now a minimal ache at the base of my neck. Remembering my bald spot, I steal Chase's baseball cap, and make it sit loosely on my head to try and cover the mess. As I walk with Jay and Joanna to the center, I look around. We're somewhere near Minneapolis, Minnesota. At least that's what Chase says.

The last few days have been quite hectic and nerve rattling. The fear of being stopped by all of the passing State Troopers, combined with the worry of APBs being put out for our arrest, has really put a strain on all of us. We pulled in late every evening at hotels and left early in the morning for the past two days. Chase pushed hard when he was driving, not wanting to stop unless it was absolutely necessary. He wanted to get as much distance between our old place and where we were heading. Now we guessed we were about three hours away from the Plover, Wisconsin area.

I hoped to be there before we called it a night, but Chase was tired of driving. He also rationalized that it would look funny if we pulled up in Plover and showed our Wisconsin driver's licenses showing Plover residency. I had to agree with his train of logic.

Therefore, Chase had decided we were going to gas up here at this Trucker Stop, as Jay called it, and find a hotel to call it a night. That's why I'm walking against a cool breeze holding his hat on. The thought makes me smile as we come through the doors.

The warmth engulfs me as we head for the restrooms. Seeing a payphone, I long to call Kim and see how she is. Deciding that peeing had to come first, I usher the kids the rest of the way in. Closing the door, I rest against it due to the dizzy spell walking even these short distances sometimes causes.

For some reason, my mind again wanders down the path of the dream I had had of the other world yesterday. I remember the awesome feeling of calm control as the waves died down by my waist. Not consuming me as it would have anyone else.

"I could use some of that power now," I muse aloud.

"What power?" Jay asks as he zips his zipper. "You know Batman has power. I'd like to have power like his someday."

Smiling at the thought, I stop, then frown. Maybe he already does, but we don't know it yet. All I can offer is the typical Mommy phrase of, "We'll see, Dude." Seeing Joanna is now done using the toilet, I move to help her fasten her snaps. "Let Mommy help, Baby."

Giving the toilet a quick flush so I can go, I watch. Again I flush, almost mesmerized. The flow of water, the movement. The potential energy it has. It seems to signify something, but I don't know what.

Jay's little hand tugging at mine brings me back to the restroom. "Are you okay, Mommy?"

"Sure, Dude. Why?"

"Cuz you've been standing there forever. I thought you had to pee." Jay pretends disgust, throwing up his young hands. "Locked up in the bathroom with a mom who falls asleep standing up at a Trucker's Stop. Ugh." He rolls his eyes at me as he taps his foot, eyes on the door.

"Okay, okay. I'll be done in a minute."

Once done, I quickly wash my hands so I can open the bathroom door and rid it on my children. "Come on, slowpokes." Holding the door open I hear loud giggles from the kids as the burst out of the restroom. "Slow down, Kiddos!"

"Hurry up, slow down." Chase is beside me. "They don't have a walk button yet. I think we forgot to install it." He points to some pretzels. "Want some?"

The thought of eating another pretzel after munching on them for days makes me give him a dirty look. "Gourmet pretzels. How pleasant. Should I buy some candles too?" My eyes bat for affect.

"Get in the car," he teases. "We'll stop and get something after we get settled in the hotel." Calling to the kids, he signals it's time to go.

"Can I call Kim real quick?"

Chase looks at me. "They'll be tracing calls. I don't think it'd be a good idea."

"Please," I beg. "Just a quick wrong number call so she knows we're still okay?"

Chase still says it'd be a bad idea, and heads for the car. Looking back at the beckoning phone, I sigh. Knowing he disagrees about calling, I wonder about the feasibility of making a call and it not being traced. Shaking my head with disgust at even trying to rationalize it, I turn my back to the phone and walk out of the travel center.

The kids are already in the car, and Chase has started the engine. Looking down the dark road, I wonder how far well have to go to be safe. I don't like the idea of running forever.

Chase pulls into a Motel 6. My Jay chirps up with a "They really do leave the light on for you!" seeing the front desk light on through the window. Chase smiles as he says to stay in the car while he goes to get a room.

"Will this one have a pool?" Dude questions like he has for every hotel on this "adventure".

"We won't be using it if it does, Jay. We still don't have swimming trunks for you." Rubbing my face, "And no, you will not go using your underwear."

"Aaww!" Dude sits back to pout.

Slowly, I shake my head at his antics. "Sorry, Little Man. Maybe we'll have a pool at the next place. If we do, I'll definitely get you some trunks, okay?"

"I want to swim now!"

"Well, I'm sorry." Seeing Chase returning to the car, I warn, "And don't go making Daddy angry about this either, or you know he won't let you go swimming for a long time."

Chase reaches the car and opens the door. "Okay. We're to the back again." He gets in and starts up the car. "There's a good place to have breakfast up the road she said." He slowly pulls around. "Unfortunately there is no swimming pool here either, but it's cheap."

Jay mumbles in the backseat, but with a quick "Dude" from me, he goes quiet.

When the car is parked, we get out. Again I stretch, even though it's only been a few miles since we gassed up. "I think I'm ready to hit the hay."

Chase opens the door and we play follow the leader as Chase leads us down the hallway a bit to our room. He opens the door and we unload our meager belongings. Seeing the phone, I long to give Kim a call to let her know that we are okay. Again I ask Chase.

"I don't think it's a good idea, Bec." He stretches out his back and neck. "They are probably expecting that."

"What if I call using a pay phone, like the one in the lobby? I'm sure they have one. And I can use a calling card, so we'll be good to go. They won't be able to track that will they? I mean, I'm calling into an 800 number for the calling card."

The look on Chase's face isn't so sure. He knows how close of a friend Kim is to me though and he slowly consents, but with. "But keep it short. And don't say anything about us."

"Then what do I say? 'Oops, I'm sorry. Guess I dialed the wrong number?'" My snap is loud even to my own ears.

Chase leans back against the bed. "Well, sure, that'll work. Just keep it under two minutes, and let's hope they can't trace you." He closes his eyes, signaling he's done talking about it.

Giving him a last look, I leave the room. Heading down the hallway I think of what I'm going to say. Knowing Chase has a valid point, that the government probably is tapped into the phones of anyone who knows us. *Maybe I should make it look like a misdial, and it'd be a coincidence that the person I wanted to reach is named Kim too.* Imagining the look on Kim's face is almost as good as knowing how she'll play along with it. Spying the pay phone out of the sight of the hotel's surveillance camera, I breathe a sigh of relief. Taking my calling card out of my pocket, I lift the receiver. Carefully dialing the numbers per the directions on the calling card, I wait for the time to enter Kim and Dennis' phone number. Finally hearing the prompt, I enter their home number. My fingers rap on the edge of the pay phone as the line rings once, then twice.

"Hello?" It's Dennis on the phone, and not what I have expected.

"Uhm, is Kim there?" Trying a bit to disguise my voice, I hope he doesn't blow it. Listening hard to the muffled voices, I can't make out anything. My fingers continue to rap noisily as I plan my message.

"Hello?" It's Kim now.

"Hello. It's me. So surprised hearing a man's voice in your apartment." The pause I give is intentional.

"Excuse me?" Her voice is cautious.

"Ya, I mean after that last guy and all the problems you had with him screening all your calls, the drinking and the guys always over. Oh, but is this one doing that too?"

"Ma'am, I'm afraid you have the wrong number."

With my voice less disguised. "This is Kim, right?" I only wait a second for her to say "yes". "Oh, well, *nice*." Again a purposeful pause. "What are the odds of that happening? I call to tell my friend Kim that I'm okay, and I get a Kim. But like, the wrong one. How embarrassing."

Kim's voice is now accepting, "Yeah, well, that happens sometimes. Can't think of any times it's happened to me, but I'm sure it's happened to someone, sometime."

"*Nice.* Well, like I said must have the wrong number. Still need to let my friend know that I'm okay, ya know?"

"Oh, I follow you completely. Have a good…whatever." She sounds like she's about to laugh.

"Yeah, you do the same. Night."

"Bye," and Kim's line goes dead.

Carefully, I hang up and look around. A smile light on my face in the hope that Kim did understand what was going on with my call. It sure sounded like she did after my "Nice" was said. In fact, I'm pretty confident she knew it was me, and so I head back to our room for some medicine to help with the returning pain, and a good night's sleep.

Knocking on the door, I wait. Part of me wonders how Chase is going to react.

"That's gotta be the shortest timeframe you two have ever talked." It's no really what I was expecting, but I'd take it that he wasn't too upset. "Weren't they home or something?"

"I could lie, and say that they weren't home." Heading for my new purse, I take out my medicine. "Actually, I pretended to have the wrong number. I think she understood though." Going into the bathroom, "Dennis answered, and I used that as a means to say that I had the wrong number."

From inside the room, I hear Chase's "Whatever."

Swallowing the pill, I wonder if he's really upset or not. Sticking my head around the corner first, I gauge his posture. "You're upset, aren't you?"

His tense face barely lets out, "Think you're risking an awful lot just to bullshit with your friend."

My shoulders sag. "I am not BSing here. I needed to let someone know that we are okay."

"Should have called you parents then." His voice is sarcastic.

"I'da thought they would have expected me to do just that." My anger starts to rise. "It's not like I told them, 'Hey Dennis, it's Rebecca. Tell Kim that we're heading to Plover, Wisconsin.'"

"Hmm." His sarcastic voice is infuriating.

"You know, whatever." My hand faces him as I turn towards the other bed. "Goodnight!"

Jodie M. Swanson

CHAPTER 23

For two weeks now we have scoured the Plover, Whiting, and Stevens Point areas for a decent place to live that is within our limited budget. We had decided to enlist the aid of a real estate agent that worked both the listing and the rental property sides of the house. He was nice enough do even take us out for dinner as a "thanks for choosing me", an unheard of thing with realtors I gathered. The next day we started. Our search had resulted in the viewing of probably close to a hundred properties on paper as we decided what we wanted to do. After checking out over thirty different homes for sale, and about sixteen for rent, we realized we may not want to purchase just yet. My anger over so many days wasted didn't ease up our search for someplace nice to stay.

Chase thought maybe we could still afford own something, and went looking towards mobile homes. Perusing seven mobile homes for sale, and eight for rent, we decided to go somewhere in the middle. I thought our agent was going to drop us with all of the switching we were doing, but he hung in there. The last two days we checked out close to a dozen apartments for rent.

Most were too small, or dumpy, to suit our tastes. We decided we couldn't afford too much, as we need to start our lives out fresh. So considering all of this, we decided on a fair sized two bedroom apartment near the University of Wisconsin-Stevens Point campus for now. The sigh of relief on the agent's face about an hour ago was obvious as we signed a six-month contract for the apartment. Right then and there we were handed the keys, so moved our meager belongings in.

The rent for the apartment, which was attached to a main house, was only a nominal five hundred fifty dollars a month, but we knew that the next six months would be the longest of our lives as we waited to ensure I was free from the agency's grasp. We knew if we had to flee, we'd be able to pay to break our contract.

And the place wasn't real bad or anything. Actually, it showed lots of promise. The small fenced yard would look two hundred percent better if someone actually tried to take care of it by mowing and pulling weeds. The small rusty swing set was going to be taken out within a week, per the contract we just signed, so that wouldn't be an eyesore or health hazard much longer. The sidewalk needed some tender loving care in the weed-pulling arena, and that wouldn't take long. The front flowerbeds also needed some serious weeding.

On the inside, the living room had just been recarpeted, and walls repainted, so it looked new. The small kitchen had some facial needs, but was still a working kitchen with a stove and refrigerator. The bathroom had been remodeled a few years back and was still in good condition. Both bedrooms were of decent size, but needed some paint. We decided that the kids were going to get a bunk bed since there was space for one in their room, and obviously they'd both need beds.

Chase just left to sign us up for a home phone. He was glad we wouldn't have to sign up for electricity, as our rent covered that as well as water. Knowing he'd also have to get a phone, he said he'd bring back some dinner.

Having a last look out the living room window, I decide to start weeding. Knowing that it will take a while, I work the kids up to the idea of pulling a few weeds out in the backyard. So, kids in tow, we head for the back door to tackle the small area as we wait for Daddy.

Chase thanks the man before him as he sticks the receipt in his pants pocket. He wonders if he really should have signed up for the long distance, as he fears that it will be too much of a temptation for Rebecca. He had though, and hopes it wouldn't kick him in the butt later. He wants to make everything look as though they were a normal family settling down. Besides, he needs to be able to contact people too.

"She *better* not do anything stupid."

Chase heads towards the Center Point Mall, with the intent of purchasing a phone. Pulling into a parking space, he sees some sale signs in the windows of the entrance to the Shopko. Deciding to stop there first, he heads in. A sign on the wall says that they are hiring stockers and a late night janitor, so he heads to Customer Service for an application. Asking one for him and for one for Rebecca, "What's the starting wage?"

"Minimal wage for stockers." The lady continues sorting her receipts as she talks. "Have any experience in being a janitor?"

Chase thinks of all of the crap the military finds new GI's to do. "Some. Why?"

She looks up a bit to size him up. "Night shifters make a little bit more. Just put on your application what you want, and they'll give you a call if you're selected." She goes back to her receipts.

Chase looks at the applications and realizes he doesn't remember half of the stuff he'll need to fill it out, nor what to put as previous employment. "Thanks. I'll bring these back later, so my wife and I can turn ours in together."

She just nods and continues with her receipts.

Chase turns away and heads towards the electronics. As he passes Women's, he thinks of the limited wardrobe they all have, and decides to make use of the special sales the signs are advertising. Grabbing a plain dress, two dressy blouses, and some pants he heads for the lingerie. After picking up a couple more items for Rebecca, he sidesteps over to the grab some more underwear and socks for himself. Seeing Men's on the other side of a rack, he gives in.

By the time he pulls up to the cashier's check out, he has some more clothes for the whole family, a set of curtains he hopes will work somewhere in the house, some shampoo and conditioner, toilet paper, a frying pan and a sauce pan, two small pillows, two blankets, two kids' sleeping bags, and of course the phone. Realizing the size of his cart, and the estimated value of its contents, he wonders if he'll be questioned on the amount of purchase.

"Lots of good deals today, huh?" The cashier starts ringing up the items.

"Yeah, been listening to her complain about needing these new things so long, I thought I'd finally break down and get them." Chase starts to laugh, then clears his throat.

"Yeah, I hear that," the cashier carols back as she swipes the items before the scanner.

Chase looks around as she continues ringing in the items. Seeing a local paper, he adds that and some gum to his pile of goodies. "Can't forget these," he jokes.

"Nope." She runs the next item. "Want them all back in the cart to take to your vehicle?"

Chase looks around waiting. After another minute he sees counter space on the checkout table. "Getting quite the workout, aren't you?"

She smiles and says that she's used to it. Placing the last item in a plastic bag, she presses the total button. "That's two hundred seventy-three dollars and fifty three cents, please." Chase tries to hide his cough. "Guess you should have given in long before now, then it wouldn't be so much at one time," she jokes.

"Guess I'm just stubborn." Chase reaches into his wallet and pulls out six fifties. "That teaches me a lesson." He waits while she swipes each bills with a counterfeit money pen, then makes his change. "Thanks," he says as she hands him the money.

"You have a good night, okay?"

Chase tells her to do the same, and pushes his cart out the doors towards his car. As he passes a pay phone, he knows he needs to call Jay Strebeck as soon as possible so that he can find out what information to put on their applications. He still has the cell phone in the car, but wants to be sure they have less of a chance of tracking them.

Placing all of the bags into the trunk, he heads back towards the store. Seeing lots of people congregating at the phone, he decides to head further into the mall to see if there is another pay phone around. After going into the main part of the mall, his eyes light on a set of "vacant" pay phones. He heads for them as he digs for his wallet. After opening it, he finds Jay's card, and sees Jay's friend's phone number on the back. Deciding to use the other number, he enters the numbers requested on the calling card, then those of the friend. And he waits.

The phone is answered on the second ring. "Hello."

Chase now feels very awkward. "Hi, I'm sorry. I have your number. It was given to me by a man named Jay Str…"

"Okay, okay. Hope you are getting settled in okay, Michael, isn't it?" The man's voice seems haggard.

"Yeah, we're fine, but need some more information on things like employment history, and the like." Chase wonders if he's got the right person.

"I'll have someone contact you. Do you still have the cell phone?"

Chase nods, as if the man can see him. "We do. But I need to pass on some information to…uhm…"

"Okay. What information did you want to pass?"

"That Be-, Tanya has agreed to the hypnotherapist. And…"

The man's voice interrupts with, "I'll be handling that one. So let's start with that. I need to know where you are at."

Chase wonders about the security of this man's position. Thinking of a way to check and verify this man's knowledge, Chase responds with. "We're living just north of the city on the licenses."

"Are you in the town with the go-carts and water slides?"

Chase shakes his head. "I don't think so." He feels panic rise within him.

"So the one with the campus then." It wasn't a question, just a statement."

Chase feels a little more at ease. "Yes."

"Do you have a phone yet that he can reach you on, or do you want him to use the cell?" The man's voice now seems robotic, but quick.

"Have a phone. If you know where we are, then you know the area code." Chase hears affirmation in the receiver, then gives the last seven numbers. "He can call if he wants."

"And the hypnotherapist will call you at home. Her name is Monique." The man's voice starts hurrying. "Can you call me back?" The line goes dead.

Confused, Chase just looks at the receiver for enlightenment. He wonders if he should call back. After about a minute he decides to. Going through the whole series of numbers again, he waits.

"Michael?" The old man's voice returns.

"Yes."

"Sorry. I want to be sure all calls are untraceable, so had to cut you off. Hope you can understand." He clears his raspy throat. "I will contact the individual who gave you my number. I will set up everything you need. Your friend will contact you, and will have the employment history information to give to you. Less risky this way."

Chase nods. "Okay."

"Time's coming up again. Please don't call me again. We're done. Understand?" His voice sounds a bit hurried again.

"I do."

"Good. Bye, and good luck." The phone goes dead.

Chase hangs up, and stands there in thought. Looking at the people passing by, he wonders if he's ever going to survive this thing with the agency. The loops and turns that they were all involved in were many. He reaches into his wallet and looks for another number to call.

Once all of his calls are done, he remembers he is supposed to get something for everyone to eat. Heading quickly to the car, he looks at the car's clock. It ius showing almost six in the evening. Shaking his head, Chase starts up the car and pulls out of the parking lot.

After driving around for several minutes, he decides on Burger King. Deciding a Double Whopper with Cheese would really hit the spot, he orders big for the rest of the family too. He offers a friendly smile to the nervous teenaged boy in the window. "First night in drive-thru?"

"Third, and I don't like it. Hope I got everything okay for you."

"I'm sure it's fine." Chase hands him the money and drums his fingers on the steering wheel. The young man reaches out with his change and food. Chase again gives a slight smile. "Thanks. Have a good night."

As he heads out of the drive-thru, he sees the campus dormitories. "Gosh, we really are close to the university."

He drives down until he finds the familiar streets, trying to find his new apartment. "Oh for crying out loud!" Chase continues to circle the blocks until he sees a sign with his street name on it. "About freakin' time!" Pulling in, he sees an unhappy Rebecca looking at him through the window. "What?"

She opens the front door. "Get lost?"

Chase mumbles under his breath as he grabs the food. "Maybe!" he shouts as she heads towards him. He hands her wanting hands some drink carriers. "And maybe I went shopping for some things." He closes the car door with his rump. "Or both!"

"Let's eat. The kids are famished."

Chase follows, and notices the walkway is cleared of weeds and grass.

Once all of the food is laid out on the floor, he mentions asking for applications, and realizing they would need the employment history. He tells Rebecca that he called from the mall's pay phones to talk with the friend Jay told him to call before they left. Seeing her face he asks, "What now?"

"Oh, nothing." She sips her Dr. Pepper. "Just think it's okay for you to call someone, and you couldn't call me to tell me where you were."

"I had the stupid cell phone, Bec!"

"Tanya," Dude says as he stuffs some fries in his mouth.

"Whatever!" Chase runs his fingers through his hair. Hearing some chuckling, he looks back at Bec. "What?"

"I love you too, *Michael*." Rebecca's face now lets him know she has been kidding. "Lighten up!"

Chase just stuffs some fries in his mouth.

"So? What you get us?" Rebecca's voice interested.

Chase swallows and raises and eyebrow. "You guys? I didn't get you guys anything. I got blankets and pillows and clothes, etc. But it's all for me."

Jay and Joanna look in disbelief. "Uh-uh."

"*Maybe* I got you something too. We'll see after you eat all your dinner."

CHAPTER 24

Jay Strebeck sits down after presenting his piece concerning what action the agency should take on Rebecca's disappearance. He had said that the investigation so far had turned up nothing. No bodies had turned up. No friends nor family were aware of the missing family's disappearance or whereabouts. And the home showed no sign of people on the run. He briefed the room of fifteen others that in his opinion, the continuation of a search would be a lost cause. His verbal confession of fearing some misfortune had befallen the family mixes with other persons involved with the investigation.

As he rearranges the papers before him, he wonders what has happened to the Stewarts. He has been waiting for over two weeks to see if they had settled somewhere. The call verifying such had yet to be relayed. Nervousness has eaten at him for the last few days, to the point of sleeplessness. He was glad this meeting was set for early evening in the hope it might drag and distract him in an effort to rest against the insomnia's hold.

So far the meeting is everything Jay had hoped. At first, Gurness had addressed the group by saying he appreciated everyone's efforts. Then he proceeded to start the meeting with the facts. Adam, who was sitting next to Jay, did his best *Dragnet*, "Just the facts, Ma'am." Snickers from the people nearby drew Gurness' disapproving look. Since that time, not much interesting except that most were tending to believe the search would be for nothing.

Jay is glad of that, of course. Yet, his mind continued to drift off to their plight. Trying to pay attention, or at least appear to be, he listens to Gurness ask Captain Roberts for more information. As Roberts stands, Jay rolls his pen across the papers now sorted on the broad table.

"Unlike some of the individuals in this room, I feel Rebecca and family are still alive and well. For some reason, this disappearance sits uneasy with me. Having visited the residence myself, I agree that all the signs of uprooting are not present. But as has been mentioned, there's no bodies, no credit card usage, and no ransom notices." He shakes his head as he sits down. "It's not the norm. It's bizarre."

Gurness gives Roberts his full attention. "What do *you* think has happened?"

Roberts shrugs. "I couldn't even begin to make assumptions on that. Perhaps I feel this way because I've never gone through anything like this before. Maybe I feel this way because of my involvement, and refusal to accept failure in this." He places his hands on the papers before him. "My opinion is that this search needs to continue, maybe only for a little while." Slouching back he adds, "Maybe then I'll feel as most of you all do on this."

Gurness chews his lip in thought. "I can understand you're being concerned for your reputation Captain Roberts, but laying that aside, how do you feel about all this?"

Roberts looks down, then straightens himself some. "How does one feel when you find out a friend has passed away?"

Maxwell chips in. "You considered her a friend?"

Roberts shakes his head in annoyance at not being understood. "No, of course not. Yet, by knowing all we do about her, I feel…disbelief. Do you understand what I'm getting at?" Seeing some confused looks. "I guess you don't."

Adam speaks up. "I know how you feel. Having worked as her Case Leader these past few years…you feel the numb disbelief of it take a hold of you."

Roberts just nods in agreement, and slackens against his chair again.

Gurness looks at the two men. "I guess those feelings can get trapped with the job. But the real issue is where do we go from here?" He looks around the room. "Any suggestions?"

The sound of a cell phone ringing makes people do a mini-scramble. After two rings, the sound stops. Jay quickly opens his briefcase, and verifies that it was the new phone with caller-id that rang. Recognizing the number, he wonders how to excuse himself.

"Mr. Strebeck?"

Jay turns towards Gurness. "Sir?"

"Was it yours?"

"Yes." Jay sits up straight. "It may be nothing, but I'd like to see, if that's okay?"

Gurness looks a little annoyed, but grants him leave.

Nodding, Jay quickly exits the room, phone in hand. He walks down the hallway, and takes the stairs down a level. Finding a secluded corner, he dials the number. After a second ring, he looks around to be sure of privacy.

"Hello?" The raspy voice is music to Jay's ears.

"What's the news?"

Some clearing of the throat proceeds, "I have received a phone call. A man gave me some information for you."

Jay fumbles to find a pen and some paper. "Go ahead." Finding none, he opts to write on his arm, where his clothes will cover it.

"Two towns north of where documentation was for. Here's a number."

Jay writes it all down. "And an appointment?"

"Told the man you would be bringing him some information."

Jay laughs. "Did you? Okay. Are they settling in then?"

"Needed employment history, and I'm still networking that." The throat tries to clear again. "The material you need is waiting for you in the usual spot. Time's short."

Jay listens to the click on the phone, then redials. Hearing it get answered he speaks, "It's me. The money will be sent to the regular account." Jay hears distant voice mixed with the man's affirmation, and continues. "And any other information, street, etc." Jay again uses his arm to transcribe the information.

"I'll talk with you soon, my friend." The raspy voice clicks off again.

Jay puts his phone away. A smile grows on his face. A deep chuckle forms in his throat, and he looks around to be sure no one is watching him. "Hot damn!" Hearing distant voices again, he quickly quiets down. Shaking off his sudden good mood, Jay knows he needs to head back to the meeting.

As he approaches the stairs, he hears more voices heading his way. On his third step up, he sees Gurness and Maxwell coming down. "Is it done already?"

Gurness nods. "We're meeting tomorrow morning for a continuation." That said, he pushes past Jay.

Maxwell pauses for a moment. "Yeah, as soon as you left, two other people's phones went off." He laughs. "Gurness got pissed and said he'd see all of us at eight in the morning." Still laughing, Maxwell heads down the stairs behind Gurness.

Jay goes up the last few stairs to head down the hallway. Passing Roberts, who is on his phone apologizing to the missus, Jay laughs. As he enters the room, Jay's eyes find Adam reclining in the chair. "You okay, Adam?"

Adam offers Jay a small smile. "I will be, when this is all over." He sits up and looks around. "So, did you help?"

Jay slowly turns. "I have helped search for her, haven't I?" Jay's face challenges Jay to say anything more. "What more do you want?" Jay grabs his briefcase and turns to leave.

"I thought we were partners."

Jay stops, and slowly turns. "I'd say colleagues, maybe friends. Don't ever consider yourself a member of the things I do." Jay looks around a second before he whispers to Adam, "You may regret it later." Putting out his hand as an offer to shake, Jay smiles to Adam. "I'll see you in the morning."

Adam takes the hand. "In the morning."

Jay releases and turns again down the hallway. Hurrying down the steps, a plan comes to mind. With all of the paperwork already waiting for him, he'd step up his plans a few weeks.

This favor owed to him had been a big one, but he fears he has asked too much within the last three weeks. So much went into switching people's lives and histories. New birth certificates and sometimes marriage or divorce decrees had to be done up. The time involved in hacking into state licensing facilities, and coming up with the materials was sometimes costly. And to not do it for just one person, but also an entire family, Jay felt a special "bonus" would be included in the regular payment for services rendered to the old friend.

Reaching his car, he sees Maxwell driving over. "Feel like dinner? My treat?"

Jay looks inside his car as he places the key into the door lock. "Sure. What do you have the money for? I'm expensive."

Maxwell chuckles. "Whatever, I'm just tired of eating fast food by myself."

"Lead the way, Dan," Jay calls out as he gets into the driver's seat. "I'll follow."

As Maxwell pulls away, Jay smiles to himself. *What better way to escape than to have someone fill my tummy first.*

CHAPTER 25

Adam pulls into his drive later the next morning. He is concerned about Jay as the man hadn't shown up for the meeting this morning. Adam had left this morning's meeting to get Jay's billeting number, per Gurness' request.

As Adam walks through the front door of his house, he sees the mail already stacked up on the counter. Passing by, he notices a plain white envelope with Jay's handwriting on it. Adam's hand slowly reaches for the envelope, his heart pounding in his ears. He sits down, and turns the envelope over to open it.

Inside he reads the first of the many typed lines, and starts reading again for clarity.

> Dear SSgt Adam Michner,
>
> It has been said that there are times when the mind and the soul long to rectify some wrong committed. I can't think of when nor where I have heard such as thing, but I know it must be true. My mind and soul have tried to do just that.
>
> I have a strong feeling that you have been on the wrong side of an unjust battle, and trying fearfully to extract yourself from the agency. Beware! The agency is strong. Far stronger than you or I ever could be. But, isn't is also said that sometimes a single mouse can do damage to an entire harvest? Think on that. Take heart in that. There are many mice within the agency. We mice aren't giving in or giving up, we're moving on. We're trying to do some damage. I hope that makes sense to you.
>
> My time with the agency has proven that the government is very, very vicious. Some of it you are now aware of. Even

though everyone knows the government is corrupt, no one dares to do anything about it. A very small handful of people now dare, myself included, to rectify all we have been a part of. One by one, we are disappearing from the strong hold the agency has over our lives. One by one, we are impacting those hurt by the government. One by one, we mice are causing some damage.

I know it sounds strange after the talks we've had, but I have now had enough. Having been a part of what killed my beautiful wife, I hate myself. Only lately do I feel worthy of being the husband she had thought she married. And I think you know what I mean in that. My aid to a select group of persons was my way of damaging the agency in a way to reciprocate the way they have damaged me and my life. My offering aid was also a way to cleanse my heart, mind, and soul, from the dirty corruption of "government life."

Your wish to one day meet and maybe help a case has come true. Your compassion helped push me to take these final steps. And I wish to thank you for your help.

Your "case" is safe, which I'm sure you guessed before now. They are such an innocent family to be jerked around and caged like monkeys. Now, they are free. Free to live as they thought they were before we came along. She isn't going to be a lab rat, but a human with feelings. Her assurance of such has helped her open up to me and her possibilities. Rebecca is more in tune with some special energy, more than many people ever hope to be. I have offered my assistance to help her figure out just what everything she thinks and feels is for. They have accepted, so I must go to them.

You may be wondering how I am doing all of this. My partners are with me. Does yesterday's conversation ring a bell? It should. My partners are vastly talented and located in strategic positions. During my time with the governments and the agency, I have acquired many loyal favors. All of them are being used now to help me help someone else. I could not ask such things from someone like you, to whom I owe.

Angela calls for me lately, and I want to go to her with a clear conscience, when my time comes. At night I hear her last words, and long to hear her forgiveness. I pray that I will when I see her again.

One last thing, I have given you this as an explanation to a friend. Do the right thing, always. Now with this letter, and with your future with the agency. With your family. Never look back with regret.

-A friendly mouse

Adam reread parts, realizing happy tears have come to his eyes. He sits there, rubbing his face, and holding the letter in his other hand.

Standing up Adam looks around. "Where does one go from here?" He looks around his place with a sense of bewilderment and wonder. Things seem so much more achievable now, so much more in perspective. Suddenly, he wants to talk with Cathy about planning their future.

Seeing Jay's billeting number still on the fridge, Adam thinks he'll go ahead and try it. Several rings confirms that Jay is gone. After talking with the individuals at the billeting office, he knows that Jay is paid for two more nights, but that's all they would offer. On the reverse side of the billeting number was Jay's business card. Seeing a cell phone number there, he tries that too. Hearing the recording saying that the person didn't have voice mail that was set up was a signal that Jay has given up his ties. He is in hiding too.

Adam sighs. Grabbing the letter again, he heads for the door. He looks around again, not really wanting to leave his home to report not being able to reach Jay. The feeling of being railed doesn't suit well. "He didn't have to say anything. But he did." With a smile, he shuts his front door. Laughing a bit, he feels the honor in being the one to deliver such a message.

Getting back in his car, he heads back to the meeting.

Adam raps once on the door to the meeting room. Hearing Gurness call for him to enter, he opens the door. Sensing many eyes on him, he looks to Jay's chair and says, "Sir, there was no answer at billeting. He hasn't shown up yet?"

"Does he look like he's present?" Gurness all but snaps.

"Well, no Sir. Maybe he's already on his way?" Adam quickly takes his seat.

"He better fricken hurry his arse up." Gurness sits heavily into his chair.

Everyone sits quietly as they wait. After about ten minutes of silence, Gurness cusses. "Who's seen Strebeck last?"

Adam raises his voice. "I saw him after the meeting last night when he came for his stuff. Said he'd see me in the morning."

Maxwell chimes in. "We had dinner last night. We were joking about getting food poi-son-ing." Maxwell's face goes a sickly gray. "Oh jeez."

Gurness orders Maxwell and another civil service agent to call the local clinics and hospitals to see if Jay's there. "I don't want to waste much time on this either!"

"Yes Sir," Maxwell offers lamely.

Adam squirms in his chair for a second as he wonders how long they'd stall with that. He hopes Jay was far, far away, and not lying sick somewhere.

Gurness pounds his fist on the table. "Now I have more missing people! What is going on here?"

A "Sir?" from an officer on the other side of the table.

"What?" Gurness almost snaps.

"Is it possible *she* has gotten him?"

Gurness pounds the table again. "By God! She better not have done anything to him, or so help me, she'll rue the fricken day!" The room stays quiet as explicative curses flow from the older officer's mouth. "We'll have to see what those two lame brains come up with."

The room tries to contain its snickers.

"Sir?" This comes from an older female civil service agent. "Did you want to go over these lists now as we waited?"

Adam looks around. "Lists?"

"Hand the Sarge one of those." Gurness waves his hands like some King to his vassals. "We were about to go over the phone calls made and received for all of family and friends, looking for anomalies, or whatever."

Adam takes the papers and begins the perusal, listening to the comments people are making around him.

CHAPTER 26

Jay Strebeck takes the exit into Stevens Point, Wisconsin. He is tired of driving, and ready to put all of the past he can behind him.

It had taken him only two hours to trade his Honda Accord in for a newer car, a little Neon. He did it in Montana, where people would be less likely to start looking, and had tossed the old plates in the trash, saying he'd need new ones for Montana anyway. The dealer hadn't asked any questions, used to making trades for new residents Jay supposed.

Seeing a Perkins as he goes past a few hotels, he decides here is as good as any to get some lunch. Pulling in, he wonders how far it is to where "Michael and Tanya" now live. He has to admit that at first he was surprised to hear Chase say that he thought they might as well head off to Wisconsin, already having the driver's license for the state. But now that he was here, Strebeck thinks the area is fairly pretty. Jay knows that the winters in Wisconsin and fellow northern states were reported as "wicked" and "never-ending", but right now it didn't seem to be such a bad area.

Wisconsin has some niceties, like any other state. The sun shines bright in the cloud pampered sky. The lawns are all green or full of color. The drive through the wooded areas has been nice, but Jay is disappointed in having seen only one deer way off in a distant field. Dairy farms littered the views from the interstate. And quaint small town were welcome distractions from the monotonous chore of driving.

Jay pulls into the parking lot, ready to stretch out his tired form. His back aches due to the newness of his car's seats. He makes a mental note to check out the Big K next door when he finishes with lunch. As he waits to be seated, he looks to see if Rebecca and family are present. Not seeing them, he follows the hostess to his table. After a few seconds an older lady asks what he'd like, and Jay tells her to surprise him with one of the skillet meals with a diet drink. She coughs out a laugh, and tells him it'll be right up.

Jay's mind whirls as he thinks again about what he's chosen to do. He knows people will be looking for him, as they were looking for Rebecca, but also knew he'd never be able to live in peace trying to get out any other way. With any luck, he'll be considered a missing person, and then forgotten within a few months.

"One can only hope." Jay reaches for his diet drink as the waitress carefully sets it before him. "Thanks."

"Your food will be out shortly." And then she was off flittering away to check on other patrons.

Angela loved watching the interaction between people in different places, and Jay can see why. The theatrics that sometimes went on was comical. Angela used to say that it was the friendliest and bubbliest waitresses that were the poorest and one's with the most aches. Jay had bet her the only ones who knew for sure were those aching waitresses. It was a joke between them, and thinking of it he misses her even more.

The meal came and is eaten with little thought on taste, but more on Jay's new life. He has settled on a new name of Jay Thomas Stone, newly moved from Racine to Stevens Point. His new age is forty-six years old, as that is an easy pass-off. He chose his history to be of little value, so he could blend in and not be easily noticed or be someone in high public view. He has chosen to have a limited college education, and the modest grades one could easily believe versus his real higher background and grade point average. In a sense, his regrets not being able to flaunt his accomplishments, but the ideas of being something and someone new did intrigue him. This way, his existence would blend, be hard to distinguish from others.

"It'll be great." Jay surmises as he wipes his face. He waves to get the waitresses attention.

She skips over, and produces the bill with a ready smile. "Thanks for coming by." With that, she flits away again to check on her other patrons.

Jay pays the cashier and waits for his change. Seeing a payphone, he reaches into his pocket for the slip of paper he had transferred Chase and Rebecca's info on. Thanking the cashier for the meal, he heads towards the payphone, change ready. He dials the number and waits, holding his breath as the line rings.

"Hello, Kirkland residence." Chase's voice comes through strong.

"Hey there. It's Jay, Jay *Stone*. Remember me?" Jay pauses, waiting for a reply. Hearing none, he continues. "I am in the area, and thought I'd drop by. Thought I'd let you know what's been going on since we last spoke."

The line is quiet for several seconds.

"Jay *Stone*?" Chase offers a small chuckle. "Of course I remember you. You need directions, or want me to come get you?"

Jay breathes a sigh of relief. "I'd like for you to lead the way, if that's okay?"

"Sure, where are you?"

CHAPTER 27

Jay Strebeck rubs his face as tiredness holds him in her grasp. For three consecutive days he and Rebecca have met with his friend Gabe Walker for hypnotherapy. The first day was three hours of getting acquainted and checking Rebecca's mindset. After figuring she was ready for the real sessions, all three decided that time was of the utmost importance, so they had met the following day, and again today. Already she had been put under, so to speak, and the mumbo-jumbo was irritating.

He put his eye back to the camcorder to verify that she was still in the viewfinder. Seeing her creased brow Jay waits for Gabe Waters to get down to business.

Gabe speaks again, "Rebecca? Are you more comfortable, now?"

"Some." The voice is distant, even to my ears.

"Can you tell me where you are? This special place?" Gabe is writing his chicken scratch notes as he watches her face.

"Here, where the wave has come. I'm on the beach. I'm her, but not like I usually am."

Gabe jots something. "How do you mean, not like you usually are?"

"Usually..." A breeze comes over me, cool, and clear. "Ahh. Can you feel it?"

Gabe shakes his head, and looks towards Jay. "No. What?"

"The breeze off the water." Inhaling, I can smell the water while the sound of seagulls tickle my ears. "Can you hear the gulls?"

Again, the looks between the two men. "No. Tell me."

The energy comes and plays with me, the warmth of it surrounds me. "Oh, it's here! I can feel it coming."

Gabe quickly scratches on the paper. "What is it?"

"Energy. The stuff of dreams and magic." My voice still sounds distant, but enthusiastic.

Jay ensures Rebecca's in the view of the camcorder again. "It's ready," he whispers to Gabe.

"Can you show me it?" Gabe asks softly. "Can you tell me it, so I can share it with you?"

Instantly, the room goes cool, and Jay whispers that he has goosebumps into the microphone for reference. The men rub their shoulders and arms as they watch the woman smile.

"It'd like that." The energy swirls and floats around me as I put my hand out. It comes in and through me...like water. "It's peaceful, beautiful."

"Tell me what it looks like." Gabe pen moves.

"Like...mist. Like floating, swirling...fog. Like this." The hand moves again. Jay stares as Gabe jumps back. Fine swirls are emanating from the sitting female form. They grow thicker and flow around her, soft almost transparent. "Can you see?"

Gabe whispers, "We can."

"So odd. Usually I can't do it without *being* her." Looking around I see the sky darkening. "Sun's going down now." My eyes scan the area. "Oh wait! It's Shadow, and she's...with someone. They're heading this way."

Gabe looks at Jay for a second. Seeing a confused shrug he asks, "Who's Shadow?"

"Our friend. She was there when no one else was. She was being shunned for being kind, so I made her so no one could hurt her."

"How's that?"

"Invisible. No one can hurt what they can't see. Most forgot that she existed within days of my doing that. She became as her name is." A smile touches my face for a second. "It's Derk."

"And who is he?" The sound of Gabe's pen is loud.

"Derk, he is...one who touched magic."

"I'm not sure I understand."

Smiling I watch their approach as they talk. "He was on some tour with dancers and stuff. I saw him on the beach when one of the waves, you remember the waves?"

"Yes."

"He saved a little girl." My voice goes soft.

"How noble!" Gabe's pen moves again.

"Yes, very." My eyes take him in. With a sigh, "And nice looking too."

Gabe offers Jay a knowing look. "Oh-ho, a crush!"

"Yeah, no, well, I don't know. Too much time's gone by for me to really care I think." My voice comes as a distant whisper.

"Too much time?"

"Alone." Again a whisper.

Gabe writes that the mist is disappearing as the swirls aren't seen as clearly.

"That's not true, Gaberon." My eyes find him sitting in some room in my mind. "It's hiding."

Gabe turns to Jay in surprise. Seeing Jay's prompt. "What?"

My smile curves deviously. "The mist, the energy. It's not disappearing. It's ever-present. It's a constant. We choose not to let you see. It's figuring you out, as I am." My voice sounds powerful, challenging.

"I have nothing to fight you with. I'm offering a way to see yourself in another light." Gabe scribbles quickly, eyes darting to the lady in the chair.

"Shadow. Derk." They address me, but Shadow sees me, as me.

"It's you!" She steps closer, as Derk does. "You are the one she talks about."

"I am. Where is she?"

Gabe interjects. "Who are you talking to?"

"Who's that? I can hear someone." Shadow looks around, and then back to me.

Putting up my hand to both of them. "Gabe, I am talking with my friend Shadow. Shadow, I am Rebecca, and the one she talks about. I am learning on me, of me, and this...ability, the energy. My friend, Jay, sits there also, in a corner."

Gabe shoots Jay a bewildered look, as Jay had come in late, yet quietly, to record the session hopefully unaware. "Rebecca? What do you see of us right now?" Gabe silently gets up and maneuvers around the room, to behind her.

"Well, you are behind me and reaching for a book. Jay sits off to my side, with that camcorder, seeing if he's getting all of this. Why Jay? What good will it do? Is this for the agency?"

Jay speaks up, "No, Rebecca. It's for us, to help learn more about you. I promise it's not for the agency."

Wanting to know for certain what he is about, I let me go, energy guided.

Jay feels me there, and grabs his head. "What are you doing?"

"Ssh, relax." Visions of past individuals in the therapy and observations, and the view of his wife. "Oh, this must be Angela."

"Get out! Stop it!" Jay shrieks in outrage.

Visions of shock experiments, cell-type rooms, wires, and pain. "Oh Jay, forgive me for doubting you." But I wasn't ready to leave yet. There was the most painful memory before me. In a second, it replayed three times before me, the ten minute argument he had had with Angela, followed by finding her body. My eyes find him as I let go. "I'm so sorry. I had to know though. I had to. I've been wondering if everything you said was true."

Jay turns towards the door and leaves.

"You are using it! Did she help you?" The phantom voice comes to me, bringing me back to my place on the beach.

"No. She's not here." My eyes scan the deep purple of the skyline. "I think I need to talk to her. Where is she?"

Shadow shrugs. "We've been looking for you, her."

My eyes drift to Derk, and his eyes on me. "Hello Derk."

"God, it's amazing. You get more, I mean, she gets more interesting all the time." His eyes aren't mean, they're glowing with interest.

"My best to you and Shadow. We've wanted to say so, but…jealousy keeps us aloof." My voice sounds hurt.

"Rebecca told me you were married, had a family." Shadow sounds confused.

"I…do. But I can feel her, am her, when we…are connected. I guess I can say now what she cannot." *Jealousy still burns.*

"Jealousy over what?" Shadow steps closer, the sound of sand moving is disturbed by the sound of a pen on paper.

"Gaberon, please."

"I need to Rebecca. It'll be clearer when you are back with us," Gabe offers.

"As if I'm ever away." My eyes refocus on Shadow, "What was that?"

"Why are you jealous? Over me?" Her voice sounds disbelieving.

"I, she is jealous. You have…," my eyes look down. "Can we have a moment please, Derk?" When he steps away a few steps, I lower my voice to Shadow. "I cannot explain this…this jealousy I still feel seeing you two together knowing he was interested in me, her at one time."

Shadow's eyes search mine. "We're not together Rebecca. We talk, and mostly about you, how aloof you, she…whatever. He is interested in her, but with her always shutting down, he can't get through to her."

"He called you beautiful." My voice sounds hurt.

She steps to me. "Rebecca? You are connected, aren't you?" She touches my face as she thinks. Her presence is around me, in me. *He wants you.* "Where is she?"

I don't know.

She shakes her head. "You are the only one who would know. She's been silent, gone, for days. When we saw you, we thought she was back." Her hand rests on my shoulder. "Find her. She needs you, and us. I know it."

Nodding, I call out, "Gaberon. I need some help."

Gabe scribbles again as he asks, "What kind of help?"

"How do I find a friend, the other me?"

Gabe shrugs, "I guess you need to go to your other favorite place.

What else do you really like?"

My eyes dart to the water. "The power of the waves." My feet start moving through the sand as I head to the water's edge.

"You cannot be serious." Derk's voice is scared.

My eyes drink him in as I vaguely ask, "Is it her that you seek?"

His light on mine, "There's something she has that I need."

My eyes challenge him. "What?"

"Her. Her spirit, her aloofness. I'm tied to her somehow." He has met my challenge. "It's hard to explain."

My face is bland as I look at him. "It's understood. We got you with the dance."

He shakes his head. "No, the beach, the wave, and the boy."

Looking at Shadow, I think, *Stay here.* The waves beckon me. Taking the necessary steps, I reach the edge of the waves. "Are you here?"

Silence greets me.

Please, are you here?

What do you want? Her voice is desolate, sad, like her childhood.

To talk to you. Can you see me? I'm outside of you! My voice tries for chipper.

The sand shifts a few feet away. *Well, blast it, and damn it too. Guess no one needs me now.*

Ah, invisible. Why didn't we think of that before?

Too proud. The sand shifts some more.

Sitting next to her, I sigh. *Derk likes you. Told me so.*

He wants Shadow.

You. Sighing, I rest my head way back. *I don't have much time. I'm with some people, they're helping me channel this.*

It's not hard when you get used to it.

"Rebecca?" Gabe's loud voice comes through.

Who's the loud-mouth?

Smiling I offer, Someone who's trying to help, I guess.

Oh. Her voice is almost interested.

Will you meet with me again? I miss your company.

Why? Why would you miss me?

Aren't we one? I'd be missing what helps make me...me! Come out, please. Shadow misses you. She's worried.

I've heard her. I thought she was feeling guilty. Her offer is weak.

She never feels guilty.

"Rebecca!"

"Hush now, Gaberon."

Gaberon? Her laughter is audible, and Shadow heads our way. Damn.

Oh you wanted to be seen, heard. I need to go now. Visit soon? Please?

Her sheer veil falls away. *I will. Thanks.*

Smiling, I wish to hug her, but somehow know I cannot. Looking at her, I see myself. Sometimes it's neat seeing me as others do. *Together then?*

Always. Guess I better cool her down to a simmer. She address the approach of Shadow.

"Rebecca!" Gabe shouts.

"Com-ing!" My sing-song voice comes clearer.

"You need to come out. Time's up."

Gotta go. My eyes blink, and Gabe stands before me. "What's the matter?" The room feels chilly, and I rub my arms to warm up. "What happened?"

Gabe rubs his upper lip, then squats before me. "It's hard to explain, but you needed to come back. The session's have a maximum time that can...span. Or threshold of 'output'. You breached that some. How do you feel?"

"Fine."

Gabe looks into my eyes and nods. This he tosses over his shoulder, "Room's warming back up."

Seeing Jay, my mouth drops open, then snaps shut. "I'm sorry. I don't think I've ever done that before."

He just nods.

Sitting more forward, "I'm serious. I don't know how I did that."

"I can understand why you did, but I'd prefer you not do that again." There was no smile on Jay's face.

Slowly I nod. "Okay."

Gabe interjects, "How are you feeling?"

"I told you, I'm fine." Rubbing my arms again, "Why'd you cool it down in here anyways?"

Gabe smiles as he stands. "You did that. Been downright chilly for the past half hour. Can you stand?"

Nodding that I could, I do. "See? I'm fine."

"Good, wait in the hall again." Gabe reaches for his notebook.

When do I get to see what you two are coming up with? My mind sounds snarly as I head for the door.

"Soon," Gabe offers.

I didn't say anything. A smile pulls at my lips.

"Yes you did. And I promise that you...," Gabe continues.

"Gabe, she's thinking it, not saying it." Jay turns the camera to get Rebecca in the view again.

Gabe purses his lips, then smiles. "Well, that shows that I'm a bit rusty. Now get out, Missy." His voice is teasing.

Nodding I smile.

It felt neat to have done that again after so long. The one time with Jay, and the other with Chase, and they had been so brief. The feeling of awe still sits within me as I wonder how it is done. Thinking on that, I sit, and wait for the two men to discuss my session. Yawning, I close my eyes for a quick "power nap" as Chase calls them.

CHAPTER 28

Jay again ensures Rebecca is centered through the viewfinder of the camcorder. The three days since they had their first view of the energy she had sent had been very interesting. They had seen the room warm up the past few days instead of cooling down. Gabe figured it was her way of resetting the controls on the energy's output. Every time they had seen the swirling floating mists hovering about her form. When she moved her hands to do some menial task asked of her, it moved with her, not her cutting through it as one would fog or smoke.

Jay watches the pen move on Gabe's paper, knowing he did a good thing by bringing Rebecca here. Gabe had been impressed with some of the occurrences with the sessions. First off, knowing his full first name, without it ever being told to her. Then there was the visualization of the energy. But in all, the session in which she cooled the room had usually taken longer with other individuals than it did with Rebecca. Her breathing had gone down as if in sleep, the regular way. But her body still had moved fluidly. A good sign, if Gabe good be believed.

Gabe was sure that she was more focused and centered than any other case he had worked on. He had made note that most of the more powerful individuals all stressed that they had a double who helped them out, came to them in dreams, or felt another presence when using the E.A., Energy Ability. Jay remembered some, especially with the "suicide" of the man he was helping coach. The man had stated that they were tired of the games, not that he was tired. He had made reference to going to a better place where they couldn't be touched or hurt any more. That had been Jay's only real experience with "dual system personality ability" as Gabe termed it. Until now, with Rebecca.

"Jay?" Rebecca addresses him from across the room and span. "The phone."

Jay looks to Gabe's desk wondering what she's talking about. The ring that erupts from his jacket surprises him. "Thanks." Seeing her softened smile, he turns to take the call out in the hall. "Hello?"

The raspy voice on the line was a surprise. "It's me. Did you give anyone my number?"

Jay quickly thinks. "Only the couple, the ones I'm with. Why?"

There's a cough. "A man, called himself…Adam, contacted me just now. He had lots of questions."

Jay panics as he whispers aloud. "Christ. He's good." Rubbing his face, Jay starts again. "Where are you?"

"Payphone in a nearby town. I'm leaving the area for a while to see what happens. I don't like this kind of stuff. You know that." The sound of wheezing follows.

Jay nods. "I know. What did he say?"

"He introduced himself, and waited, like I was supposed to know who he was." The voice pauses for explanation.

"Adam is the guy who was the case lead for this individual," Jay supplies. "He's on our side."

"Are you sure about that?"

Jay nods again. "Pretty sure. I left him a note saying I was leaving, and trusted him to do the right thing."

"You shouldn't have. You know how influential the agency is." The raspy voice wheezes before it continues. "He wanted to know where you were. I kept telling him he had the wrong person, that I had just got the number he had called only a few days ago."

Jay waits for a second to see if there is more. "What did he say?"

"He asked that if you called me to tell you things aren't good, that they are thinking foul play. He also said that the search is still on." A cough follows.

Frowning, Jay sighs. "I see."

"Look, I owed you lots." There's a raspy silence. "Maybe I owed you too much, but this is too scary now. I don't want to be in this anymore."

"I understand. You've done so much, thanks again. Those past employment histories were great! The husband got a job right away." Jay hopes divulging that information will call down the old friend.

"Glad to hear it, but…Jay?"

"Yeah?"

The raspy voice is to the point. "I'm done. The debt is repaid, okay?"

"Okay." Jay feels a sense of loss. "Thanks for everything." After a long pause, "Any news for you yet?"

There's a raspy laugh. "Nah, they said any day now this stuff will have me."

Jay listens to the raspy wheeze and sighs. "I'm sorry."

"Not your fault. You've done more than could be imagined. But, we fought it hard, didn't we?" Sadness tinges the wheezing.

"We did."

"Well, guess I better get going. I'm serious about the debt thing."

"It's been repaid. It's done, I swear." Jay holds his lip between his teeth.

"I guess this is good-bye then."

Jay nods. "Okay, good-bye." All he hears is silence, then a click.

Slowly, Jay puts his cell phone away with a small smile. Despite his regret and sadness over what else was said, he knows his intuition about Adam has been correct. "Guess Adam's on our side after all." Still, knowing he just lost a valuable contact, Jay feels a loss. *So many losses since I started with the agency. They've seen so many. Why haven't they gotten the hint yet?*

Jay looks as the door to the room where Rebecca and Gabe are working out specifics on her abilities and control. He slumps down into a leather seat as he stares at the door. "One saved."

Thoughts of his first months with the agency brought back the hideous visions Rebecca had "seen" a few days past. Lips purse in remembrance of experiments done in which Energy Persons, or EPs were shocked, injured, and isolated for weeks to see the effect of such things on their energy levels and patterns. Some people were horribly mutilated in an effort to ensure "accuracy." Some lost fingernails, others lost ears, toes, or fingers. Others were cut, left bleeding, to see how quickly they could heal. One individual was robbed of sight to see how it affected everything. Amazingly, most of the cases had enough personal strength and pride to survive. Many chose not to.

Looking back, Jay can't even remember how he really got started with the agency. He remembered reading on it in college, the whole "classified" discovery of personal control and energy displacement. He recalls some of the interviews with professors and agency members, some still around, others long gone. Thinking on it, Jay wonders if he blocked out most of it, due to his fascination with the idea.

The government had really been off when trying to discern the origin of the energy fields. But that someone had actually been able to pinpoint the specific fields enough to measure them! The thought made Jay frown in self-disappointment. He'd never come up with anything like that. He wouldn't know where to start, only how to be a part of.

"But I can help end it." Jay stands and heads for the door. As he reaches for it, the doorknob moves. Standing there, he watches in amazement, as if this is the first time. The door opens, and Jay steps forward hearing Gabe complimenting Rebecca.

"Well done! Most can't do that for months." Gabe smiles in acknowledgement of Jay's return.

"It's easy when she's helping." The feeling of wholeness, an "oneness", surrounds me. This completeness is due to my parallel part being with me, guiding me.

Simpleton. Ask him for something harder.

"We want something harder."

Gabe smiles, "Ah, but do you know how to do it without her help?"

"Why would that be important?"

Gabe puts the pen to his mouth in thought. "What if something happened to her, and you needed to open the door?"

"I'd use my head," a smile helps finish it. "And turn the knob with my hand."

Gabe makes a face. "Smarty pants."

Nice one.

Thank you. "I guess I haven't ever needed to do these things, but always dreamt that the ability to was…right…there. It's just on the tip of my tongue, right around the corner, or just forgotten by waking up."

Gabe nods. "I guess you're right in that you probably won't need them." He thinks a moment.

"No, too easy." My voice interrupts his thought.

Gabe raises his eyebrow. "You think so?"

Swiping at an errant hair, I pause. "Yeah, I think so. Jay's was too easy last time, even though I'm not overly sure how I did it."

What? You read someone's mind?

Yeah, Jay's the other day. Why?

I don't even do that. Never thought to I guess.

"Re-bec-ca." Gabe's sing-song voice gains my attention. "How about you decide then. Let's let you push yourself? Set your own limits."

Should I show you how I did invisible?

Nah. Just…like when we get directing the energy. You know, letting it move… us, I guess.

Her laughter comes, a demented, funny sound. *Hold onto your pants, Gaberon.*

"Why should I?" Gabe looks nervous.

Jay takes his seat, eyes on Rebecca.

"It's coming. Wanna see it, how it does it?" My voice sounds so distant again as the energy swirls and forms itself around me. Moving slowly, as if in slow motion, I feel light, weightless, and know now is the time to ask to be moved. Lifting a heavy thought-filled, hollow hand, it lifts me, and I can turn as if a dolphin playing in the water.

"Oh my God." The hushed words are Gabe's.

Told ya. Her smile is evident in her mental tone.

"Haven't seen that yet." Again, they come out barely audible. "How are you feeling?"

"Wonderful. Light, in control. I am relaxed. I imagine this is how it feels to be in space. Weightless, and relaxed." My head falls back in agreement.

Jay stares in wonder, then double checks the camcorder's view. "Christ."

Opening my eyes, I am out of my chair and off the ground. Slowly I cause my form to shift, and my angle is now one where I can better see both men. The wisps of energy swirl around my, hold me. "Look at me, I'm a sorceress." With a wave of my hand, I gently take Gabe's notebook from him. "Wanna see a trick?"

Holding the book about four feet away, I move my fingers, and the pages start moving, in time with my fingers. Back and forth the pages move, following the slightest asking of my fingers.

"What else?" Gabe's voice is small.

With my open hand facing him, I smile. "Relax." Slowly moving my hand upwards, he rises from his chair until his feet dangle about two inches off the floor. "Ever want to be and astronaut? Maybe you should've worked for NASA."

Laughing as he looks at his feet, and then carefully he tries to move his feet, "Or maybe you should have. They probably would have saved millions using you versus the anti-gravity equipment they used."

Lowering my hand slowly, Gabe's feet come in contact with the ground once again. "Touchdown. So what did you think?"

Gabe nods. "That was amazing. Very nice, and the control…well that is definitely your strongest ability so far."

Jay quickly steps up. "Do you do that a lot in your dreams?"

"I do." My eyes take in his face. "What's on your mind, Jay?"

He sits on the chair I was in minutes ago. "I have some questions now, okay?" At my nod he continues, "Can you tell me more about your dream life? Like the wave experiences? I know you've told Gabe some, but…I think I'm wondering about the waves. When do they come?"

My face frowns, and the energy shifts. "They just do, and have always come, that I remember. Then the one I've told you about when I was about seven."

"What's your earliest memory of this dream world?" Jay quickly asks.

Flashes of the dream world life and memories flicker in my mind. "As a kid, I remember…going to bed late, and having a weird dream of flying. There was a…little kid who helped teach me how to fly, who came to me when I was sleeping." Looking down at him, "Does that make sense? I heard my name while I was sleeping, opened my eyes, and there was the kid. It seemed so real."

Gabe looks toward Jay, "What are you getting at?"

Jay puts up a hand. "Rebecca, do you remember things that happened to you when you were an infant?"

"I see...no, like an idea of a bubble. The energy was in my bubble, and reaching for me." Making a face, I lower some. "Pain, I think. A squeezing pain. Seems like I'm watching a movie, almost ya know. Like it didn't happen to me."

He knows something, or is thinking something. Her voice is a hushed whispered thought.

"Jay?" Gabe distracts me. "We need to talk." Turning to me, Gabe smiles and tells me to come back, to let go of the energy. He heads out of his office, Jay in tow.

Feeling the firmness of the floor under my shoes, I let gravity take control. The weight comes on and I realize how heavy I really feel. Taking a seat by the window, I feel the exhilaration felt after doing the levitation in my dreams. My body tingles and I feel so aware.

Wonder what's up. Should I go check it out?

She's already on her way to see what they're talking about, so I just wait. The realization that so much has come clear to me in the last few months is foremost in my mind. Memories of strange dreams throughout my childhood came to replay in my head. As I sit there, I wonder about the people I see passing by on the sidewalk, if they've ever had dreams and thoughts like mine. Part of me says, "If they did, they'd be sitting in here too."

CHAPTER 29

The backyard looks much better now after the rusty swing set has been removed. The weeds aren't the dominant plant, and color speckles the small area. The tree in the yard next door lends spots of shade as the kids play. They're engrossed in their role playing, so I let them be. The time to reflect is welcome.

Ssweeh.

A soft breeze like sound in my ear alerts me to her presence, again within me. Funny how I can pick up on it better now with Gabe's counseling. *Hey. Where have you been? Been wondering if you were going to let me know what you've found out yesterday afternoon.* My fingers move hair away from my face.

Sorry, but I felt I needed to talk to Shadow about all this. Thought she may have some good ideas. She gives an exasperated sigh.

Smiling, *Oh, back to talking to Shadow are you?* The breeze has moved my hair again. *What's the deal?*

The deal is…I think we need to advance you further out of these sessions you've been having. Her matter-of-fact attitude is aggravating.

And why's that?

Again a sigh, *They were discussing your abilities, and were trying to find a way to access some agency information about a case. Jay thinks he had seen some information about water experiments and dreams influencing weather systems, somewhere. Something about the agency still has the equipment first used by the government when they were trying to locate the energy pattern origins. The equipment hasn't been used in years, but if the agency looks into using that as a means of finding you, he feels that what you did yesterday may have tipped them off, or can, or something like that.*

"What?" My thoughts whirl. "But what has that got to do with…like him asking me about the waves coming?"

Couldn't get in his head. Apparently Jay felt it was significant. Did you ever tell them that I was told the waves came after I was born?

Not that I'm aware of. Why? The hair is getting more aggravating.

Well, Shadow and I discussed the waves, and my calming the last wave, at some length. We think that, one, yes...my presence and moods affect the water, enough to cause the waves. Two, that the energy is weather related, or the weather is more energy related than is normally thought. The idea of weather patterns, energy systems. Does this make any sense?

"I don't get it."

There's this...feeling, static...that sometimes happens with the energy I feel. I call it harmonious interjection, Shadow calls it screwing around with the energy. It's the... synchronizing of energy with preset patterns, "future" if you'd prefer, is how I can best describe it. Like the pattern of things is preset, and the energy of it can be tapped? At least this is what I think. She pauses. Like a slight foreseeing, then causal manipulation.

"We can change the future?" Some of me denies the possibility, when the other parts of me wonder if this is true.

Uhm, more like...influence, not really change.

"There's a difference?"

Her sigh is loud. *Shadow's so much better at this than me.* Her frustration is just as loud. *You know in the dance, with Derk? The...thought, then it happens? It plays off the idea of what was already happening, then give it another shot of energy. There was a choreography, a certain way to move, and I helped influence the dance with my thoughts. I didn't really change the outcome, just the way it ended.*

"I'm still confused."

Okay, forget it then. That's not really that important. What we came down with is that you are still a captive, though by "conscious" submission. You are still under observation, to find out what they can about what you can do. Right?

That thought has been playing around with me for the past week or so. Being subject to their questions and viewing. *Yeah, somewhat. But at least it's my choice to be there.* Denial creeps in the back of my mind.

Fair enough, but when will it end? She gives a pregnant pause. *They are going to want to push you more and more, to test you. It's basically the same as what the agency would be doing, right?*

With a nod, I concede.

The tension tickles my neck as she pauses. *This won't ever end, unless you do it. You only dreamt of this stuff until I helped make it real. All that you can do is because I've extended...myself, my thoughts, my abilities. Shadow thinks if I can help develop you more, than you can find a way to end this.*

"How?" My eyes gaze at my children as they continue playing, oblivious to the conversation I am having with myself.

Oh, I don't know. But, with some coaching, you can do what I can. What you've been dreaming about doing as you sleep. You've known the "know" is right around the corner.

"Let me think on it." My mind feels full, confused.

If it were me, I'd want revenge.

"Revenge." The word sounds harsh, but it triggers all the things that have recently transpired. We were relocated, lost all of our possessions, friends, and family. The anger fills me. The more I think, the more I agree. "Are you going to help me?"

Shadow approaches. "Hey, you. What she say?"

"She didn't know what I was talking about with the idea of preset patterns and influential energies." Rubbing my face against fatigue, I continue. "Can you believe it took a while for her to even think she is a victim? That she has cause for revenge?"

Shadow remains silent and still.

"We toyed with some ideas, after which, she agreed she was wanting revenge."

Shadow arches a brow. "Ideas? Like what?"

Waving my hand through the air, "Implanting a virus in their mainframe of computers, but I'm not too sure what all of that really means." Seeing Shadow's shrug I continue. "We talked about writing a letter, and some other weird stuff. I don't know what she really wants to do. She said she's going to talk to Jay, and then we'll get together some more."

Shadow nods and turns away.

"Where are you going?"

She turns. "Derk wants to see you. He's in your…house."

The words catch me off-guard. "Derk?" She takes a few steps. "Wait! Where are you going?"

She tosses me a look over her shoulder. "I have an appointment with your father." She heads back to the stony steps.

For once, I can actually feel my heart pounding. It's been years since my throat has felt this tight. Derk is in my tiny shack of a house, and my only real friend is going to talk with my father. She acts like nothing is amiss about any of that. Watching her, I wait to see if she looks back, but she does not. Nor does she before she's out of sight.

Her words are loud though. "Coward."

Anger hits me. *I am not.*

My feet strike angrily across the sand as, in denial, I head for my hole. After reaching the step, my anger has given way to a supreme case of nerves. As I slowly take the steps required, my mind laughs at Shadow's antics. She knew I'd do just this, that I am too proud not to take her up on her challenge. One stair at a time I go. All the while wondering what Derk is doing in my crummy abode. The thought of his opinion of where I lived slows me down even further. And as I stand in front of my doorway, I pause. Long seconds stretch as I wrestle with my thoughts and nerves. Long minutes, and I knew I am losing, and so I take the last few steps until I am in, and looking at him.

He's sitting calmly on my mat, as if it was the most natural thing in the world for him to be doing. He looks up at me, and I don't know whether to be angry or run to throw up in the bushes outside. He stands, and I begin to think running outside is a very good idea, as there isn't much room here. Somehow, with Shadow, the space never seemed to be a problem.

He sighs. "I'm glad you finally were able to make it through your door."

My eyes dart to my portal, then back at him.

"I was wondering if you were even going to come. Shadow did say she'd find a way to get you here though." Again that smile.

Swallowing the nerves lodged in my throat, "What did you want?" Mentally I curse the crackling in my voice.

He looks around. "So this is where you live?"

Looking around, I see it as he must. It's horrible, dirty, like I am a beggar. The floor is dirt-caked in places. My little cupboard is all busted and worn, and adorned with cobwebs. My meager stack of dishes all chipped or scorched. And as a crowning point, my bare light bulb dangles from above like a yellow flare. "It is." Again my voice crackles, though he pretends not to notice. "And it's ugly, I know."

He looks at me, then shrugs. "Things could be worse." He looks around, and I want him to stop.

"What did you want Derk?"

Those eyes, like during the festival, captivate me. "I'd like to talk with you."

My eyes blink, then blink a few more times. "Talk with me?"

"Yes." He sits back down on my mat, and seeing my odd expression, stands back up. "Sorry."

"It's okay, it's just that's…uhm, it's my…"

"Your bed, right? Sorry. It's just that I'm more comfortable sitting. Is that okay?" He waits for my reply, so I nod. He sits, and looks at my expectantly. "Are you sitting?"

Looking at the small mat, I realize that Shadow and I have shared it when talking many times, even though it was so small. Yet sitting there next to him would be almost like sitting in his lap. "I prefer to stand."

Again, that sigh. "Why are you still trying to put space between us?"

"I'm not." The denial is too loud, even to my scared ears. Trying again, with more calmness, "I'm not."

He smiles. "I've been talking to lots of people," and he gives me a look. "About you. Many people have hurt you, haven't they?"

"Duh." Immediately I realize what I've said, and my hand covers my mouth. "Oh my gosh. I'm so sorry." Mortification turns my cheeks many shades of red and pink.

He is looking down at the floor. "It's my fault." Then he looks up. "I apologize."

"For what? My obnoxious mouth and rude manners? I can admit my faults and be responsible for my behaviors." My voice is slightly tainted with irritation, so I try to ensure he believes my sincerity. "I'm the one who is apologizing, and through no fault made by you."

He smiles broadly. "Well, I do believe that is the most you've ever said to me!"

"What?"

He smiles and laughs. "I said that that had been the most you had ever spoken to me at one time."

Not sure how to take his humor, all I can offer is my lame, "Oh."

"Now, we've established you were indeed hurt." Seeing my guarded face he adds, "By many people. But I have some questions for you. Okay?"

"Why do I feel a set-up is taking place here?" The try for a joke sounds a bit weak due to my nervousness.

But he laughs, and I offer a small smile. "Shadow said she had been traveling, as a runaway?" At my nod, "Why did you open to her?"

The question throws me. Blinking I think for a few long second. Feeling his piercing eyes on me, I look around. "I guess because she opened to me, and stood up for me."

"Haven't I tried to do that too?"

His question demands my look, though I quickly take it away again. "It's different."

"Why? How?" Derk leans forward a bit, interested.

"I was younger, hurt, weak. She needed to hide from what she ran away from. I needed someone to...care. It was a mutual thing then."

"And it's not a mutual thing now, with me?"

My eyes lock with his. "Why would it be?"

He sighs and slumps back. "You're pushing me away. Did you do this with Shadow too?'

Reflecting a moment, I nod.

He clasps his hands together, and brings them to his forehead. "Okay, let's try this then." His hands come down. "I find you a very interesting person. I feel for the...pain and...anguish that you have felt. I was hoping, and have been trying, mind you, to have some sort of mutual relationship with you. I am...," he searches for a word as he looks around my domicile. "I am...disheartened that you haven't even tried to...act friendly in turn.

You act to me as others have acted towards you, in a sense."

My mouth opens to call him a liar, but it snaps shut first. Bile sours my stomach. What he says is true, and I am suddenly filled with humiliation. There's nothing to say except, "I'm sorry." I do so, looking into his eyes so he knows I'm sincere. My hand comes to my mouth, and I rub my lip with my knuckles as I look down again.

He slowly stands and as he does, nervousness fills me. "Let's try this again." His hand reaches out, and I step back. "Hi. My name is Derk."

"What?" Disbelief echoes in my voice.

He smiles, and pushes his hand out further. "Hi. My name is Derk."

Glancing at my right hand a moment, I think. Raising my gaze to meet his, I stick out my hand. "Rebecca."

CHAPTER 30

"Who are my friends and who are my enemies?"

Jay Strebeck looks up from folding his clothes on the floor. He regards me a moment before he speaks. "Who are your friends?"

"And my enemies." My voice is bland, even though I am irritated.

He sets down the shirt he finished folding. "I take it you are talking in reference to the agency?" He looks up at me for confirmation, so I nod. "Well, technically, everyone in the agency is your enemy in that they want to lock you away, run tests, and wires, and stuff like that." He gives me a look to see if that is sufficient.

It's not.

"I want names, descriptions, instances." My voice is giving way to my hostile thoughts. For almost three days I have been thinking about what Two had said, and now my wont for revenge is burning. I am going to get some answers tonight. "I want to know how many people, what they do, where they work, and how that affects me. As I see it, you are the only one who can give me that information."

Jay stands up, and shakes the stiffness out of his left leg. The looks on his face tells me he's still wondering what to think of my asking, especially like this. "Okay. I guess you have a right to know."

"Damn right," quickly I look to make sure my munchkins didn't hear that. "Darn right, I have a right to know. These people have turned my life upside down! And for what? A phenomenon that some people share, though in different levels or whatever?" At the last word I realize my voice has risen. "I mean, what really is it that they have a problem with here?" My voice is more in control again.

Jay sits down at the small dinette he and Chase had picked up two days ago from a garage sale. "Gabe's job was to determine if certain individuals, such as yourself, were able to...," he uses his hands now, "to damage, or...

weaken the government and its defenses."

My bland look says I'm not following him.

"Okay, take for instance you, say you were an experimental, a person he was to test. He needed to see a list of your abilities and non-abilities, as they were termed, to assess your...destructive potential. Either against the United States, or for aiding the United States against others."

"But what if I didn't know I had these abilities? I mean, I didn't! The government was the one who fu..." a quick look to the kids. "The government was what flubbed by letting me know I could do things."

Jay nods in agreement. "True."

"Had no one told me, I'd still been seen as a threat, though. Correct?"

Jay nods again. "Correct."

"And why is that? One would turn against the government then, I would think."

Jay only nods, trying to see where I'm going with this.

"Okay, so you leaked it, but if you hadn't I would've been 'collected', as you call it, to be experimented on?" Seeing a nod, "Where would they have taken me to?"

"To a military installation in New Mexico, or one in Arizona. There are two sites. One for stronger leveled individuals, such as yourself. That one is in New Mexico, and is high security, high experimentation. The other is for weak levels, just to determine possible scales and if there are any abilities." Jay sets his hands down, signaling he thinks that completes what needed to be said.

"What are these installations called?"

Jay looks at me before answering, then asks, "Why?"

Offering a smile, "Just curious." Seeing him shrug it off as I had hoped. "So, tell me again how they determined these energy levels and sources."

Jay leans back and brings up his hands as he speaks. "An older gentleman named Roger Schumbert had been assigned with some detail to see if the Russians or Japanese had any new weapons we needed to... defend ourselves against. He ran tests on water pollution, checking for toxins and poisons, abnormal parasites or microbes, and radiation. He checked food, and soils, and waters, and clothes, and toys, and...you name it, he probably checked it. He became obsessed with the idea that he might miss something, and delved further into energy levels, etc. When he was able to measure energy levels, he discovered the anomaly that I told you about, the high-energy emission levels in certain areas. Convinced that someone had manipulated the sun's rays or something like that, he was assigned to gather more data and discover the sources. Sometimes it was weather related, such as lightning, uh...circulating weather patterns, the collision of fronts, as better explained by meteorologists.

"On one of his experiments he was reading some minute readings when someone approached him. His instruments went hay-wire! When the instruments returned to the readings that they had just been giving off after the individual was leaving. Schumbert called the man over. As the man approached, the instruments were alive with readings. Schumbert then refocused his attention on people. That's the short and how of how you were discovered, and how the agency has progressed through the years."

My mind focuses. "Is he still alive?"

Jay frowns and shakes his head. "He died of an apparent heart-attack about, what…eight years ago."

"So who heads it now?"

Jay goes down the list of people and experiences with each one he knew personally, or stories of the others. He went on to give brief descriptions on some of them when I asked, and soon he is a fountain of flowing information. He volunteered so many names I know I'll never remember them all, no matter how I try.

After a bit, I wonder, "Is there anyone who works for them still, who would be considered my friend?"

Jay shakes his head. "Not really. Most are dedicated to their good government retirement plans or 'the cause'. Some, like Drake and Adam and I aren't happy seeing what's going on."

My ears catch the familiar name. "Adam? As in the one who did that bogus survey?" Seeing Jay's nod, "So why is he still there?"

"He's military. He can't just up and leave. At least not until his enlistment is up." Jay cocks his head. "You sure are full of questions. Why is that?"

Trying to control my facial features, "It's good to know who I'm up against, and how many right?" Smiling at Jay's laugh and nod, I thank him for his time. "Well, I guess I better get these munchkins off to bed."

Amidst the repeated "I don't want to go to bed" and the "But, I'm not tired", I ask Jay how much longer he was going to be shacking up with us.

"Well, I'm going for that interview on Thursday, in two days. And with any luck I'll be able to find something and be out of your hair by the end of the week." Jay smirks. "Why? Can't wait to be rid of me?"

"No." My face is an exaggeration. "Just like having the help with the kids is all. Was wondering how much longer we'd have the extra hand."

Strebeck smiles and heads to the bathroom to prep for another night of blankets on the living room floor.

After tucking my children in their bunk beds, I kiss them and remind them how much Mommy loves them. With big strong hugs and wet kisses, they tell me how much they love me back. "Momma's baby dolls."

Together, they chime, "And daddy's baby meatballs!"

"Sweet dreams, kiddos." The door is shut, and some protests erupt.

"Not another word," I call through the door. "It's bedtime." They quiet down some.

Entering my bedroom, I see Chase is still passed out. I know he has only a few more hours of rest before he heads off to work in the morning.

He was able to land a decent paying job as a shift supervisor at the Wal-mart. He has to go in early to relieve the night shift manager. Gazing at him, I feel so much pride. *He's a good man. A good man.* Carefully, I kiss his cheek. Hearing Jay leave the bathroom, I head in there myself to freshen up.

As I look in the mirror, I wonder if I can go through with what I've planned. Part of me is scared beyond belief, and part of me prays everything will go as Two said it could. Knowing if things didn't work out that I'd never see my family again is what scares me the most.

My son's duffle bag still sits under the bathroom sink, filled with a hundred dollars and a few amenities I nabbed from the hotels. Knowing I won't need much, his small bag will do nicely.

Jotting a quick note on a piece of paper, I know that I am ready for when Chase's alarm rings in little over three hours. I'm going to settle this, or give it my best shot.

CHAPTER 31

The loud monotonous rrr-rrr-rrring of the greyhound bus hurts my tired ears. Even though I have been on this bus for the past three plus hours, I haven't been able to nullify the annoying sound of its engines. After getting on the bus at five o-clock this morning, I wondered if this was a mistake, my "returning to face the enemy." The thought that I have no one to blame but myself is a falsehood. I have the agency, the government and its henchmen, to blame.

A Minneapolis-St. Paul, Minnesota, stop is next on the route, and a thirty-minute layover awaits me. Deciding that at the next stop in twenty-some miles would be a good place to make some calls, and give my ears a rest, I begin to stretch. Feeling a few snaps and pops as I hear them tells me that stretching is indeed a very good idea, and that I'm getting old.

Before long the bus is slowing down for the next city. The tall buildings, not really skyscrapers, mingle with the smaller buildings of the Twin Cities, and I find the contrast interesting.

"Wow! What's that?" An awed sigh comes from a passenger up ahead of me, by the driver, as we pass some golden horses on a building.

"That's the capitol," the driver volunteers.

Ssweehh.

And I smile. *Hello Two.*

Where are we?

On a bus back to Idaho. I said I was going to do this. After a moment, *Are you here to help?* My breath is held a moment as I wait for her response.

Yeah, like I'm going to let you have all the fun by yourself? Like you can do it without me? Her mental chuckle is genuine. *Thought you might need some backup. You know, some moral support and stuff.*

Swallowing another nerve ball in the back of my throat, I nod. "I appreciate that," my voice a soft whisper.

As the bus finally slows to a stop, I reach for my son's bag. Seeing everyone getting up ahead of me, I decide to sit and wait for the pushing and shoving to ease up. Another lady gets the same idea as me, and we share a raised eyebrow at the scene before us. "All this pushing and shoving," and I shake my head.

So do something about it.

Smiling at Two's challenge, and knowing she's expecting the energy, I call out, "It's going to be thirty minutes whether you push each other out of the way or not." Seeing a couple evil looks thrown my way, I shrug, "Might as well not kill each other getting off."

A few more dirty looks, but some finally ease off the aisle.

Okay, not exactly what I had in mind.

The line then files methodically out of the bus, and I stand in turn. Knowing there is only about a safe fifteen minutes to stretch, get something to snack on, and make my calls, I make my way through the dodging people and crowds to the pay phones. After many "Excuse me", "Coming through", and "Pardon me" phrases being said, I feel the energy ask.

Patience.

Raising the receiver, I slowly press zero for the operator. Hearing the male voice prompt, I ask to make a collect call to my residence in Stevens Point. "Please hold while I try the number for you." The line rings, and I hear the operator cover a yawn. As Jay Strebeck's voice answers, "You have a collect call from, caller state your name...." After saying my real first name, I wait while the operator finishes his speech, "Will you accept charges?" After hearing affirmation from Strebeck, the operator disconnects to leave us to our privacy.

"Where are you?" Jay sounds pissed.

"How are the kids?" My counter shows I'm not willing to discuss it.

"Fine, but asking about you." He tries again. "So, where are you?"

"Give them lots of love for me, okay? Have you talked to my hubby yet?"

"No, but I will." Jay's voice is filled with threat.

"When you do, tell him not to be angry. Tell him I love him, and hope to see him soon." Pausing to hold the chunkiness in my voice, "I gotta go. Thanks for watching the munchkins for me." And I hang up, take a deep calming breath, and head for the snack stand.

Stepping off the bus, I stretch with a loud yawn. It feels strange being here again, knowing what I do now. There's a strangeness, a tenseness in the air. *Or am I imagining it? I wonder.* The views of the mountains are calming, inspiring so they are afforded my long gaze. Last rays of the sun filter over the mountains in the distance, and they feel so familiar.

"Ma'am?" The driver looks around, and tips his hat. "Have a good day, Ma'am." He quickly mounts the steps of the bus, and closes the door.

"Thanks." Even though the driver's already putting the bus in gear, it feels right to thank him for his assistance. He wouldn't have even had to address me if I hadn't had to run away. If I hadn't had dreams, and supposedly some abilities. If the Agency had never been formed to begin with.

As the bus pulls away, I half expect to be jumped by the Agency's henchmen at any second. Slowly, I look around as the wind pulls my shortened cropped hair. Running my fingers through the tresses, I miss the feeling of my longer hair. But now my wisps didn't bangle in the glory of the mountain wind as I wait to be collected. My trimmed tresses only flap. With a sigh, I remember having Chase trim to trim my hair to hide the hideous chunking done to my hair when the implant had been removed. The flat cut he gave me was proof he'd never be a good stylist, though he was given my loving thanks as the fairly flat bob did a decent job at masking the shaved area around my healed head wound.

The weight of two full days' worth of grime makes me whine. I need a shower and a beautician. Smiling at my own joke, I give another quick glance. Seeing no one, I guess it's time to call Kim to have her pick me up.

Standing in the department store's parking lot, a lone pay phone is visible to my tired eyes. My feet make quick work of the distance until the phone is in my hand. Reaching for the change needed to place my call, I pull out my last few crumpled bills and small handful of change. Carefully picking through the lint, I scan the area again. I press Kim's number and wait.

"Hello?" Her voice is like rain to a desert.

Trying not to cry, "Hi Kim. It's me," I say, not even trying to disguise my voice. "Can you pick me up? My ride left me at the Shopko off Fairview."

"I'll be there shortly." The line goes dead.

Looking around, I wonder if Kim's line is still tapped, and if I just gave my location away. Deciding to watch from a distance, I head to a small eatery about a block away.

The soft bell sounds as I open the door, announcing my presence. The smell of stale cigarettes overpowers any delicious aromas of the food being served. A stout waitress acknowledges me. "Smoking, or non?"

"Non." But I have to wonder if it'd really make a difference as the spirals of lit smoky treats fill the small space. "And near the door if possible? I'm just waiting here for a friend to get me."

She nods and signals to take a split-seated chair to my left. "That work for you?" At my nod, she asks what she can get me while I wait. A menu comes with her spoken words.

Without taking it, knowing I don't have a lot of time before Kim arrives, "Just a Sprite, please."

The waitress nods and makes a face as she heads behind the counter. As she fills my glass, I turn to look out the window. Her setting the glass down in front of me startles my gaze back inside the small cafe. "That'll be a buck, please," she offers with a cheeky smile.

I offer her one of my own as I reach for my small wad of bills in my pocket. Carefully, I untangle a single dollar and offer some dimes as tip, and hand them to her, before I take a sip. The cold soda scalds my throat as it goes down.

"Thanks," she offers as she leaves again.

My eyes move from her to the view out of the window. After a few sips, and several minutes, a few cars slow down and enter the Shopko parking lot. My heart pounds as I watch the cars then drive the perimeter of the building, circling a couple of times. One car's occupants enter the department store. After a few swipes of the parking lot, they spread out, and one head's my way.

Why did I want to be near the window? Mentally I kick myself for calling Kim. *Knew it was tapped.* Finishing my soda as I watch the car slowly cruise by, I wonder what I should do. *Idiot.* Standing, I open the door for a quick look, then proceed to follow the car that just passed by, and head towards Kim's place on foot.

As I walk I see the car's front at a corner about a block ahead. Holding my breath and trying to act natural, whatever that is, I pray it turns away. Luck is not with me as the car's blinker indicates it's indeed heading back in my direction.

Damn it! Act natural.

The car turns my direction and begins its slow approach.

Trying to act relaxed, I casually toss my trimmed locks, hoping the agency won't recognize me, if it is indeed the agency. My confidence is short lived as the car stops beside me. Allowing a curious glance, my eyes light on the man talking on this radio as he looks back at me. Giving him a slight smile and nod, I continue walking. The car then pulls along side of me and I hiss out my breath. My feet keep moving steadily as I hear the car's door open.

"Miss?" The man calls to me, one foot still in the car.

Oh crap! Oh crap! Slowly I turn and try to look confused, or interested. Anything but guilty, "Yes?"

He's a little taller than me, and now out of the car, approaching fast, a picture in hand. Within a few feet of me he stops, and unconsciously I take a step back, while he looks at the picture in his hand, then at me. "What's your name Ma'am?"

"Excuse me?" He receives my best "annoyed at the interruption" look.

"What is your name?" He is tense. Even the muscles in his face are tight.

"Why?" My eyes see the other cars approaching, and I know I am out of time and luck. There's no chance of escape now. And this isn't how I wanted it to go, not at all.

The man again looks at the picture, confidently comparing it to me. "Is this you?" With that, he thrusts the photo in my face.

Slowly, I take the photo from him. It is a picture of me, holding Joanna taken a few months back. Seeing my little girl, I wonder how she is, and am jealous he has a photo I do not.

"Ma'am?" The man insists on an answer as another, balding, man approaches cautiously.

"Sure looks like me, doesn't it?" It's not an answer, nor is it a confession.

A third car pulls up, and I recognize the driver as Adam, my interviewer. Slowly, I turn to face him. Feeling surrounded, I step towards his approaching form. Feeling the other two men corralling me, I shake off their reaching hands and toss them an irritated look. With the photo still in my left hand, I offer Adam my right. "I want to make a deal with you."

Adam Whatever-his-last-name-is just stands before me. His shock is evident. "What kind of deal?"

A hand at my arm demands my immediate attention before I can return a statement to Adam. "I am turning myself over to you, and only you, and on set terms." Sensing the balding gent is about to grab my arm, I turn light lightning. "Touch me again, and it's assault, moron. So, keep your hands to yourself, Maxwell."

Maxwell looks stunned as he takes a small step back. "How do you know my name?"

Adam just stands before me. His shock is evident. "What kind of deal? What are your terms?"

Squaring my shoulders, I begin. "For starters, my family is to be left alone...forever. No trying to find them, ever...period." My voice is firm despite my insides are shaking worse than Jell-O during a stampede. "Second, no wires, no torture, no prison cells, and I'll cooperate." Hearing Maxwell grumble, I pierce him with my most menacing look. "Third, keep Maxwell, and Gurness here, away from me." Seeing Maxwell's raised eyebrows, I continue, "I'd hate to be provoked into hurting someone. And fourth, I would like some information as to what is going on." My eyes meet Adam's. "Do we have a deal?" I take in the total of five cars now surrounding me and pray whatever it is they think I am capable of is enough to scare them, to keep them on their toes.

Adam looks at Maxwell, who only makes an angry face. Then Adam turns back towards me with a tentative smile. "And what about this information you already know? What do you know?"

My stance and voice challenge with more courage and conviction than I really feel, "Lots."

"Who told you?" Maxwell's voice practically snarls.

Sparing him an exasperated look, "Who told me what? That I'm special? That I feel some sort of...power when I sleep? And that the knowledge of how to use it is shown to me in my dreams? Think about it for a moment, will you? Why would anyone need to tell me anything? Why do you even waste your time to ask?"

"There's a good...friend...of mine that's...turned up missing." Maxwell throws it out like bait.

Taking a few deliberate seconds, I blink. Feigning realization, "Oh! You think I did something to your friend? Or that I know about your friend? Why would I? I don't know any of you, but I've learned about you. The only one I know, or have met, is him." My finger points to Adam as my eyes hold his, "Have we got a deal?"

Adam looks at the other two, seeking approval. The first man to have approached me speaks up, "We will do what we can. But I can promised that no one will bother your family." His eyes bore mine, "You have my word."

Looking at him, "And I ride with you to wherever I need to be taken." Seeing Kim's car go by slowly, her face a twist of anger and disappointment, I offer a small smile directly at her to comfort her as she passes by. Then, looking at the barrage of cars and men surrounding me, "But first, can we get something to eat? I'm starving."

CHAPTER 32

This place is everything Jay said it would be. My tired eyes continue to take in the view as I am driven past the guarded gate. Military working dogs patrol the plain desert landscaping. Some of the dogs bark as the car passes by.

"I dare you to tell the dogs to quiet down," Maxwell goads.

My eyes take him in. "I'd rather sick them on you." Somehow my features remain as blasé as my voice.

His face becomes an evil twisted smirk. "All freaks should be shot, you know."

Jews being slaughtered. Indians being massacred. Calmly, I return a look of serenity despite my seething anger. "And why would you say that?" I pause, reflecting. "Jealous?" Barely blinking at the man's sputtering, I smile. "Ah struck a chord, did I? It's a talent I have, the ability to piss people off. Comes with being a woman." That's something Kim would have said, and I know she would be proud of me in this moment for saying so.

Maxwell raises his hand as if to strike, his face mottled red with anger.

"What are you doing? Stop it, Dan!" My savior at the moment is the man who had stopped me last night, Gurness. "You started it, now back off."

Maxwell's hand drops, but his voice raises. "One of these days, Freak!" Seeing my want to challenge him, he stops me. "Adam doesn't have any say now, Honey," he drawls. "He doesn't know how involved I am with some of you 'Experimentals.'" His voice drops to disgusting, "I get very involved."

Turning my calm eyes to look out the window, I take a deep calming breath. "I'm not afraid of you.'

"You will be," he sneers.

177

"Oh!" My eyes find his splotched face, "Yes, Master Yoda," I drawl out.

Gurness snickers in my favor, "She's got spirit Dan. Ya gotta admit that." His laughter continues to fill the car the last few seconds it takes to approach the huge main building. It stops as the car is put into park.

"Welcome home, Rebecca," Maxwell tries again for another poke at me.

"Vacation, really. It'll be a nice break from the kids. Will I be given a tour?" I try to force a jovial tone.

Maxwell grits his teeth and jumps out. "Sure! I'll give you a personal guided tour of the whole *compound*, including you very own secluded, isolated, padded cell!"

Relaxing my shoulders, I offer a brilliant smile. "Oh, thank goodness! Comfy room all to myself, quiet and alone! This is better than I had hoped." My hands clasp to my chest happily. "This is better than I had read about in the brochure! And the customer service here isn't half so bad, Maxwell excluded, of course."

Another man approaches while Maxwell stomps off. This new guy opens my door for me and I get out. He takes another look at the vanishing form of Maxwell. "I don't know what you did, or how you did it, but you really got to him."

These two men seem friendly enough, so I address the new guy with a smile. "And who are you?

"Jamison," he offers his hand as he speaks, "Rob Jamison."

Carefully examining his proffered hand, I raise my eyebrows. "Are you sure you want to touch a freak?"

He laughs, hand still offered. "Heck, I've read your file. You're harmless. Witty, but harmless."

Pumping his hand briefly, I smile. "Maybe."

"Come on. I'll take you to your comfy, isolated *cell*," Gurness says as he indicates the way, turning only to verify I'm following. Jamison walks beside me, like a sentry.

As we pass through the second set of doors, I feel it...angry and hot...the hostile energy here. *Back off. Just back off.* The saying comes from an old Steven King book, and as I say it to myself, it rings true. Then I counter with, *I'm here to help.* More faces look my way, and I hear names but don't bother to tie them to anyone. Seeing Jamison pointing I try to catch what he says. "I'm sorry. Could you repeat that?"

Gurness turns and sees me about twelve feet behind him. "He said this is what we call the West Wing. You know, Admin, Security, Personnel, Physicians and the like. He points in the opposite direction, and my body goes numb. "That's the East Wing."

"What's there," I hear myself almost whisper.

Jamison shrugs, but his body is stiff, "Electrical...stuff."

My eyes dull as the energy speaks, and I repeat it. "The Shock Shop."

My guides just look at me. Jamison cannot hold in his surprise. "Uh, yeah. How did you know that's what we call it?"

Shrugging, my answer is, "I can feel it. Guess I heard your wish to call it that." My eyes meet his, "And I will not let that kind of stuff happen to me."

Again my guides just look at me, wondering what to say. After a few seconds, Gurness turns and calls over his shoulder, "I'll show you around some more." For the next half-hour, I have seen most of the compound and some of its staff. Then I am escorted to my room. It's very small, with a twin bed up against the white, unpadded wall. A small dresser is next to it, sporting a small wind-up clock. The small window barely allows any daylight through the bars and panes. White walls, and the off-white bedspread, emphasize the starkness of the room. It just reeks of "desolate" and "stark."

Turning to Jamison, I try to smile. "Not exactly the Holiday Inn, is it?" And rudely my stomach interrupts, sounding its discomfort and unease. Trying to laugh, I ask, "When do we get to eat?"

He checks his watch and sighs, "You already missed lunch, but dinner will be served in about an hour. We'll bring you to the cafeteria then."

"I think I can find it, thank you."

Gurness frowns, "Not really an option." He looks around, "Oh, and yes...uniforms."

"*Uniforms?* You've got to be kidding me."

Gurness shakes his head. "Nope, all in-mates are required...."

"*In-mates?* I am *not* an in-mate." My temper is rising fast. "So no breakfast this morning, no lunch, no television, no family, no freedom, but *uniforms?*" The energy all around is ready, asking, heavy with my hostility. "Oh! Leave me alone!" I turn my back to the two men and wait. Hearing the door shut, my body sags onto the small bed. Exhaustion consumes me, and I am off to sleep.

Before me are some of the Agency's top, and very rude, henchmen. From Strebeck's description, I am able to place a name on three of the five involved in this "interview." A big, burly man they did not identify stands at the door, like a guard, while they people before me go over rules and my need to follow codes of conduct. Feeling this is a false formality, I sit quietly through it, gritting my teeth at their cold behavior.

A man named Roberts asks, "Do you have any questions?"

Carefully, I think, not wanting to lose this chance, but wanting the right words to come out. "Yes, actually, I have a few." My eyes meet

Maxwell's first, then back to Roberts. "First, what is it that you hope to learn or...benefit from, by my being here?"

All the looks before me are cold. Roberts clears his throat. "You will undergo a series of tests, interviews, and...experiments."

One named Patterson addresses me next, "We are here to establish the full extent of your abilities and capacities."

Roberts adds, "We also need to determine if you are a danger to yourself...and others. We must verify you are not a threat to the government of the United States, and...."

My hand flies up to interrupt, "You think that by keeping me locked up, in seclusion, and performing experiments on me like I am some *lab rat*, that there *won't* be hostile thoughts towards you, or the government?" Their faces remain neutral. *"You people are your own threat!"* Seeing nothing further offered from them, I quickly think. "When do I get to leave?"

The snort and chuckles from Maxwell are what I expect. As is Roberts', "You don't."

"Oh, I see. So in turn for my acting like a lab rat for the rest of my life, I get a small undecorated, drab, desolate room to use. Is that correct?"

Patterson nods.

"Well that hardly seems fair."

All of them nod.

Throwing my hands up in the air, "I see how you all really care here. Forget the Code of Conduct you all just read off." They barely blink. "And if I refuse testing?"

Maxwell and Patterson smirk as Roberts throws down, "We have ways to make you assist in this, if necessary." Another chuckle from the two men.

Two, give me strength. "Then let the games begin." My eyebrow raises theirs, while silencing the mirth. "We're ready for you."

Patterson coughs, "We?"

My eyebrow stays raised. "Maybe you all haven't been properly briefed about me. When you worked with me, you work with someone else too."

Patterson frowns a bit, "How so?"

"The entity, my dream-like self, connects with me when I need her. And she's much more powerful than I am."

They all seem to shrug this off as Maxwell snorts, "Are we supposed to be afraid of you and your imaginary friend?"

"Are you stupid enough to not be?" My challenge is as loud as his. I lower my voice, "You all aren't really that stupid, are you?"

"Enough!" Roberts bellows as he stands abruptly. "Testing for you, Miss Imaginary Friend, begins at 0800. I suggest you get to bed and rest up. You'll need to be at your best for this."

I slowly stand, watching the five cronies file out.

You handled that well, Two gushes out.
Gee, thanks. So? What do you think? I ask Two.
Her laughter rings in my ears, but not my heart. *This is going to be fun.*
Easy for you to say.

Jodie M. Swanson

CHAPTER 33

"I said, lift the cup!" Maxwell shouts into the microphone. His loud voice reverberates through this small room I sit in as he stares at me from behind the two-way mirror on the wall.

Offering him an annoyed, slanted glance, I calmly say "No" yet again. For four long days now they have pushed and poked trying to get the data they hunger for. And for four long days I have refused to comply with their requests and orders. I have yet to participate willingly.

A series of explicative words fills the room. "Lift the fuckin' cup!"

Two's mischievous whispers have me walk over to the cup, saying "Okay" loud enough for Maxwell to hear. Reaching out my hand, I let it hover mere inches from the cup filled with what used to be ice water. Hand poised, I slant him a look. "No need to cuss, Moron. You want it lifted? Here." Using my right hand, I pick up the cup and dump its contents. "Satisfied?" In disgust, I throw the now empty cup at the two-way mirror. "Mission accomplished." Then I turn around and head back across the room, back to the mirror again.

"Goddam it! Use your mind and do it!" Maxwell sputters.

Poor Maxwell's pissed, Two chuckles within my head.

Thoughts of Biology and Physics come to mind as I slowly face the mirror. "As I understand it, *Mister* Maxwell, I did use both my mind and energy to lift that cup. I did what you asked." Then I present my back once again.

From behind the mirror, I hear Jamison snicker. "She has you there."

Maxwell silences the transmitter and cuts Jamison a dirty look before focusing on the calm lady before him. "Take her to the Shock Shop. Now."

Jamison stops laughing, "Come on, Dan. Most in-mates are rebellious at first. Leave her alone."

Maxwell curse, "She's a freak, and a flippin' arrogant bitch. She's been uncooperative. Now, take her, dammit!"

Jamison frowns and backs away, knowing Maxwell is above him, and that he must obey. He takes his key ring from his belt loop. "This isn't going to help," he mutters.

Within seconds Jamison opens the door to my experiment room. He cannot make his eyes meet mine yet, and I feel myself go cold.

"Well?" His eyes finally meet mine. "I take it we're going somewhere?"

Jamison only nods, then opens the door. "Come with me."

But I don't move. Instead I look at the mirror, piercing it as I ask, "What now?"

Maxwell's voice echoes, "Punishment."

"Prick," I toss as I am escorted by Jamison from the testing room. Following him as he weaves through the halls, I sense it, hot and angry. My feet stop cold. "No way, Rob. I'm not going."

The sound of footsteps approaching has me look behind me. Two members of security are heading our way. The look in their eyes cannot be mistaken. Thoughts of *One Flew Over the Cuckoo's Nest* war in my head as they come to stand beside me. Suddenly, I feel small beside the men ready to take me on.

Let them, Two hisses.

This is my body, not yours! I remind her.

"Miss?" One of the Security henchmen calls as he steps closer.

"Just follow me, Rebecca. It won't be so bad," Jamison lies.

Hotly, I turn. "*It won't be so bad?* Have *you* ever undergone this? Huh?" He meekly shakes his head as the two goons roughly take my arms. Trying to shake them off, I feel the energy rise. "Let me go! You'll regret this!" The goons only laugh and pull me along, Jamison in tow. When he meets my look, he lowers his. "Coward! How do you sleep at night?" My struggling feels useless, but the energy is mounting. I feel Two is at the ready. *Not yet. I can do this. They won't take me there.* "Please," I implore again, "Please let me go!"

"To late, Freak." It's Maxwell's voice coming from behind us. "You need to be taught a lesson."

The energy is practically scalding as I am drug along. "Help, Two. This is not good."

Her presences is surrounding. *Let it take over! Let it go!*

"Who are you talking to?" Jamison asks.

The energy is screaming, deafening, clawing to have a go. It reminds me of the intensity I felt in Two's dream world when her mom was killed. So hot and furious, like a living beast filling the space around me. I look at the two men dragging me, "Oh, you are in for some *serious* trouble now."

184

And I speak to the energy, *Come on. I need and welcome you.*

Instantly it flows, searing and angry. My eyes feel heavy, lethargic. My body feels light, and in control. It lifts me, safely, in its airy hold. The wispy swirls emanate, fast and think, like a heavy smoke cloud reaching for the hands that hold my arms.

"Holy Christ!" The one on my left releases me and bolts. The remembrance of Firestarter again plays in my head, and with the thought, a blast of searing energy pierces him, knocking the bulky man to the floor. He panics at Maxwell's feet, feeling the hatred and control of the energy pushing down on him. "Help me!" As it squeezes him, "Oh god, somebody help me! She's killing me!"

And he's crushed. Gone.

The other henchman finally let go. Maxwell harps on him to get a hold of me again. But his eyes are too wide, "Mother Fu-"

"No cussing." My eyes meet his. "It won't help, and it's vulgar." With a wave of my hand, he is thrown against the wall, only to land in a limp pile.

Maxwell calls for backup and tranquilizers, and I turn to face him. "You're jealous, aren't you? You just want all this power." He just stands a mere ten feet away, looking nervous for the first time since we've met. "You want a feel?"

"Huh?"

My hand raises, "Try it on for size."

It flows, lifting him, slowly. He casts bewildered eyes towards me. He struggles to move his hands and legs, so I allow it. His awe does nothing for me. The energy is the one tricking him here.

"Feels good, doesn't it?" My taunt brings his looks back to me. "*Doesn't it?*" My calm facade gives way to the underlying anger as I lower myself to the floor. "Doesn't it? Tell me, *Dan*, how *do* you sleep at night? How do you feel good about yourself as you push people until they break? Haven't you ever cared about anybody? Didn't your mother love you as a child?'

He just looks at me, mouth clamped shut.

The thought comes, knowing people are coming. Giving Jamison a quick look, my hand goes up. His too is raised in a sign of protection. "I want to walk. Do you want to join me?" Already I have turned, mentally pulled their forms through the air behind me as I stride down the hall towards the Shock Shop.

"Freeze!" The command is quickly followed by, "Holy Shit!"

There are about nine of them behind you, and I think six armed on their way. Two ahead, and the rest are coming from behind.

Two, you really are good back-up. Thanks. My feet continue moving forward.

"I said freeze!"

You're welcome. I'm impressed by the way. This is neat, watching you and it together like this. Her mental voice is tinged with awe.

So, you're not helping?

Not yet. No need. You're doing great so far. But what do you have planned? In a quick instant my thoughts are her. She whistles. *Oh boy. You're going for the kill shot, aren't you?*

Slowly, I turn to face the man still shouting for me to stop. "Death to the Agency." My voice might not be loud, but it's menacing, and still the group. "And to all its henchmen."

I never was the violent type before. I've always been against people who hurt others. My self-warring comes to a quick stop. *But then again, I have been for the death penalty of murderers. I just never thought I'd commit murder myself.* The distant voice of self-awareness plays with my emotions.

Ah, but you aren't going to murder anyone. The hostile energy they have created has done it. It's getting even. Getting revenge. Understand? You are just an innocent bystander caught in the fray. Two's voice of reasoning penetrates. *They've done it to themselves. You are just the channel. Don't deny it its revenge.*

My hand goes up. "Okay, you all need to come along too."

Together, we all head towards the two individuals who have just come into view. As I walk, the rest float along behind me in petrified silence. The two brave men raise dart guns.

And behind you, Two warns.

A thought comes to mind of the protective cocoon during the waves I faced as her in my dreams. And it's there, surrounding me. A bubble of wisps and swirls now encases me with a see-through shield about a foot away from me in all directions.

Good idea, Two coos.

Thanks!

The dart guns fire. In a surreal moment where time seems to stop, I see the darts come. And stop. They are suspended in my bubble, so I reach out for one. The barrier won't actually let me touch it, so I mentally crush it. Then with a quick look, the rest of the darts snap and crack apart, then fall to the floor. More darts fly, but they too meet the same fate as those on the ground at my feet as I continue down the hall.

The energy immobilizes the people as I get closer, freezing them where they stand. It's still so angry and hot, unappeased by this resistance. It begs for more, and asks me to follow.

Let's go.

A few minutes later, I find myself before some large wooden doors. Their edges are lined with rubber, and I know I have arrived at the Shock Shop. With a flick of my wrist, the huge doors fly open revealing the pent up hostile energy. It intermingles with itself as I stride forward, bringing along the hostages. With a quick look, I understand what each device is designed for, and my heart lurches at the lingering stigmas I feel. I swallow so I don't hurl.

Before me is a torture chamber they would have been proud to have in medieval times. Ten electrical chairs and six electrical beds line themselves against a dark wall. A series of suspended wires connected to hooks indicates another painful method used. A tank full of swimming eels is along a long metal tub on a wooden table. Other wooden chairs complete the area, and my eyes have taken their fill. They know there is so much more around this space, but I don't want to "see" any more. I squeeze my eyes shut tight, and take deep breaths.

"What are you going to do now, Freak?"

Shaking my head, I face Maxwell. "You aren't very bright, are you, *Dan*? First, no one in their right mind would insult someone who has them as I have you. Second, what do you think I'm doing? I'm letting the energy have its way with you." My hand waves and they all fly off to different torture area within the room. Some of them to areas I haven't even seen yet. The energy straps them in and secures them with its wispy strains. Once they are fastened, my protective cocoon disappears.

"For Christ's sake, Rebecca!" Jamison screams in panic. "My name is Drake! Mike Drake!"

The name strikes a memory, and the energy releases him. Strebeck had told me there were still moles in the Agency, and his friend Drake was one of them. Slowly I walk over to where he is now free standing. "Is that so?" At his nod, I ask, "And why should I believe you?"

"Because Jay told me he told you about me." He looks at me then shakes his head, "He knows you're here and is on his way."

"Dang it!" I think of my kids alone with Chase. "When did he leave?"

Maxwell's voice booms, "What's going on here? What are you saying? That Strebeck was a mole?" A finger flick from me and he is silenced. I don't look to see how.

Drake looks at Maxwell, then back at me. "He's on a flight here. He should've already arrived. He'll be here any minute." He looks at the door. "It's only a matter of time."

My eyes look around, seeing some of the scared faces of the people "strapped" down to their own torture devices. "So? How does it feel? To be the one sitting where you are now? Do you like it?" Several forms of "no" are seen and heard. "Was the pay worth it?" With that I walk out of the room, slamming the heavy doors shut behind me.

Drake quickly opens a door and follows me. "What are you planning on doing with them?"

Slowly, I turn to look at the big doors, then to him. "Me? I'm just going to allow the energy to get its revenge. Where's the circuit breaker?"

"Oh no," he shakes his head as he catches my hand. "No way."

Frowning, I look at him. "Okay. Where's the main computer?"

Drake makes a face and I can feel his tension, his indecision.

"Let me make it easy for you." With that said, Two and I mentally grip his mind. His shout of pain echoes through the halls as I search for the areas in his memory I want to find. "I'm sorry," I offer, "I don't know how to do this without making it hurt." Having my needed information, I release him. "Sorry."

"Damn it!" Drake leans against the wall and holds his head. "What are you going to do?"

"I'm putting an end to lots of careers with the government." Taking a couple of steps, I pause and look back. "I would leave this area if I were you. Like now." My feet quickly move down the hall towards the main doors and the West Wing. The big wooden doors of the East Wing open before me with a wave of my hand, and close behind the stumbling Drake.

The lights flicker around us, and distant sounds of screams are heard. Drake stops cold, eyes wide in realization. "Oh my God."

"Keep moving, or it'll want you too." My voice sounds uncaring as I make my way to the small door, but I know I do care, a lot. Putting my hand to the knob, the door unlocks, and I can twist it open. My eyes dart to Drake as he stands next to me. "What?" I ask.

"So, are you like some channel for this...this energy?"

I pause long enough to ponder his question. "Some people are mediums for spirits, aren't they? I guess I'm a medium for energy. Two taught me that."

I did?

"I can hear her," Drake whirls around. "I heard her! Where is she?"

My eyes meet his. "She's traveling with the energy, I guess. She and I are linked, somehow. Her friend thinks it's a link of the parallel worlds. I've just realized it's a link of the energy. For some reason we are different people, but the same person, from different worlds, or realities."

That was deep. Her voice is soft and quiet as she continues, *And that makes so much sense.*

"Now, if you are truly wanting to end this, as Jay said you might...leave. Leave and never come back to this. It'll all be over soon." The door gives way, and I walk in.

Hearing his footsteps, the distant sound of the front door, I sit before the main computer of the compound. Not recognizing anything on the screen before me I panic. "Help me. All I know is how to use Microsoft Word and how to log onto the internet."

What are you talking about?

The energy comes, and the monitor comes alive with information. Instinctively, I put my hand near the screen as my file pops up. In a second, it's gone, flipping through the pages and pages of individuals the

Agency is, or has been, messing with. The energy stops with the files, and goes the main programming prompts. Again I feel lost as codes and commands appear. Hundreds of thousands of commands flash before my eyes in a span of minutes as I wait before the screen, having never touched the keyboard or mouse. Suddenly, there is a stillness to the screen. A lone page the energy has settled on. Leaning forward, I note the energy seems to be scanning this page repetitively.

"What do I need to do?"

My hands rise, and gently come down on the keyboard. Suddenly, my fingers are flying over the keys, and I know the energy is in control. My keyboarding finesse is hunt and peck, and this looks like keyboard flying. My fingers wipe through commands, and soon there is the sound of the modem. A screen pops up, asking if I wish to continue, and the energy doesn't move my fingers. It asks, wants to be sure.

With my right index finger poised over the Enter key, I whisper, "Make it all go away." My finger hits the key.

The dialog box says "OK" a split second before the screen starts flashing codes and numbers. Another dialog box pops up indicating a computer virus has been detected. Message after message flash one on top of another announcing programs and files with fatal errors.

Oh, you are so good, Two hums.

The computer screen goes blank. The lights flicker. The urge to leave intensifies, so I follow Drake's footsteps out the front doors.

As the hollowed boom of the door sounds behind me, I sense a power surging through my body. The cocoon reappears. For long seconds, the energy courses through me, and I feel myself levitate with the power of it. Images of Jesus on the cross is how I imagine I must look to Drake as he watches some twenty feet away, his mouth catching flies. A strong feeling of loss and panic emanate through the energy as it returns through me. The feeling of people, then not, comes and goes in an instant. Then pulses from my body land upon the compound's walls. Splattering of mortar and brick shower my cocoon, and I close my eyes.

A huge explosion, and a fiery wall of heat lift me off the ground.

Two! I'm falling! Help me! I'm falling!

And blackness surrounds me.

Jodie M. Swanson

CHAPTER 34

"Rebecca?"

The voice is barely a whisper as I wade through the water. A dolphin jumps within a hundred feet of me. My hand goes up at the sight, and I scan the water's surface. The sun feels so warm as I reach up and stretch against the crick I now feel in my neck. The sound of seagulls dances across the waves, and I look up and greet them. "Hello, you noisy pests," I joke. My hand tries to splash water their way.

"Rebecca?"

The voice is a little louder now, and the gulls are gone. Blinking in confusion, I turn around looking for the source of the voice I hear. There is no one within my eyesight. Calmly, I call out, "Who's there?"

"Come on, Rebecca. Wake up." It's a male voice. "Wake up!"

The concern in his voice worries me, but I wonder why I'm being told to awaken. *How silly. Of course I'm awake. I'm standing here in the ocean after all.*

Something's moving me, I sense it, though the water stays the same. "What's going on here?" Part of me wonders if it is the dolphin playing some sort of game with me. My hands don't find anything, not even water, and again I feel movement this time around my shoulders.

"Come on, Rebecca. Come on! Wake up for me!" This is a new voice, still a man's. Strange, it sounds vaguely familiar.

The firm repetitive pressure on my chest is explosive. My lungs feel tight, like they are about to burst. Or as if I have been pushed under the water I am standing in. Panic. *I'm suffocating! Help! Help! I can't breathe!*

Her hands are suddenly on me. *Come on, Sleepyhead. Wake up! There you are. Where have you been?*

Her face looks a little worried. *Looking for you. You need to wake up, now. Please. Wake up! Wake up! Please!*

My eyes open and Strebeck is leaning over me, hands moving quickly to my shoulders. "Damn, you don't need to shout," I croak out. Weakly, I try to sit up, and Jay quickly offers his support. "What happened?" My eyes are still trying to focus.

Jay Strebeck's sigh shares his relief, then he gives me a big old bear hug.

"Ow, ow!" My body feels horrible, abused and battered. "What happened?"

Drake steps into view, and now I recognize the voices calling to me earlier. "Have a look."

Slowly, my eyes finally focus on the ruins of the compound. Smoke rises, and the feeling of death fills me. My last conscious thoughts come back, and my jaw drops. Struggling to stand, both men at my sides, I look around. Approximately three square miles of compound, people, fence, and military working dogs are gone. The impact of it makes me sit down again. "Oh my God." Nausea rolls in my head and my stomach.

Strebeck holds my wrist, telling me to relax as he takes my pulse. He's watching me closely, so I turn my face towards him. He smiles. "Found ya."

"Didn't realize we were playing hide-and-seek," I squawk out.

He chuckles, then turns serious. "You shouldn't have gone without me."

"Didn't realize I needed your permission, *Dad*." My voice comes out as a hoarse whisper as I think of how much like Kim that sounds. Sighing, my eyes take in the view again. The compound is down to the ground and any fires are minimal. "How long did it last?"

Drake snorts his laugh, "What the siege, or just the destruction?"

My eyes meet his before going back to the remains of the building, "Both."

"Are you saying you don't remember?" Drake sounds incredulous.

Carefully, shaking my head, "I just want to be sure. It seemed like, only...like ten minutes before I touched the computer. Then the cocoon, and the power pulses. I think I blacked out."

Drake offers a small smile as he addresses his friend. "It was *amazing!* The control she has is *amazing!* She said she feel is she is a medium for energy, and I believe it. She was grabbed by Willis and Henry, to be taken to the Shock Shop, and all hell breaks looks! Maxwell starts calling for backup, and insults her." He continues his recount of the story as I listen and remember. "...and made this steamy-looking bubble appear around her, like some sort of force field. She drug us all to the Shock Shop and strapped us in."

"I didn't do that," I interrupt with force. "It did. The energy did, not me."

Drake rolls his eyes and continues with the recap, "Thinking 'This is the end'...and then she's telling me to get out while I still can. She was inside by herself for all of five minutes before she came out and...started attacking the place! Light just burst from her, hitting everywhere. And she was up in the air, levitating! Geesh, it last...I don't know, maybe...fifteen minutes tops?" He looks at me. "It was unreal."

Jay pats Drake on the back. "It's over now. At least, I'll almost bet it is. Come on!" He helps me to my feet. "I'm sure alarms went off, and the fire trucks and military noses will be here soon. We need to get going."

My feet feel shaky as I make my way to Jay's rental car. Drake heads to the driver's seat. Jay sets me in, then goes to the other side to side beside me. "You're still cold." He takes off his jacket it wraps it around me. Closing my eyes against the hurt, and opening to the warmth of the jacket, I sag into the seat.

Drake looks in the rearview mirror seeing the sleeping form. "She okay?"

Jay watches Rebecca's neck for the light signs of a pulse. "Yeah, I think so. Let's get going."

"Is she sleeping?"

Jay nods, and sighs. "That was close. She had no pulse and no breathing for a while there. We almost lost her."

Drake apologizes, "I didn't know if I could touch her. Sorry. I guess I froze. Then I saw you pulling up, right after she fell. It all happened so quickly." He puts the car into gear and applies some gas. Then he looks into the mirror again. "I think Dan was going to kill her. He was following, and he usually doesn't do that."

Jay nods and offers a smile. "She got under his skin, huh?"

Drake smiles, "That's an understatement. She was quick with retorts and comebacks. She was hysterical. Dan just had enough of her, and...and I think he was really going to do some damage, or kill her trying."

Jay just nods and looks at the woman sleeping peacefully. "You did good calling me when you did."

For a few minutes they travel in silence. Drake keeps looking back. Rubbing his jaw he sighs, "So, do you think it's over?"

"What?"

"The Agency? Is it finished?"

Jay looks back out the window, a peaceful feeling settling over him. "If she got into the mainframe back there, it probably is. There's no way of telling what she's done without finding a place to gain access. Either way,

I'd find a new job if I were you."

"Thank God," Drake carols.

Jay smiles in turn. He looks out the window, and wonders if he can contact Adam when they are safely away from here to find out what information he can.

CHAPTER 35

My eyes look down at the moist granules of sand at my bare feet. Slowly I take another step towards the water. Offering a quick look over the water, my gaze returns downward. My toes dig deep into the sand, nervously. The surf is so close, I know. Finding the strength, I take the last few steps, until I stand in the water again.

The energy bathes me with serenity and peace.

Sighing I sit down in mere inches of waves, a sense of calmness soothing me.

"See? I told you," Derk calls out from the water that holds him from the waist. "It isn't just for looking at, or the waves."

"But this is different water," I protest. "It's not the same."

Calmly, he strides towards me. As he approaches, my gaze lowers. "Coward. Come on out here where it's deeper."

Frowning at him, I stand and take a few more steps towards the deeper water. My eyes scan the chilly water's surface, looking for a reason to flee. So absorbed in this I didn't realize he was beside me until he takes my hand. "Relax, Rebecca."

My eyes meet his, and I offer his a tentative smile. "Okay."

It seems so strange, this kindness and appreciation. I almost don't know how to take it. He had come shortly after One had left my safety, and asked me to follow him. Following him, I was surprised to see my father outside my shambles. My stance had gone rigid, ready for the confrontation. He had looked as uncomfortable as I, and Derk prompted him to say whatever it was that he was going to.

The words, "I'm sorry," hit me like a bold of lightning does a flagpole. For several seconds I had just stared at him, my mouth parted in surprise. The surprise still lingered on my face as he offered a nice, new set of clothes. My trembling hands had taken them as a whispered "Thank you" came forth from my lips. Then, with a terse nod, he had mounted the stairs, leaving me with a mix of odd emotions as I watched him leave. The sense of finality seemed to reconcile the pain I had harbored for so long.

Derk had then told me he want me to leave with him, and tried to take my hand. My reaction had been to snatch it back. Fear of the unknown and of not being accepted made me say I wasn't leaving. His calm look and patience had me believe that I could live happily somewhere, and with him. That thought alone took a long time to comprehend as I looked at his handsome face.

"Wait, did you say 'with you'?" My voice had been a croaked whisper.

"If that's okay, that is. I was kinda hoping we could spend some time getting to know each other and stuff." He offered a crooked smile.

"Where?" I had asked. "Where do you want to go?"

His arms had spread wide. "Wherever!" Just somewhere else, so you can begin anew." He had sensed my hesitancy, and offered. "Just try it. If you don't like where we go, and what we see, you can always come back."

My eyes had searched his, and I had slowly nodded. His broad smile caused one to curve my face.

Now, here I slowly turn where I stand knee deep in water, only hours from my old home, and feeling a memory of One's life creep into my head. A family, a man who cares and respects me, just like in her life. The realization that this is for real has me turn and face him. "So, you really want to get to know me?"

He smiles, and steps closer, "I do."

"Lesson One, I might take a while to adjust to things."

He takes my hand, "Okay."

An evil, playful grin comes to my face, "Lesson Two!" With a quick shove he falls backwards with a big splash. He comes up sputtering and swiping at the water in his face. His look is murderous, "What the hell was that for?"

Innocently I smile, "I have a playful side. That was Lesson Two."

The look on his face switches from one of anger, that of incredulous. "Oh, you brat! Come here!"

And with that the chase is on amidst the laughter and the waves.

Adam answers the phone on the third ring with a groggy "Hello?" He sits upright in bed, then checks to see if Cathy has awakened. Seeing her sleepy, questioning look, he puts up a finger. "Where are you?"

"I am near Oklahoma City. I just have to know, can you check to see if it is all...over?" The voice sounds tired.

"The search? Of course it is..."

"No," Jay's voice interrupts. "I mean if it is *all over.* The whole thing, done."

Adam is up and out of the bed, heading down the hall in his boxers. "The Agency," he hisses in the mouthpiece. At the kitchen, he toys with a pen on the counter.

Adam listens as Jay recounts some of the events of the past few hours, though some of the details were twisted to protect the innocent. He doesn't know one vital person is being kept form the story. "So, we think in essence, the computers killed the Agency. Is it possible for you to go to work and check the computers and whatnot?" Jay's pause is pregnant, "It's important."

"Sure, how do I reach you?" Adam snatches a piece of paper and quickly jots down the number Jay offers. "Okay, I'll call you back as soon as I know something."

"Be careful, wary of tracing." Then he hangs up, and the line is dead.

Tiptoeing back into his bedroom, Cathy asks in a voice muffled by comforters and pillows, "What's going on?"

"Friend needs some help," he says as he pulls on a shirt. "I'll be home before you know it." He quickly bends down and pecks her sleep-puffed cheek. Then he leaves with a pair of pants in his hand. Quickly, he finishes dressing and leaves the house, anxious to find out what is going on. The ride to the base is quick, so Adam pulls into the nearly empty parking lot about ten minutes after leaving his house. He is surprised to see Roberts and Gurness' cars already there. Locking his door, he heads for the building. Once inside, he hustles down the hall, feeling much like a spy. As he nears his office, he sees the two men sitting quietly before a computer's blank screen. He hides himself, but listens to hear their conversation.

"And this is all we have had not for the past six hours. It's like the system is gone. There's nothing." Gurness is talking as he points to the screen. "It's the worst virus I've ever seen. It's definitely targeted to our systems, and there's no way to bring it back up." Gurness runs his fingers through his thinning hair. "All of the programmers are stumped."

Roberts rubs his face. "And how did this happen?"

Gurness leans back, his tired face getting a rub itself. "There's more. We've lost all contact with the Agency's two test sites. The people who were sent to discover what happened are saying that it's a massacre, like a strike attack occurred on both of the compounds. No survivors yet. God, I'm glad we came back here."

The look on Robert's face mirrors that on Adam's. Robert's voice is barely audible. "So, where do we go from here?"

Gurness shakes his head. "We can't go anywhere. All the in-mates and staff were killed. All programs and research lost."

Roberts looks around defiantly, "We have printouts, files, hard copies..."

Gurness holds up a hand to stop the barrage of comments, "So what? We've lost all the in-mates and controls. We've lost all the personnel who were working with them. With no one to research, and no researchers...we're out one government agency."

"So, who bombed the facilities? Who's claiming responsibility? And how did they know about this?"

Gurness frowns. "For years, we had wondered if there were spies or moles somewhere in the Agency. I guess we were right, not that it matters now. There's no way for us to find out who was who at this point. The DNA testing may take months. The people involved are probably long gone already. People have a way of disappearing if they want to."

"Where did the planes come from?"

Gurness laughs sadistically, "There's another problem. An air strike with no aircraft detected."

"Some aircraft...a secret aircraft...one that we don't know about?" Roberts looks at Gurness with awe.

"That's what we are focusing on now. Who and what," Gurness nods.

Adam has heard enough. Carefully he exits the building and heads to his car. The Agency is done, finished, and brought to an abrupt end. He can't believe it. The amazement of it makes him pull over to the payphones by the Shoppette, the base's gas station slash mini-mart. Quickly he pulls out the scrap of paper with a number on it. His fingers tap on the booth anxiously as he waits for the call to go through.

First ring and "Hello? What did you find out?"

Adam quickly recounts what his spying had disclosed. "Both compounds were destroyed. Roberts and Gurness were convinced it was an aerial assault." Adam also relays that there were no reports of survivors. Adam hesitates, then asks, "How did you know so much already? Are you one of the spies they were talking about?"

Jay hesitates in answering, "There are no spies, Adam. There wasn't an air strike."

Adam calls Jay a liar, "I heard them. They said it was an air strike."

"Were there aircraft detected?" Jay prods. "No, they're grasping at straws."

Adam notices some headlights approaching the Shoppette. "Oh crap! It's Roberts. I gotta go."

"Adam, wait!"

"Yeah?"

"Be happy. You can start looking for another job," Jay jokes.

"Right, thanks I guess." But the line is already dead.

"Adam?" Roberts calls from the pumps as he gets out.

Adam pretends like he just sees him, "Oh! Hey Captain Roberts, you're up awfully late."

"As are you. Everything okay?"

Adam shrugs, thinking quick, "Yeah, just needed to get some Motrin for my kid with a fever. You know."

Roberts offers him a weak smile. "Sorry to hear there's illness in the house. But, weren't you on the payphone just now?"

Again, quick thinking. "Ah yep, had to call the missus and check to see if the AAFES brand is okay. Forgot my cell phone. You know how women are, quality versus price. I don't know why she just didn't go get it herself."

Roberts just nods, "Well, have a good night. See you in the morning." With that he turns back to gassing up his car.

Adam hurries into the Shoppette and buys the medicine, fearing Roberts will be looking. He trophies it out as Roberts enters to pay for his gas. "See you in the morning, Sir."

Once in his car, Adam smiles broadly. "I'll be free in a few weeks. In two weeks I can start my terminal leave and be done with this place within two months. I'll be free." And he pulls out of the Shoppette parking lot, a small smile still on his face.

Jodie M. Swanson

CHAPTER 36

"Mommy!"

The excited screams of my children as they race towards me brings tears to my eyes. Dropping to my knees, I scoop them up, bestowing quick loving kisses on their precious heads. "Oh my precious little munchkins! Mommy's missed you so much!"

"Bec?" It's Chase's voice as he comes from the bedroom.

My watery eyes meet his, "Oh, Honey!" Quickly I find my feet and fly into his welcoming arms. "I have missed you."

"You are so stupid! You could've been hurt! Killed. Then where would we be?" He holds me tight.

"You'd be in the local restaurants trying to find another maid," my voice whispers out against his neck.

He pushes me away to look into my face, then pulls me close again. "I have been worried sick. Are you okay?"

Offering him my big teary smile, "I'm fine."

He cups my face as he kisses my lips. "You've cut your hair some more."

"Couldn't go around sporting that butch job you gave me, could I?" Seeing him judge it, I ask, "Do you like it?"

He nods, "Obviously the person who did this has a lot more talent with scissors than I do." He ruffles my cropped hair.

Jay Strebeck comes in next and offers Chase his hand. "Told you I'd bring her back. She didn't need me after all, though. She was all done by the time I pulled up."

Drake knocks at the door, "And then some. I was there."

My eyes find Drake's, "Save the story for when the kids are in bed, okay? Honey," I turn to my husband, "this is Mike Drake."

"Mike," Chase offers his hand. "So, can I hope that this is never going to happen again?" His eyes are on me, accusing, and I'm slightly surprised.

"Darn straight," Strebeck chuckles. "She destroyed the Agency to the core."

My eyes roll as the terrible twosome try to hear what happened. My eyes rest on Strebeck, filled with accusation and the threat of dealing with me if he lets out too graphic of details. "Sorry kids, another time. I want to play with you. I have missed you," and take their small hands and lead them to the back door. For the next half-hour I hold my children in my lap as I answer their young questions with censored answers for their innocent minds. I cannot keep from running my hands through their hair and giving them hugs every few minutes.

"Will you go away again, Mommy?" My little angel asks as she sighs against my chest.

"Nope, I don't think so. You guys got so big when I went away. I think that deserves...a tickle tackle! Rrrraaaarrr!" And two loving cuddly kids scramble and giggle out of my reach.

It's late. Chase, I mean Mitch, is sleeping beside me on the mattress he acquired while I was away. The kids are sound asleep, and kisses stick to their clean faces as they dream. Jay and Mike left two hours ago saying they were going to get rooms at a cheap hotel a few miles away. But I cannot sleep. My mind still thinking and remember, won't rest.

Jay Strebeck had told me it would take time to get over this whole affair, but I doubt I ever will. Every time I had drifted off on the way back home, I had visions of the energy and the things that were done. The finality of it was unsettling. There is no regret, just a hollow series of realizations. The energy had used me, and I had let it. Two was right, I knew, that it was having revenge, and that I shouldn't take it personally. But how does one not? I knew that even innocent people were killed, and that the energy had let them die. But why?

Jay had said that maybe it was the only way to totally bring about an end to the Agency.

I guess he could be right.

Well, if you think about it, it does make sense in some sick way.

And you are no help, whatsoever.

It's nice having a conversation with myself again. Part of me misses Two's wit. *And I'm not witty? You heard Drake. He said I am comical and good with retorts.*

But I know it's not the same.

Carefully, I ease from the sheets. Going out to the dining room table, I sit down. My son's notepad sits before me, and I slowly open it and look at the pictures he's used to fill the pages. A smile lights my face as page after page are renditions a mother can always be proud of. Turn the last art-filled page, and a sense of purpose fills me. Spying a pen on the counter, I snatch it up, and begin.

As I sit here, I am faced with the memories and visions of many people, and a few days of hell. Part of me doesn't know where to start. This story is so long in the making. So maybe I should start somewhere in the middle. You see, I have weird dreams, dreams in color and in sequence of another world, another day.

Maybe I should start there, with one of my dreams. And this is indeed what one of my friends told me to do, write all my dreams down. But you see, it goes far deeper than just my dreams. So here we go:

With a smile I realize that indeed this has all just been a series of days, another series of days. My pen flies on to aid in telling my story.

Another day. Adjusting my leather boots and get the kink out of the material, then grab my long trench coat. With a flick of my hair, I pass through the small portal of my small dumpy home.

Did you enjoy this book?

The journey continues with

Another Time
Another Place
Another One

Follow me on
Facebook - http://www.facebook.com/jodiemswanson
Twitter - http://www.twitter.com/jodiemswanson

Jodie M. Swanson

Made in the USA
Lexington, KY
15 April 2017